THE
DEVIL'S
ALL-AMERICAN

SHAKIR RASHAAN

COVER DESIGN by Woodson Creative Studio

PUBLISHED BY NEBU PUBLISHING, LLC

PRINTED IN THE UNITED STATES OF AMERICA

ISBN 978-0-9986640-2-6

For my Beloved...

"Moral wounds have this peculiarity - they may be hidden, but they never close; always painful, always ready to bleed when touched, they remain fresh and open in the heart."

Alexandre Dumas – The Count of Monte Cristo

ACKNOWLEDGEMENTS

25 September 2018
2035hrs (8:35PM)

They say that you can't look back, that the only time you should look back is so you can see how far you've come. Well, if that old adage is true, then consider this my way of bucking the trend of sorts. Not only did I look back, I went back to an old project and made it anew.

This was an older project from six years ago, when I wanted to challenge myself to write a book where I could—for lack of a better term—restrain myself a bit. If you've been around me for any length of time, that isn't exactly my strong suit LOL.

At any rate, I sort of re-wrote this book, including some of the real-time issues going on today: the NCAA scandal that involved improper benefits to star players, the #MeToo movement, and other things to give this book a new feel for the present time. (To my diehard readers, I didn't change the book *that much*, but it is still worth the read because I added some elements to give the novel a more romantic feel.)

I have more than a few things up my sleeve coming for 2019, but I can't say what that is just yet. I have to leave you in some sort of suspense. I got to have a little fun LOL.

So, you know what comes next, so let's get to it?

To my mother and father, thank you for your continued support of my literary career, the ups and downs, the failures and successes, and I hope this newest book gives you a reason to brag about your literary genius children.

To my sister, Rae Lamar, although you've temporarily (hint, hint) put the pen down to handle other affairs, know that when you decide to get back in the mix, your big brother will be there waiting. I love you.

To my Beloved, there's not much more to say that hasn't already been said in the past, but it bears repeating: I love you more than life itself.

These people I have to thank because I can do that!

To Naleighna Kai, J.L. Woodson, and N'Tyse, thank you for being such an integral part of my literary journey and success throughout. I thank you from the bottom of my heart.

And finally, I'm going to end this in the usual fashion because we'd be here forever while you had me gushing over folks, so do me the usual solid and insert your name in the following statement;

I'd like to thank _____ for the support and love. I hope to continue to put books out that you will always want to tell your fellow bookworms about.

Thank you and God bless,

THE

DEVIL'S

ALL-AMERICAN

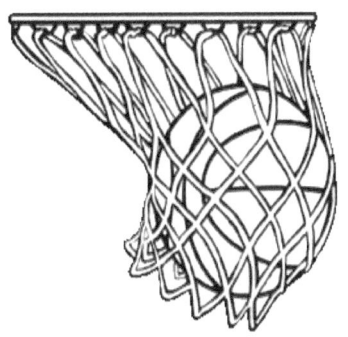

PROLOGUE

My name is Keenan Ellis, pleased to meet you. I'm the starting point guard for Tempest State University in Virginia, one of the most successful basketball programs in the country. We're going into this season as the consensus top-ranked team in the country, riding a forty-game winning streak and the status as the defending national champions, with the whole college world gunning to take us down.

You know my face; I'm on every pre-season All-America team you can think of and a lock for the top pick in the NBA Draft after I finish my college career. I even have a nickname that you can't help but remember: White Chocolate. I picked up that nickname in high school, thanks to my biracial heritage; my father is African-American and my mother is South African.

Yeah, I'm sure that has you scratching your head, but when your mother is a doppelganger for Charlize Theron, then you'll understand how I got the nickname.

Being me has its privileges, too. Not to say that I'm all that, but…okay, yeah, I'm all that. I could be on the cover of several different magazines away from the court based on my fashion sense alone. It ain't nothing to see a model on my arm at different events that I get invited to. I ain't gonna say nothing about the other perks that I get either; well, you know, violations and all that. But let's just say, I get a pretty penny for the extraordinary plays on the court, if you feel me?

All I need to do is win my second straight national champion-ship and break the career scoring record and I'll go down as one of the greatest ever to do it on the college level. Next stop, multi-millions in the pros.

All my dreams are coming true, so you would think I would be on cloud nine, right? Well, I would be, and under normal circumstances, I should be, if it weren't for a deal I made during my junior year with this dude by the name of Lucius B. Prince, or L.B. was what I called him, I would be able to enjoy my spoils without looking over my shoulder.

Man, I remembered feeling the pop when the forward went low after I broke loose for a dunk and he knew he wasn't gonna block my shot. It was the game against Trent State right before conference play when I tore every ligament there was around my knee. The coaches and training staff were all but convinced that I was done, and my teammates wondered if I could even walk again without a limp.

The doctors were even less helpful, telling me if I wanted to be stubborn I could still play, but I would pay a severe cost once I retired. If I continued, even with proper care from my physician, I wouldn't be able to walk without a cane after my playing days were over. Despite the advancements in sports medicine to deal with injuries like this, I was gone for a year.

My parents tried to sound encouraging; my dad had worked for the railroad all his life, and mom stayed at home to take care of me and my little brother, so I knew that they had a stake in what might happen to me. Dad tried to sound diplomatic, saying I still could get a decent education and do some good with my life.

I wasn't trying to hear all of that. I was going to take care of my family so they didn't have to work again. I told them all to go to hell; that I wasn't done yet. I was so frustrated I told the hospital staff that I didn't want to see anyone for the rest of the night, including my family. I needed to be alone, the fear and uncertainty of my future feeling like someone was squeezing the life out of me.

I was stuck in my private room, watching the four walls and listening to the machines as they conspired to drive me insane. I pleaded with God to explain to me why I was going through this pain. Why had He punished me? What did I do to Him?

Tears began to flow as I shouted out for someone to help me get my life back. I didn't want the one that everyone swore I had to live—a life without basketball. I shouted into the darkness, desperate to get the frustration out of my system. "I want my life back!"

I didn't know what I expected after that. The silence was deafening, eerie didn't quite explain how quiet it was in those moments after. The only noise was the incessant beeping of the machines that checked my vital signs.

I thought I heard something a few moments later, but it was hard to tell since the pain medicine they had me on made me feel like I was hallucinating. I didn't trip out too much; the nurses had already checked on me, and there wouldn't be a need to get a visit from anyone for at least a few hours. I settled into my bed and closed my eyes to try and get some semblance of sleep before the next rotation came through to poke and prod for the next round of blood work.

In the next instant, I heard someone shift the chair next to my bed and sit down, startling me in the process. The pain meds had me loopy, so I couldn't tell if I was awake or in a dream state. All I knew was when I looked to my left, there was this dude lounging like he had every right to be there.

He was a well-built dude, looked like he'd balled back in the day, and he wore a Tempest State t-shirt, so I had him pegged for a booster or an alumnus coming to see about one of their stars.

"How badly do you want to prove all of them wrong? Are you willing to do anything to get your old life back, Keenan Ellis?"

"Anything, whatever it takes."

"Remember that when the time comes to settle up. Remember your promise to me."

I didn't think anything else about it as I went to sleep that night. I thought he was some crackpot agent that wanted me to sign with him or something. Little did I realize what he'd done and the aftermath of that action.

About a month after the surgery, the doctors and the coaches were in absolute shock over the recovery, and to a degree, I was, too. My leg was as good as new, and no one could figure out how it happened. All of that confusion soon faded when a pretty chocolate sistah came into the hospital room with flowers and a note on the card.

Anything is possible ... give 'em hell! L.B.

And that's what I did, I gave them all hell.

I didn't have a choice ... I fell for the crossover and became the Devil's All-American.

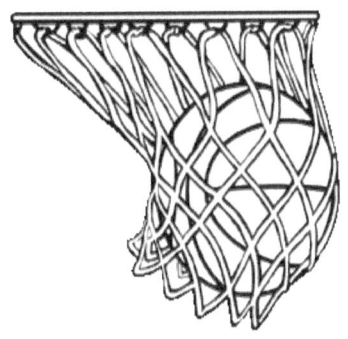

Chapter One – Genesis

"Rome! My knee! Shit, my knee!"

"Kee, relax and let the trainer take a look at it, man."

"Get me off the floor, dammit! I don't want to be on the floor like this!"

"Keenan, let them take a look, all right?!"

I wished they'd left me unconscious. The pain was unbearable. My knee was the first area to grab my attention, and when I went to try and grab it, my shoulder made its presence known. I must have hit the ground harder than I thought.

"I need to pull Javi and Jarmon out of the fight with the Trent players, let the doctors take care of you!" Rome yelled as he raced toward the melee.

I was already on the stretcher as I heard the medic giving me instructions. "Keenan, buddy, try not to move, okay? We'll get you back to the locker room so we can evaluate you there. Do you understand me?"

I gave a strangled-sounding "yes" as they rolled me off the floor. I didn't know what happened, all I knew was my lower body was tied down tight, and I couldn't move my head from side to side. I didn't want to feel trapped, but I didn't have a choice. I felt the urge to scream, but I couldn't hear my voice. The fear gripped me and wouldn't let me go. I'd never felt so helpless in my life.

The hush in the building scared me; I only assumed the crowd was focused on me. My parents were in the stands for this game, and so was my younger brother, Tyler. I didn't want them to worry, so I raised my left hand to wave and give the thumbs up that I was okay. At least, I thought I was okay.

Once I heard the applause in the arena I felt a little better. It felt good to know everyone hoped I would be okay. I heard Rome and Javi and Tony yelling in my direction, but I kept my eyes closed; the glare of the lights was too much to handle.

Instead of taking me to the locker room, I was diverted to the ambulance. I knew I was in trouble when I glimpsed the flashing red lights. All I wanted to do in that moment was block out as much of rolling nightmare as I could. I didn't remember much of the ride; I was still groggy from the smelling salts.

I wasn't sure if I was dreaming or not, but the sports radio host the driver was listening to freaked me out. It felt like an out-of-body experience; I heard him describe with bone-chilling detail: my body in the air, flipping head over heels and the resounding thud against the floor. I swore he was talking about someone else altogether, but he was talking about me.

Everything faded to black as I felt myself being pulled back to reality. The ambulance lights were the tell-tale sign that I hadn't dreamed the whole sequence. The pain also made itself crystal-clear that I wasn't dreaming, as my shoulder played "how fast can I go from one to ten" with my knee, taking turns on which could be more intense on the pain scale.

They wheeled me into my hospital room, the sanitized stench in the room strong enough to make me nauseous. I didn't want to be in there by myself; I hadn't suffered a major injury in my basketball life before, so I had no frame of reference to figure out what I was supposed to do. The EMTs did their best to offer their encouragement, doing their best to wait until the nurses made their way into the room to take over my care.

I turned on the television, watching the highlights of the game on *SportsCenter*, and I was smacked in the face with the play that ended my night. The way I watched the play in real-time speed, it looked eerily similar to the way I saw it in my mind's eye as I slipped in and out of consciousness on the way to the hospital. I couldn't watch anymore, using the remote to switch to another station so I wouldn't have to relive the horror again.

One of the nurses came in after what seemed like an eternity, equipped with a mild sedative to help me sleep. I was hopeful that maybe I might be able to escape the nightmares of the lasting images that I had a hard time shaking from my mind. The only thing that the sedative provided was the ability to numb the pain, so I switched the channel to Comedy Central so I could at least watch something funny to take me away from my predicament.

"Yo, Kee, we took care of Trent State for you, bro."

I awoke to find Javi and Rome in my room, along with Tyler and my parents. I was so groggy from the sedative and the pain meds being fed through the I.V. drip that it took a moment to remember where I was, and more importantly, how I ended up there. I didn't realize I'd drifted off; the last thing I remembered was watching *South Park*, and I'd managed to laugh myself to sleep.

I took a look around at the concerned faces, all of them trying to hide their reaction to my being laid up like this, with all these tubes protruding from my body. My mother never had much of a Poker face, and the way she looked over me, I must have looked like I was in bad shape.

"What was the score?"

"We blitzed them by twenty," Rome replied. "Once they took Leggett out of the game for the flagrant foul, they didn't stand a chance."

"Yeah, their university president came into the locker room after the game to offer his apologies and let us know that Leggett was being suspended by the university the next three games and he would personally appeal their league commissioner to add more games." Javi added that information. It didn't make me feel any better, but I had to live with it for now. Payback was on my mind; he meant to take me out, and I couldn't stand idly by and not say or do something.

My cellphone rang, but I didn't recognize the number. I wasn't sure if it was someone trying to get a statement, so I had my father answer the call. He chatted for a couple of seconds, and then handed the phone to me. "She says she's a close friend of yours, son."

I was confused about that reference, but it didn't take long for me to come to my senses. "Hi, pretty girl, how are you doing?"

"I'm worried sick about you, that's how I'm doing." Ariel's voice felt like the remedy I needed more than anything in this world. "What did the doctor say? The way you fell—"

Almost like they were on cue, the doctor came in along with the nurses. She had them usher my teammates out of the room, leaving me and my family there to listen to what she had to say. After a few moments, she turned her attention to me, looking like she was trying to find the right combination of words to ease my anxiety.

Considering they rushed my boys out, I took the hint that it wasn't good news. "Ariel, the doctor is here, I need to talk to her to figure out what's going on. Can I call you back once she's done?"

"I'll be waiting for your call, baby. Whatever it is, we

will get through it, okay?"

"Okay, baby. I'll call you in a bit."

I didn't want to end the call, but I didn't want her to have to hear that side of me in case the news wasn't anywhere near what I wanted to hear. My temper was legendary in that sense, and it was something I was trying my best to get under control.

The doctor took a couple of minutes for me to get comfortable before she introduced herself. "Mr. Ellis, my name is Dr. Orton, I hope you've been able to rest comfortably. I wanted to get to you and your family as soon as I could, so we could go over your x-rays."

I didn't want to hear what she had to say, unless it was what I wanted to hear. "Just give it to me quick, Doc, how long will I be out?"

Dr. Orton took a deep breath, realizing that I was rushing her ability to settle into her bedside manner. "You're looking at six months at least, Mr. Ellis. You tore your medial collateral ligament and your anterior cruciate ligament in the fall."

"I can't be out that long?!?!" I shouted. The flood of emotions raged from every pore I had. "You can't brace it or something, or what about the experimental treatments over in Germany? There has to be something that can be done, please."

She looked over at my father and shook her head. "You're going to need time to heal, whether you like it or not. We can get you back on your feet in a month, but after that, the rehab is going to be long and painful, I won't lie to you. We don't ever want to rush these things, especially if you want to continue your basketball career."

"I can't be gone that long, Doc. I *won't* be gone that long." The anger continued to pulse through me. I refused to believe her, I wouldn't accept what she was telling me. This wasn't happening to me; it felt like a nightmare that I couldn't escape. "There's got to be another way."

My father placed his hand on the doctor's shoulder. "Ma'am, can we have a moment with our son?"

"Sure, Mr. Ellis, take all the time you need." She turned to me, her eyes pleading with me to try and calm down. "I'll have the nurses to check in on you in a little while."

I looked over at my little brother, watching the tears streaming down his face. I turned away from him as fast as I could; I forgot he was in the room. He looked up to me, and I felt like I had somehow been diminished in his eyes by even being in here like this. I felt ashamed; I'd let him down on so many levels it wasn't funny.

It was silent for a few moments before Dad spoke. The words he chose were meant to cushion the blow, and if I wasn't so emotional, I might have listened to him. "This storm will pass, Keenan. You have to trust in God that you will get through this and come out of it stronger. You will be a better man, a better player for it."

I had anger in my heart because I felt I did not deserve this. I glared at Dad, letting the tears flow. I didn't know what else to do, my desperation had reached critical mass. "You're bringing up God, Dad? God saw what was about to happen to me and sat back and let it go down. What did

I do to that dude to have him try to take me out? He could have killed me!"

Mom interjected. "Baby, you didn't do anything wrong, and I don't know what came over that boy to do something like that, but your father is right. We taught you that even in times of strife, God will help you see through the despair and show you the light."

"We'll get through this together, son." Dad leaned in, grabbing my hand in an attempt to console me. "This might be a lesson for you to learn from Him."

Those last few words were my breaking point. A lesson? What possible lesson could I have learned from this? If anything, it was a quick clinic on how to not be the nice guy in a situation. I should have buried Leggett the first chance I got before he could get me. If I'd done my job, they would have had no choice but to take him off me and put someone else on me to try and stop me.

"I don't want to learn any lessons, Dad!" I didn't care what I said anymore. I was so incensed, I saw red. "I refuse to believe that this was meant to happen to me. For what? What lesson am I supposed to learn? That I'm not meant to use my God-given talent to take care of my family?"

"We have been okay before you got to this point, Kee, and we'll be fine after, too," Mom explained, her calming voice resonating in my ears. "I know you're angry, but let it pass."

"I need to be alone right now," I resigned. I was exhausted from everything. My emotions were all over the place, and I couldn't calm down from the darkness in my heart. "I can't deal with this, not yet. I just need to sleep."

"We'll leave you be, son," Mom kissed my forehead before they left. "We'll check on you in the morning."

Tyler grabbed my hand, hugging me as gently as he could to keep from causing any pain in my shoulder. When he lifted from me, I saw a nervous smile on his face. I realized that he really didn't know how to handle me in that moment. We were always close; he was my shadow. I wanted to explain to him why I felt the way I felt, but the words were not there for me.

Before he left me, I tapped my fist over my heart four times. He nodded and did the same; it was the silent gesture between us when we were growing up, an unspoken understanding that we would get the chance to talk when things calmed down. I was the cooler head under normal circumstances. Tyler was always the more high-strung between us, so, watching me lose my composure was a complete reversal of fortune for the both of us.

He mouthed the words, "I'll holla later," before they closed the door, leaving me alone in the room with my thoughts, which became more troubling by the moment.

The rhetorical questions to God flowed faster than a waterfall. Why had He punished me? What did I do to displease Him? Did He send Javon to rip my dreams away?

The tears wouldn't stop falling. I wanted this nightmare to end. I couldn't live without playing basketball. It was as necessary to me as breathing.

I wanted to show them all. I would get back quicker than any of them thought I would. I was not done, not by a long shot. I'd show the basketball world how I got down. I didn't come this far to be shut down by some fluke incident. I was stronger than that.

While I lay there, thinking I had things figured out, the flip side of the coin presented itself: my game would undergo a drastic change. My vertical jump would be cut in half. I would have to develop a mid-range game to compensate for not being able to rise in the paint. All of the holes in my game that I could cover up with my athletic ability would be exposed in ways I hadn't imagined. My game was always played above the rim, what was I supposed to do now?

Insecurities presented themselves with the force of a wrecking ball. Would I be welcome back to the team after I went through rehab? I'd seen this story happen to other players, and college athletics was still a business. They would have to replace me, even if I could come back at full strength. But that would take a year. Would Coach Bolden even want me then?

Nah, I couldn't go out like that, but what choice did I have?

In a fit of rage, I took one of the vases and threw it against the wall. The porcelain shattered into hundreds of small pieces, sprayed out against the impacted area. I yelled out into the darkness the moment I heard the crash. "I want my life back! This isn't how it's supposed to end!"

Sleep took me quick once I got everything off my chest. It was quiet…the type of quiet where you questioned whether you were in a bad horror movie, waiting for the killer to take you out. The only noise I heard was the drip of the painkillers to keep me from really losing my mind. I didn't have the energy to call Ariel back to recap everything, so I decided I would call her in the morning, when I had the capacity to go through this emotional roller coaster all over again.

In the distance, I heard a voice, but I didn't remember anyone entering my hospital room. I tried to wake up to see who it was, but I felt a hand ease me back into bed. Then, I heard the words that would change me forever.

How badly do you want to prove them all wrong?

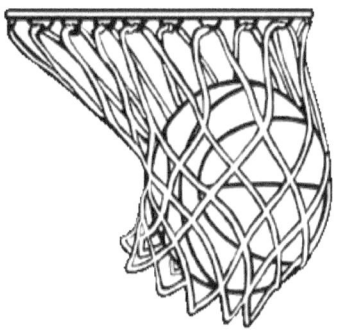

CHAPTER TWO – SOPHOMORE YEAR

"I am the greatest!"

I felt like I was on top of the world.

About an hour ago we'd beaten the fifth-ranked team in the country, Lawson State, on our home floor and on national television.

But that wasn't why I was acting a fool, though.

I exploded for a career-high forty-five points in my first game as a starter for the legendary Tempest State Crimson Wave basketball team.

I walked into one of the house parties off campus like I owned the place. I gave the fellas pound, I kissed the girls that wanted me to, and some that I did kiss didn't want me to, but they didn't want to say anything.

I…was…the…man! You couldn't tell me nothing!

That wasn't to say the rest of the team didn't do what

they needed to do to get me open and all, but it felt like I was shooting the ball into the ocean tonight. Coach Bolden even told the rest of the team to let me run wild; there was nothing anyone could do to stop me.

Some of the seniors weren't too thrilled about those orders, but all that mattered was winning. It didn't matter to me, but then again, I was on the receiving end of those orders.

"Dude, you might wanna calm all that down, you know?" Javi sounded off in my ear, trying to be all diplomatic. "You already pissed off half the squad with that mess you said to the sideline reporter for ESPN."

Rome piped up after Javi, feeling like he needed to get his words in. "I don't know why you decided to get the big head about starting, but you might wanna calm that noise before Coach changes his mind."

I balked at the both of them when I heard the suggestion. "Are you kidding me? After dropping forty-five tonight, come on, son!"

I didn't care much at all when it came to what anyone thought about what I was doing. I was on my hoops swag, and it was only a matter of time before I would be all over *SportsCenter.* I guess, in hindsight, they might have had a bit of a point, though.

When I got into the locker room, all eyes were on me, but not because I'd single-handedly put the team on the map again. I didn't pay it any mind because I was on a high, and sour faces were not on the menu. I mean, that was why Coach recruited me, Rome, and Javi to begin with. The luster on the program was beginning to dull and he needed some ballers to shake things up.

One of the juniors on the squad, Evan Tripp, had been hating on me ever since I got on campus. I didn't worry too much about him because he didn't have the talent I had or the championship pedigree, either.

I was the one coming off three straight high school state titles, *not* him.

I was the one who was the two-time player of the year in the state of Georgia, *not* him.

I was the one who had the women on campus checking for me from the minute I stepped on campus, *not* him.

It's not my fault that this dude was losing his spot to me after we got booted out of the first round of the NCAA tournament last year, it was his, and the whole team knew it.

Evan started in on me the minute I got to my locker, trying to get in my face. "You think you're real slick, don't you, white boy? You're lucky you even rolled like you did tonight, with that bullshit jumper of yours."

"Look, Evan, let me break it down for you." I stayed in my chair, never once bothering to look up to meet his hateful gaze. "Never mind the 'white boy' comment, especially when I can trace my family line back to the motherland quicker than you can. If you were handling business like you were supposed to, I wouldn't be coming in to take your minutes, got it?"

The answer to my candor was a swift right that was intended for my jaw, if it weren't for Javi's arm locking up with Evan's. Evan tried to move his arm, not realizing how strong the big man was. He glared up at him, his scowl making his face look almost contorted.

"I see now, someone's gonna have to teach your disrespectful ass some manners sooner or later," Evan remarked as he snatched his arm away from Javi. "You might wanna get your boy some act-right. I don't think he understands how things are supposed to roll around here."

Javi stood there, a look of confusion all over his face. "You seem to think I stopped you from hitting my boy for his sake. You might want to rethink that strategy, especially after you just pissed him off with that insult, bro."

Evan returned his gaze in my direction, but by then I'd already been on my feet for a couple of seconds. I had him by several inches and at least twenty pounds, and he knew better than to try me. What he seemed to forget about was the small skirmish with the football players during their season when I laid out one of their linebackers where he stood because he got pissed about his girl trying to holla at me.

Why was it always the short, bulldog looking dudes that wanna prove they ain't no punk? It was almost unfair that night; he was shorter than me, but he thought he had the advantage because he had bulk and supposed technique to take me down. Man, please!

I guess I had to teach Evan a lesson, too. I was about to give him the business, too, until Coach Bolden popped up and felt the ice in the room. He gave us both a look and shook his head. I knew it would be one of those lectures about making sure the team was first and whatever, but that wasn't on my mind, and I knew Evan wasn't feeling it from the way he kept flexing his fists.

Later for him, I had sexier fish to fry.

I sat back down at my locker, noticing an envelope with my name on it. It was thick, and it felt like a lot of paper was in it. I wasn't sure whether I wanted to open it or not, but my curiosity won out. I opened the envelope and found ten one-hundred-dollar bills inside and a note inside.

Keep up the good work. A friend of the program.

A friend of the program? What was that about?

Rome tapped me on the shoulder and pointed me in the direction of a trio of sexy Deltas that wanted our undivided attention, shaking me out of my thoughts. "Look, Kee, if you can dial that ego down for a few hours, maybe we can enjoy the evening? I mean, we can work that mess out with Evan and the rest of them nuts at practice tomorrow, you feel me?"

"Rome's got a point, and I need to blow off some of this energy before I hit the sheets," Javi concurred, motioning for one of the girls to head in his direction. "If I'm lucky, that one right there will be hitting the sheets with me."

The other two walked over, and there was an instant connection between Rome and one of them. She was pretty, I had to give her that, but it was her body that spoke with purpose before she ever said hello. She was in his personal space in seconds, leaving no doubt she was staking her claim from the jump.

Rome licked his lips before speaking, giving me the silent signal between us that he was gonna see about her. "So, what's your name, sexy? They call me Rome."

"Well, since they call you Rome, maybe I might want to call you something else." She kept her eyes engaged with his. If I didn't know any better, she was acting like either me or her soror existed. "My name is Angela."

I coughed for a minute to interrupt this groove between them. I wasn't feeling being ignored like I was some second-rate afterthought. I looked at Angela's soror and I kissed the back of her palm. "I'm sorry. I guess we need to forgive our friends. My name is Keenan, and you are?"

"Yours, if you want me. Damn, you're sexy for a white boy," she quipped without batting an eyelash. Rome and Angela whipped around toward her with looks that said they couldn't believe she was being so bold. "Oh, forgive me, my name is Kira."

If she wasn't as sexy as she was, I would have dismissed her with that "white boy" comment. I realized my skin tone threw people off, but it wasn't like I possessed any European features. Outside of my grey eyes, everything else pointed to the Motherland. I shook it off in favor of wanting to enjoy the rest of my evening. If she played her cards right and shut off that mouth, she could get it.

"Well, Kira, would you like to head somewhere quieter so we can chat and get to know each other?" I wasn't about to be deterred by her trying to take the lead on this dance. I did the driving, and I didn't compromise on that, ever.

On the other hand, I wasn't in it for the long haul; I only needed twenty minutes. "Besides, it sounds like these two might already have their own ideas."

"Sounds good to me," she replied as she cut her eyes at Angela. "Besides, Angela's handled one of her duties tonight anyway. I can cut her loose so she can have some fun."

We never got to chat.

Well, chatting wasn't on the agenda. Besides, it's kinda hard to do that when you have your tongue down someone's throat. Other appendages were in the midst of merging thanks to Kira going commando under the skirt she wore to the party. Yeah, I like them when they're easy access like that.

We were outside on the hood of her car going at it under a pale full moon. I hadn't even thought about pulling the condom out of my pocket because she pulled me in close and started for my zipper before I could think to protest.

"I wanna feel you right now."

"Slow down, let me get the raincoat."

"Don't worry about it, sexy, I'm on the pill."

"Why should I believe that?"

"Does this feel like I care if you slip inside me without a raincoat or not?"

Like a dummy I let my body do the talking. I was consumed in seconds, and her screams could have awakened the dead as they pierced the night air. I saw a few people getting a glimpse of what was going down, and I started to slow up because I didn't want campus security trying to catch something to tell the news channels.

"Come on, baby, I want them to watch, it turns me on."

"Kira—"

"Come on, daddy, take it, we don't have all night."

I threw more caution to the wind as I slipped in and out of her, steadying my rhythm so when the moment arrived I could pull out without incident.

Kira had other plans.

She kissed me deep and wrapped her arms around the small of my back, giving me no room to do much of anything but slam into her. I knew it would be a matter of moments before my body would tighten up and the eruption would be heavy. I tried to pull away, but she wouldn't let go.

"Give it to me, don't waste it."

"Kira, let me go, I'm about to—"

"Give … it … to … me!"

I let off in her with such force that I began to see colors. She bit my neck as the wave began to take her under, choosing that moment to try and stifle her screams. I don't know why she chose when she chose, it wasn't like folks couldn't hear her dramatic screams the whole time? I pulled out and attempted to clean myself off, but she licked me clean, leaning me against the side of the car while she took care of business.

"I think I'll keep you," she proudly boasted. "Especially

after you did your thing in the game tonight, who wouldn't want you as a play toy?"

Play toy? Who said I wanted to be kept around to begin with?

Nah, she got the game twisted.

I thought about reading her the riot act, but I thought better of it; she was a good piece to showcase around campus. Sure, she could brag that she had me, but she was only boosting my reputation. After all, I was only a sophomore.

"Yeah, I think I wouldn't mind having you around when I need to let off some tension," I casually mentioned, waiting for her to catch the hint that I wasn't some pimple-faced freshman dying to have his balls emptied. "Maybe your home girls might be interested in helping your boy with some tutoring, y'know?"

She must have been in some post-orgasmic bliss or something; she missed the diss I hurled in her direction. "Yeah, I think I can hook one of my girls up with you. Mia is a big fan of yours, too."

I hated basic females. They always mucked up a good thing.

We finally got dressed, and the first thing I saw as we made our way back to the party was a couple of campus officers. I froze for a moment, knowing full well we were caught. The trick didn't bother to at least work her fingers through her hair to make it look like she hadn't been run through by a runaway freight train.

"Good game tonight, Ellis," one of the officers

27

commented. "If you keep that up we might win another title."

They gave a curious a look at Kira, and I prepared for the worst. They had to know we had finished with a heated merger. There was no denying it. I was waiting for one of them to say something about it; we were young, wild, and black on a predominantly white campus. There was no way they wouldn't take us in for lewd behavior on campus.

The lead officer winked at me like I was supposed to be in on some sort of inside joke between us. "Now, you make sure you get this lovely young lady home, all right? It's after midnight, and gentlemen should make sure the women are protected on campus. Have a good night."

They walked off in the direction of another group of women to give the same speech, I would imagine, but it wasn't my concern at that point. We'd gotten away with near murder, and the officers didn't bat an eyelash. If I'd known any better, they might have gotten a peek themselves while Kira was screaming her head off.

I didn't care, though. If this was the way I was going to be handled when situations like this came up, I would have balled out during my freshman year instead of trying to be a team player. I could get used to this star treatment if this kept up, and I had every intention of taking full advantage of the benefits that came with being the man on campus.

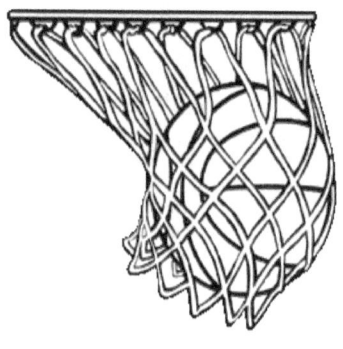

CHAPTER THREE

"Yo, give me the ball, I got this fool."

"You might want to rethink that statement, bruh."

"Keep your mouth shut and D up. I'm getting tired of hearing you talk."

"Then you know how to shut me up, right? All you gotta do is score on me, but we both know that's not gonna happen."

"You gaming for an elbow to the jaw, Kee. Keep talking, I'm gonna make you famous."

We were running some three-on-three before practice started a few days later, and Evan insisted on trying to make me look silly on an isolation play while the other four guys looked on. I ran with Javi and Rome, and Evan ran with a couple of seniors on the team, Jarmon Pace, our starting small forward, and Tony Dekes, our starting point guard. Everyone else stayed on the sidelines, enjoying the show before we went to work.

He called himself trying to use Jarmon to screen me off on a pick-and-roll and try to catch me sleeping on the switch underneath so he could use me to try and make a play on either him or Jarmon. I guess he wanted to put me in a bad spot so that either way I turned, I would get burned.

Bad career move…

I slipped over the top of Jarmon's screen and picked Evan's pocket off the bounce before he could try to go into the paint. I didn't worry about losing the point, even if he could get by me; I knew Javi would have my back to erase the shot.

I couldn't wipe the smirk off my face as I waited for him to realize I had him and he needed to come see about me at the top of the key. "Did you really think that weak-ass pick-and-pop was gonna trip me up?"

Evan's irritation rose to the surface. He glowered at me, urging me to stick to the game. "Shut up and ball!"

Okay, if he insisted…

I dribbled left, leaning Evan in that direction before I stopped on a dime and kicked back for a step-back three-pointer.

"Bank is open!" I yelled as the ball kissed the backboard before the net caressed its leathery skin. "Game!"

Evan heard the rest of the team barking and yelling, and his first motion was in my direction to get in my face again.

I stood my ground, waiting to see if he would try to invade my personal space, daring him to find out what would happen if he decided to put his hands on me. I had height and length on my side, but I didn't want to take him seriously. After all, he was my teammate, but this act was starting to get old.

"You scored big in one game, big deal!" Evan yelled as Tony tried to get between us. "Where was that so-called game at last year when we needed it, huh?"

"Wow, you needed me, is that how you wanna play that, Evan?" I stood pat, watching Tony as he tried to keep Evan at bay. "Nah, Tony, let him go, I guess we need to get this out in the open before Coach gets in here."

Javi and Rome inched closer in my direction as Tony stepped out of Evan's way. I waved them off, letting them know to stick close, but not to turn this into an "us against them" situation.

Evan decided to turn up the heat on his argument. "Look, don't get it twisted, we didn't need you or your boys, partner. We were getting it in fine without you."

I looked at Rome and Javi, and they returned the same incredulous look that I had for him. I tried not to sound like I was insulting his intelligence, but he was bordering on the delusional. "You sure you wanna roll that stance, man? Correct me if I'm wrong, but if I remember correctly, three years ago was a first-round blowout in the tournament, and before we got here last year, y'all had a losing record that put Coach out there to get the three of us."

"Man, do you really think I came off the turnip truck or

something?" His anger was palpable now. He sized me up, thinking he might have something on me that he could exploit. "You and me? There's no comparison. I'm the one who has the ring, you don't. You think you're some golden child or some shit because you got the media drooling all over you, you pretty-ass wannabe. You got lucky last night, and I'll prove it. Give me the ball."

I looked at Tony and Jarmon and gestured to them that they might want to get their friend before it was too late. They shrugged in response; they'd gone down this road before, and it was a matter of whether I was going to handle business or let him keep talking.

Oh well, if he had to go to school, he had to go to school.

"Handle your business, Kee." Javi stated. "I'm starting to get tired of his negativity."

"Yeah, gon' break him down so we can get back to it," Rome agreed as they both walked off the floor and sat on the bench. "If this is the only way we'll get any peace this season, so be it."

I put my hands up in resignation; I really didn't want to roll like that, but he left me no choice. I shot a look at him, realizing that he thought I was soft or something due to my fairer skin. "It's your funeral."

I let Evan take the ball at the top of the key, and when I got up on him, he swept his elbow before he started his dribble, catching me across my jaw. I lifted up to check for blood as Evan kept going to the basket for an easy layup.

Rome was the first on his feet. "Is that the only way you

can get loose, bruh? Seriously?"

I waved Rome off. "Nah, it's cool, Rome, this is a man's game, right?"

I winked at him, and Rome caught the hint. "Yeah, this is a man's game. Blacktop rules sound good to me. Let's see how you get down, Kee."

Since it was the usual "make 'em, take 'em," I had to stay on defense. He tried that same move, only this time I saw where the ball would end up and swiped it a few seconds later. I rested the ball between my hip and my elbow, staring him down as I took my free hand to gesture that he needed to get on defense. He had the nerve to try to get up on me while on D, trying to poke in my ribcage to throw me off my rhythm.

I pulled the same sweep move on him, drawing blood the moment my elbow connected. Evan yelled out in pain, holding his jaw to ensure his teeth were still in his mouth. Instead of driving past him, I waited for him to recover.

He looked like he wanted to take me outside the gym and get dirty. I was fine with that idea, too; the look he saw in my eyes told him that if he wanted to go, he'd better be prepared to play past the whistle. Only, there would be no whistles blown.

I kept my dribble as I waited for him to make sure he was good. "Now, we're even."

I started on the bounce and saw he was giving me the paint, like he wanted to measure me for the block if I got past him. I took the bait; I had something for him.

I backed him down in the paint, intent on grinding him

down for an easy shot. I could have smoked him from the perimeter, but I wanted to teach him a lesson. I had the height advantage, and I guess he was wondering what I was up to since I didn't settle for the jumper. I got him on the low block before I made my move.

I hooked him on the spin move and went baseline when he tried to measure me for the weak-side block. I already saw that coming, so I pulled a "Dream Shake," compliments of Hakeem Olajuwon from back in the day. I broke his ankles with the series of moves, leaving him on the floor clutching his lower leg as I rose for the dunk.

The whole team went into a frenzy by the time I dropped from the rim. I didn't bother to extend my hand to help Evan up. He was already on his feet and glaring at the sideline.

"What was that you were saying? Oh yeah, that's right, the golden child got lucky last night!" I shouted, hearing the echo of my voice bounce around the gym. "I guess you were lucky you really didn't break your ankles, because then you might actually need me, right?"

"All right, you two, that's enough." Coach Bolden was standing in the corner, to our collective surprise. "You two might want to save some of that for the next game on Thursday night, or are you too busy trying to figure out how to second-guess me again, Evan?"

"Coach, come on, I was just giving Keenan a hard time." Evan tried to spin the situation to make himself look good. "It's not my fault your favorite child is feeling himself, I had to take him to school a little bit."

"Not from where I was standing, especially considering I watched the one-on-one you two just had." Coach Bolden grinned. "It looks like my 'golden child', as you put it, just made up my mind for me on whom to start the next game at shooting guard."

Evan seethed. "I ain't got time for this. If you think he's better for the squad that I am then let's find out. I'm putting in my transfer papers and go ball somewhere else."

The gym got quiet. The standoff between coach and player had settled itself at half-court, and no one wanted to get in the middle of it.

Now, it wasn't like I didn't do my homework on Evan before I got to Tempest. He was the top scorer on some horrible teams that saw a few players jump early to the NBA, and Coach couldn't replace the talent quickly enough. He was a freshman when they won the national title, but he was a backup at the time, only playing in the title game because the regular starter broke his wrist and couldn't go that night. I guess getting that ring had gotten to his head.

Coach Bolden didn't flinch. "Well, if that's the way you feel about it, I guess you gotta do what you gotta do, right?"

Evan's eyes widened after hearing Coach say what was on his mind. I remembered this speech when he was recruiting me. *No one was above the team, regardless of how good they are.*

Realizing his bluff had been called, Evan tried to scramble to save face. "You know I was just playing,

Coach. I'm good with whatever helps the team win."

I sat back and watched. It wasn't my fight.

"I'm glad you said that, because I was serious about Keenan starting next game," Coach deadpanned. "We'll shake things up a little bit; let's face it, you've been in a slump. You'll back up Tony and Kee so I can keep your minutes and keep my starters fresh, unless you have any objections?"

Evan caught the rhetoric in Coach Bolden's voice. "No, sir, whatever helps the team win."

"Good, I'm glad we could come to an agreement." Coach Bolden closed the conversation before turning his attention to the rest of us. "All right, now that you've had your fun, it's time to go to work."

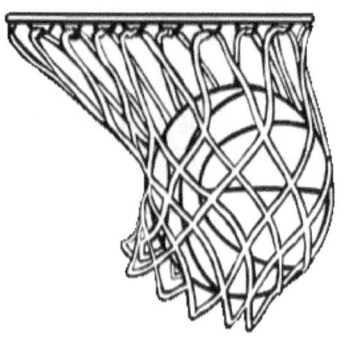

CHAPTER FOUR

"What the hell do you want, Ellis?"

I wasn't sure what I wanted with Evan after practice. I think the standoff with Coach Bolden had me feeling a bit sorry for the bum. Yeah, he put himself in that position, but he almost talked himself off the team, which would have been killer for the press that I should be getting.

I found him sitting on the stairs by the exit of the practice gym, so I took the chance, since we were alone, to try and figure out the best way we could co-exist. If that was even feasible.

"Yo, look, Evan, we need to stick together if we're going to get through this season in one piece. I don't like you, and I'm pretty sure you don't like me, and that's cool, we don't have to like each other off the court."

"Yeah, you're right, I don't like you, on or off the

court." Evan stood from the stairs, looking like he was ready to fight. His eyes were fiery, like he really had nothing to lose by telling me what he really thought about me. "I don't know what Coach sees in you, but sophomores don't start over upper-classmen. They don't. Losing my spot to you? I'd rather quit the team and transfer than deal with that. I'm the one who helped put Tempest State on the map. You haven't done a damn thing since you stepped on campus but run your mouth about how good you are."

"So, you don't like me because of something out of our control? What kind of BS is that?" I wanted to throat-punch him in that moment. My game was better than his, I didn't care at all about the system. "If you can't rock with the fact that I'm better than you right now and this is what might get you another ring, then you're dumber than I thought."

"Look, pretty boy, ain't nobody trying to hear this rah-rah you're spitting in my ear, all right?" Evan shook his head, stepping back from me to give me a head-to-toe onceover. "I can live with the fact that you might be better than me, if it wasn't for the arrogance you have on you. You're gonna fall soon, and I'm gonna be there when you do."

"You got one more time to call me 'pretty boy' or 'golden child' or anything else before I show you how gutter I can get." Who the hell did this dude think he was? He needed to be reminded of where I came from, and it wasn't some private school, fairy-tale nonsense that he was thinking about.

I grabbed him by the shirt and slammed him against the wall, watching his head bounce against the brick a couple of times before he was able to focus and realize I was over him, primed to prove my point. "Now, I'm gonna explain how this will go down: you're gonna flow with the program so we can get this title, and if you don't wanna flow with the program, then quit. You sounded like a pussy when you threatened to transfer, anyway, so maybe that's what you needed to do in the first place."

Evan tried to shake from my grip, his eyes widening when he realized he couldn't go anywhere. He looked in my eyes, trying to stall as much as he could, hoping someone would show up so I would let him go. In a last-ditch effort to sound like he still had a backbone, he tried to muscle up against my hold on him. "Oh, so you think this is how this is supposed to go down, huh? Yeah, you got me fucked up, bro."

That was the exact response I wanted from him. I took my hand and grabbed hold of his throat, ignoring his immediate reflex to scratch and pry it away. At that point, I saw red, my anger rising by the second. I saw Evan's eyes gloss over a bit, and a slick smile spread across my face. I was about to put the last fear of God in him when I heard a voice out of the blue, sounding like he was cheering me on.

That's it, teach him a lesson. You're the man, he's gonna see that soon enough. He's gonna fear you, it's the only way he's gonna respect you. He's gonna punk you until you show him, Keenan. Come on, bruh; get yours.

I almost freaked out, trying to figure out where the voice came from. In the midst of my confusion, I let Evan go, watching him fall to the floor, trying to gasp for the air I was trying to deprive him of. He crawled away from me, his eyes showing the fear that the voice in my head spoke about. The confusion he saw in my eyes was met with the trepidation in his. We'd hit a crossroads, that moment when the first one who didn't blink would have the upper hand.

Evan blinked. "Are you crazy or something? I should report your ass to campus security for assault!"

"But you won't, and you know the reason why, too." I took a step toward him, causing him to flinch in reaction. The smile crept across my face again, this time looking more sinister than I did when my hand was around his throat. "You've been tormenting me for the past year, and I've got witnesses who can attest to that. All I have to do is say I defended myself, and it's a wrap. Now, you were saying about filing charges?"

Evan cursed under his breath, picking himself from the ground, standing in front of me again, only this time, he wasn't as aggressive in his stance as he was twenty minutes ago. "All right, Kee, you got it, bro. I'll flow with the program … but when you slip up—and you will—I'm taking my spot back. And this time, you won't get the chance to get back into the starting lineup until I graduate."

I walked away from him, heading up the walkway back to the dorms, shaking my head over his insistence on being defiant, even when he knew I would have folded him up like a picnic chair for even thinking whatever he was thinking.

My answer was not meant for his ears, but I meant every word of it. *You'll take my spot over my dead body. Nothing and no one will get in my way.*

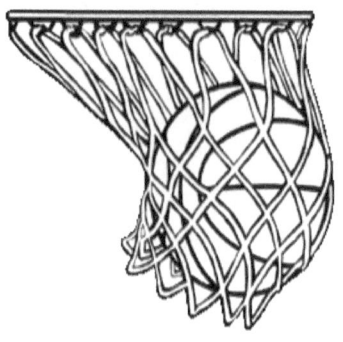

CHAPTER FIVE

"Well, hello there, how are you doing?"

"I'm doing okay, Keenan, how are you?"

"I'm better now that I've gotten your attention."

"You may have gotten my attention, but that doesn't mean you have the ability to keep it, Mr. "Future Lottery Pick." Don't think I haven't checked you out."

"Aww, come on, what could you have possibly learned that would have you acting so cold?"

I did my best to keep the attention of one of the girls on the cheerleading squad, but she was making it hard as hell to stay in her good graces. Ariel Starks was the type of young woman who had the ability to make a man follow the straight and narrow path with no regrets whatsoever. She'd had my attention ever since I'd stepped on campus, but she never gave me the time of day—until today.

"I heard about what you did to Kira Parsons after the game the other night." Ariel blushed as she mentioned it. "Word around campus is that she's claiming you for herself."

"She can't claim what was never given away," I replied. I should have known to treat that like a smash-and-grab. "So, is that the reason why you aren't vibing with me? I'm supposedly off limits?"

"No, it's not the only reason, but you're stretched too thin, Keenan. Even if I wanted you, you probably wouldn't be able to give up your harem to be with me."

"Now, that's unfair. How would I know if I don't have the opportunity in front of me?" I began to enjoy the banter between us, but there was no way I was going to let her slip from me this time around. "Have lunch with me, and you'll see I'm not as bad as the campus rumors would have you believe. Please?"

Her eyes narrowed, regarding my request for a few minutes. "I guess lunch won't be so bad. If it will get you to calm down your stalking, I can get with that."

Walking through the Quad was interesting, to say the least. All eyes were on us, but I couldn't figure out why that was the case. It wasn't like I cared all that much, I was pleased with myself that I could get her to even agree to lunch with me.

She must have noticed the stares, too. She was grinning as different women frowned at her while I smirked at the men gawking at her and scoffing at who she was with. Talk about an ego boost? Things couldn't have gotten any more entertaining, that was for certain.

"If I didn't know any better, I would say you're just as popular as I am," I remarked as we made it off campus to one of the eateries I'd had in mind. It was a quiet mom-and-pop locale where the sandwiches were to die for and the cheesecake was heaven. "But I guess when you're dealing with someone as beautiful as you are, you have to deal with their fan club, huh?"

She blushed. "That was a smooth quip, Keenan. Maybe I might have my own fan club. After all, I am a Temp-State cheerleader."

"You do look damn good in that uniform, for real." Flashbacks of her during the last blowout win were enough to cause my body to betray me. "I guess I should definitely try to impress enough to get a second engagement."

"Don't try to impress, just be you, and I think you might be surprised."

I tried to calm my nerves. As much confidence as I had on the court and in front of the cameras, Ariel had me shook. There was something about her that I couldn't put my finger on, but it was more than a conquest this time around.

We found a spot near the window, getting a view of the street and the activity going on outside of the restaurant. I couldn't stop staring at her, looking like a lovesick puppy. It wasn't a good look for me, but she had me so entranced, it wasn't out of the realm of possibility that I would do anything she'd asked of me. I shook my head at how much power I'd given to her and we'd only sat down for five full minutes.

As the waitress took our orders, I pondered over how to approach the conversation. I didn't want to come on too strong, since she'd already been predisposed to my supposed reputation on campus. I had no idea how to begin, so I blurted out the first thing that came to mind.

"So, what are you planning to do once you graduate? What's your major?" I couldn't think of anything else to ask, so I went with the cliché icebreakers. The waitress had managed to come back with our orders, so I waited for her to examine and make sure everything was to her liking before she considered my questions.

"I haven't decided what I want to do with the rest of my life yet," she replied as she took a bite of her sandwich. "I'm only a sophomore, so I have another year to try and figure it all out. My major is in International Commerce, so what I had in mind was something more global in scope. The company I've been interning with has kind of opened my eyes to things on a wider scale."

"Who are you interning with?"

"You're being a bit nosey, aren't you?"

"I'm trying to get to know you a little better."

"You're only buttering me up so you can find out what time my legs open." Her eyes bore through me like a diamond-tipped drill. "It's okay, sexy, there's no need to put on pretenses. Maybe I want you to take the edge off. It's been a stressful semester."

I didn't know how to respond to that bit of candor. She'd been blowing me off at every opportunity, almost avoiding me altogether in other opportunities, and now she's ready to have me invade her intimate space on a whim?

She studied my face, a sly grin spreading across her face. "And here I thought you were down for whatever. I guess the rumors weren't true after all."

There was no point in trying to fake like I was in on her inside joke, so I didn't try to hide the confused expression on my face. "So, I guess this was your way of cutting through the BS, huh?"

When she caressed my face, the feeling of her fingers on my skin was nothing short of electric. In an instant, I had visions of the two of us snuggling on a couch in our home, enjoying the offseason, binge-watching whatever the latest show was on Netflix, indulging in a large tub of popcorn while sneaking kisses between the slow moments of the show. It felt so real that I could feel the fabric against my palms—a little too real, and scarier than anything I'd imagined.

I broke from her touch, doing my best to try to recover from the visions in my head. Ariel raised an eyebrow as I tried to avoid obvious questions about what went through my mind and why I wasn't as jovial as I was before she touched me. In my mind, I didn't deserve the images I saw. I mean, considering how I treated women as nothing more than a Las Vegas buffet, did I really deserve a happy ending?

"Keenan, what's wrong? Your whole energy just shifted." Ariel tried to pull my face to meet her gaze, but I resisted, unable to bring myself to look into her eyes without feeling the weight of the guilt on my shoulders. "Come on, you can tell me."

She placed her hand on top of mine, and in the next moment, all those doubts and dread I felt washed away. I couldn't understand it, it didn't make sense over how her touch could have me run the gamut of emotions without so much as a word being spoken. I wasn't sure if I was in over my head or not, but something deep down told me I had to have her in my life, and I didn't care in what capacity. I wanted her, but my public persona was in direct conflict with my truest feelings.

"Do you believe in love at first sight?"

"I believe in lust at first sight. Love isn't lightning in a bottle."

"Well, I believe in it. I also believe that when I meet a woman, I know exactly how she will fit in my life within seconds of conversation."

"And how do I 'fit' in your life?"

"I need you in my life. I would love for you to be my girlfriend, but I don't want to scare you by saying that right now."

"You'd be surprised at what doesn't scare me, pretty boy." Her smile disarmed me; I couldn't protect myself anymore. I wasn't accustomed to being in this position, and maybe that might have been the reason why I was so scared. "I don't scare easily, so unless you plan on telling me you're some sort of serial killer on the low, I think I'll be okay with you telling me you think I would fit in your world as your girlfriend."

"So, will you be my girlfriend?" I wasn't sure why the words came out like they did, but I didn't regret them. I wasn't even sure if I meant them; I still had other women in my life who were there for other purposes. But I couldn't see my life without Ariel in it.

"I'm not saying no, but I need time to figure out how you fit in my life, Keenan." Ariel's demeanor was a bit standoffish, but I still felt the connection between us. If anything, it felt like she was pulling me in deeper. "My life is a bit complicated, and I'm not yet sure I'm ready to let you all the way in, but there's something about you that tells me I will be able to trust you when it's time to tell you."

I didn't take that answer as a complete rejection, but at the same time, I realized I was going to have to compete for her attention. When dealing with someone as stunning as she was, there was going to be a fan club to deal with, too, and they all wanted a shot at being the president and #1 fan. I could live with that for now. If anything, it would give me the opportunity to work out my own issues so that if and when she decided that I was ready to be a part of her world, that I would be ready for all that came with it.

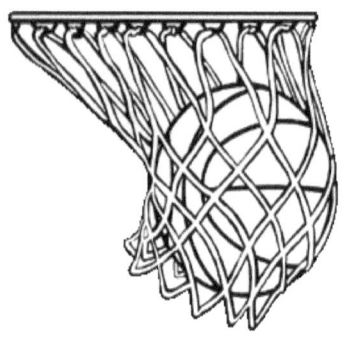

CHAPTER SIX

"So, what's on the agenda for the weekend, bro?"

"I'm about to see what's popping with the young lady I was with while you were smashing her soror, Kee."

"Man, this is the first weekend in the season where we don't have a game, and you wanna get all domesticated? What's up with that?"

"Not everyone has the ability to pull who they want, when they want, bro. There's nothing wrong with trying to see about the one who has your attention. It ain't my fault that you got too many to run through to figure that out."

I didn't know whether I wanted to start hating on this new woman taking up my best friend's time already. It was taking the air out of my ability to use my primary wingman to hit the campus, and it was only a matter of time before I would begin to resent her for it. I could have rocked with

Javi, but he took the weekend to head home for a quick turnaround visit to see his family. Either way, I felt like he could see her during the week; hell, I would even dip out the room and take Javi with me so they could Netflix and Chill or something.

I did take a slight offense to the inference that I was some type of manwhore or something, though. "I don't have a harem or a rolodex of soft legs to scroll through, bro. I'm not stretched out like that."

"So, you gonna play like you ain't smashed at least two this past week, including one of the cheerleaders after that road game we had at Tennessee?" The look on his face almost had me wondering if he had been keeping my score card for me. "Or do I need to remind you of the fabulous five that you rotate on campus, all sworn to secrecy in terms of who isn't on the roster?"

"Okay, I get it. I guess I need to slow down a bit before something comes back to bite me, huh?"

"Look, Kee, I know this new-found celebrity on campus and in the media has you gassed up and all, but I'm worried about you." He stopped putting his outfit together to face me. "Lincoln once said, 'Nearly all men can stand adversity, but if you want to test a man's character, give him power.' I have a feeling you're being tested with this next level exposure and power. Be careful how you handle it."

What he said should have stopped me in my tracks. His words were profound to a point, but I didn't think they were meant for me. I could handle the power I had when I was in high school and I had the whole city of Atlanta in the palm of my hand. For him to suggest that I couldn't handle being on the national stage was ludicrous.

"Look, Rome, I get it, there's this big brother vibe you got going when it comes to the two of us." I dropped my hand on his shoulder, staring into his eyes for a few seconds. The smile on my face was meant to assuage his concerns, but in hindsight, I didn't think it did. "And for the record, there might be someone who might make all the others fade to black."

Rome raised an eyebrow, trying to figure out if I was bluffing or not. "Word, Kee? You're serious? I might need to see who this super woman is. I don't know if you're trying to finesse me or what."

"I'm not trying to finesse you, bro. I had lunch with her the other day, but she's not sure if she's wanting to see about me yet, though."

"That's because you got too much going on," Rome replied. "You need to clear out the clutter in order for a woman to feel like she ain't got no other feminine energy to deal with. You got all sorts of feminine energy around you, that's probably why she ain't seeing about you yet."

"When did you get all relationship guru? You and Angela ain't even rocking that tight yet, and here you are giving me advice like you been married for years."

"I know what I've seen, Kee. I'm the youngest of five kids, bro. All of them are married. My parents have been married for over forty years." Rome grinned as he recounted his family tree. "You learn a lot watching all of them and how they make things work."

"So, you have no desires to flow through a few before you know who the "one" is?"

"Some people are built that way, man, I'm just not one of them. I'm a serial monogamist." He laughed as he thought about that phrase. "For real, I'm comfortable in the skin I'm in, but this ain't about me. I need you to slow down, though. If you plan to have me try to keep up with everything you got going on in case one of them shows up, I'm telling you now, I don't lie very well."

"Okay, I got you, Rome. I'll clean up the mess a bit so you and Javi don't have to cover for me and feel all dirty inside." Getting the laugh out of him helped me as much as it might have helped him. I needed to focus on my game. Everything else would come with the elevated game play, so it was in my best interest to focus on that—and making sure I stayed academically eligible, too. "Oh, and enjoy your night out with Angela. I can tell she's built for you, for real."

"Thanks, bro, I got a good feeling about her. Hopefully, this mystery woman that you're into will get you righteous soon. I don't need all this random booty taking the energy you should have for the season."

There was a knock at the door, and when I went to answer it, I was surprised to see Angela standing in the doorway. I greeted her with a smile, knowing my dude would be happy to see her, but the disturbed look on her face gave me pause. "Hello, Angela, how are you? Is there something wrong, why are you looking at me like I killed your cat?"

"You didn't kill my cat, but I'm not exactly happy with you right now," she replied. She didn't move from her spot outside of the door, which had me confused even further. "Did you really have to dog my soror out like that?"

I raised my hands in mock surrender, with nary a clue of what she was talking about. "Can you clue me in on who I supposedly dogged out? If you have information that I'm not privy to, I would appreciate knowing what you know so I can at least figure out what I'm supposed to be ducking and dodging at this moment."

"Kira, dude ... does she ring a bell at all, or do you have half the campus strung out on you?" Angela's vitriol began to focus itself, but I was still in the dark over the reason why. "You got a lot of nerve leaving her like that."

"Like what? I'm serious, Angela, I don't know what you're talking about."

Rome popped up in the midst of the conversation, looking as clueless as I did as to what was going on. He took one look at Angela and went into protection mode. "Angela, what happened? What has you so upset? Who needs to bleed?"

"Your teammate, apparently." Her eyes shot through me like a knife through warm butter. "He's been doing girls dirty on campus, including my soror."

"Okay, pause, first of all, I haven't done anyone dirty."

"So, you're going to stand there and tell me you didn't head into a storm without a raincoat with Kira?"

"That was one time, and we'd been using protection

ever since." That night came back so crystal clear it wasn't funny. I let my body do the talking, and now I was about to be caught up in some legit campus gossip. I put two and two together and realized why Angela might have been so heated with me. "Wait a damn minute, what is she accusing me of?"

"She said you got her pregnant, punk." Angela's eyes narrowed, giving a look like she wanted to rip me to shreds.

"So, this is what this attitude is about? How in the bloody hell could I have gotten her pregnant when we got together a little over a week ago?" I exhaled as I ran through the conversation before the carnal interlude between us happened. "Did she tell you that she told me she was on the pill? Did she tell you I tried to rip her off me until I could get the condom on? Or did she switch the conversation to make herself look like the victim because she found out she wasn't the only one I was smashing?"

"I can't look at you right now, Keenan. I heard you were loose, but wow." Angela turned her gaze toward Rome, almost like she wanted to lump him in with me. "If I didn't already know you were a standup dude, Rome, I would have dropped you in a second. Your boy is toxic, and what he's done is not cool."

"Let me break this down for you, Angela, and hear me when I say this." I leaned against the door, shaking my head the entire time. "When this comes out and I'm not the one you need to be mad at, I'm hopeful that you will have it in your heart to tell me you're sorry. I'm a lot of things, but if I got Kira pregnant, and I knew about it—remember, you're the one who told me, not her—I would not abandon her like them punks on the street. That's not me, but if you'd stuck around long enough to get to know me, you might have found that out."

Rome stepped between us, trying his best to insert a cooler head into the equation. "Okay, how about we do this: let Kee find out for himself what's going on with Kira and take things from there. I've known him since we moved in together freshman year, and he's not that type of dude. Let him do right, either way, okay?"

To my surprise, Angela calmed down after he said those words. She still glared at me with her final words of warning. "Do right by her, or I'll bury you. I'll get the entire sorority to bury you."

"Okay, I feel you and that Greek solidarity, all right?" I scoffed at the implication that I had anything to do with Kira and any type of madness she'd gotten herself into. I was going to find out what the real was as soon as they got gone. "But since you on that Greek solidarity, you might want to make sure your girl has her story straight. It could be all bad if she doesn't."

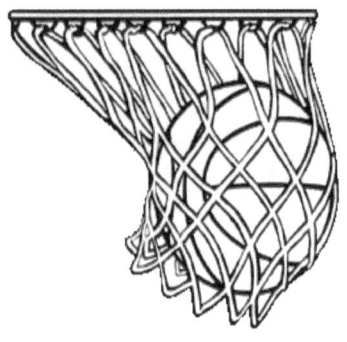

CHAPTER SEVEN

"Kee, it's true, what Angela told you. I'm pregnant."

I didn't know if I wanted to laugh or what. I looked at the phone and thought it must have been some kind of joke or some prank call from one of the Hampton radio shows or something. I mean, yeah, sure, Kira and I had been going at it like rabbits for a minute, but I made sure after that first time outside of the party that we kept it tight and protected.

I was feeling her a little bit, and had it not been for Ariel giving me time and attention as of late, I would have given the whole serial monogamy thing a try before Rome suggested it. Still, it never felt good to be played, and the fact that she was doing that and trying to play the victim card at the same time was a sad commentary.

The reason I wanted to laugh had everything to do with

the information I had at my disposal. It was damning to say the least, and it was also something that could ruin her reputation. I didn't want to be forced into revealing that information, but if she left me no choice, there would be no choice but to destroy her.

I wasn't convinced of anything she was saying, and my feigned concern showed in my voice. "So, why are you telling me? Have you checked with your doctor?"

"Oh, what, so you don't believe me?" She took the defensive too soon, which tipped me off that maybe she might have done this song and dance with somebody else. "You're man enough to smash but you're not man enough to handle the consequences of getting me pregnant?"

She must have forgotten that I was taking a psychology class this semester; this reverse psychology/guilt tripping she was doing fell on deaf ears. "On God, you act like I didn't find out about the four-on-one you did after you left me to go "study" one night, right? Or do I need to holla at that dude Karon? He was the one who called me after you were done, trying to clown me about the whole thing."

The lengthy pause over the phone let me know that I wasn't too far off the mark. Karon Blakely, the starting tailback on the football team, was all too willing to not only tell me about the little freak fest that she was a willing participant in, but even caught it on video and sent me a copy. It wasn't like I was going to marry the girl or anything, but if she was going to play hardball, she might need to know who she was playing with.

I was waiting for the explosion in 5… 4… 3… 2…

"The baby is yours, Kee!" she yelled through my earpiece. "I'll make sure you pay for the shit you've done to me!"

She disconnected the call before I could yell at her for hurting my eardrum. I leaned over to put my cellphone back on the nightstand, smiling at the delicate hands that caressed my back. Those hands felt like satin, causing goosebumps on my skin—among other stimuli.

"What was that about, Keenan?" Kira's friend, Mia, asked as she lay in bed with me. "Someone didn't sound too happy with you."

I leaned over and kissed her lips as I squeezed her hips to move her on top of me. "Someone tried to play me like I didn't have juice and ended up getting squeezed and thrown away. Now, come on and take care of business before our tutoring session begins. A brotha has to keep his eligibility, you know?"

A few days later, I sat across from the man I considered a father-figure, a man I never wanted to disappoint, but that's the position I'd placed him in. To say he was irritated didn't do his facial expressions justice. It was the first time since I was fourteen when I'd caused strife in my father's life through my boneheaded actions that I'd wished I could make it all go away.

Campus had been raging for the better part of two days as Kira's sorors were out for blood, coming at me from every possible angle. Campus radio, the paper, it was a level of dogged focus I did not account for. I was called everything but a child of God away from the public forum. It was brutal, and that was more of an understatement than anything I could ever express. It was only a matter of time before it began to affect my teammates.

I kept my mouth shut through it all, despite the intense urges to release that video to shut every hater down who came for me on social media. I was taking a beating in the court of public opinion, but I'd promised myself I would not go there. I had no choice but to weather the storm the best way I could, using practices as temporary sanctuary.

The one thing that worried me more than anything was how this would make me look in Ariel's eyes. Despite the fact that she was noncommittal with regard to whether she wanted to date me, how she saw me meant more than anything going on in the outside world. It was weird that she held so much sway, but she did. The conversation that we had was hard to go through, but she ended up believing me when she told me that she'd seen bits of the video. She did make it clear that I would have to do a lot to get back in her good graces, though.

I couldn't figure out who to be more pissed off at, me or Kira. The reality of what I was facing seemed to be out of a bad crime movie somewhere, it was so surreal. I still couldn't believe it when I read the police report: she went to campus police and filed rape charges against me!

I had heard of sore losers, but this was ridiculous. She was doing this to get back at me after she'd found out I had been intimate with Mia. I heard through the rumor mill that she had been called on her bluff about the pregnancy, so I guessed this was the next level up. The funny thing was that I was, by comparison, a low man in the pecking order. Of all the men she'd ran through, I wasn't the biggest fish that she could have gone after, but that was assuming that money was what she was after. Damn, I hated manipulation. She couldn't handle the game she played, and now she wanted to cry foul?

He studied my face before he asked his first question. "Do you know a Kira Parsons, Kee?"

I rolled my eyes, completely over this Q&A already. "Yeah, Coach, I know her...or I should say I *knew* her."

"There's not a point in beating around the bush, Kee. Did you rape her?"

"Nope, she came at me; we headed out of the party. I took her on the hood of her car, end of story." I didn't see the point of mincing words, either. If anything, the brutal truth was on my side, and if she was honest with herself, she would have seen that before she made such a critical error.

Coach wasn't satisfied with the answer, so he came at me with the report in front of him. "So, why would she file rape charges a week later?"

"Because I stopped handling business when I found out some information that I wasn't thrilled with." I tried to be polite and not call her out of her name, despite her intent to ruin mine. My mom taught me better than that. "I found out she had been rolling some of the dudes on the football team, so I moved on. Next thing I know, she's calling me, telling me she's pregnant, which is also a lie, by the way."

Coach's shoulders slumped, which was never a good sign. It meant someone wanted him to do something that he didn't want to do. "The university president wants me to suspend you until the charges can be validated or dropped."

"Come on, Coach? Isn't there something you can do about that?" I protested. "I didn't do anything. I would never lay my hands on a woman against her consent, especially in light of this #MeToo movement going on right now. I would be committing career suicide before it even got started."

"Give me the rest of the day, D. I'll try to smooth things over with the president."

"Coach, I didn't want to have to do this, but I don't have a choice in the matter." I pulled out my smartphone to retrieve the video file. "This video was taken a couple of days before I ended things with Kira. Does that look like a woman who has been raped?"

Coach watched as he observed Kira putting in some work on at least four dudes in the video. After a couple of minutes, he shut the video off and handed my phone back to me. "How long have you had this?"

"Long enough to know that I'm glad I have it, in light of the circumstances."

"You realize you could ruin a woman's life with this information."

I thought about his words for a moment. I thought about the damage this could do ever since I got hit with the visual proof that the girl I had been involved with had been all over campus with other dudes. At first, I was a little upset about it, but I got over that real quick once Mia asked to be my tutor in another subject, and she became the cushion that my heart needed to rest on.

Still, it came down to the choice: her life or mine. Like that was even a decision? My future was a hell of a lot more important than hers. I had a lot more people who were counting on me to make it to the next level, and no one was going to take that away from me. No one.

"No more than her filing false rape charges on me. She's pissed I'm not with her anymore and she's doing everything she can to ruin mine, including getting her sorors involved at every possible level. I'd get kicked off the team and lose my scholarship, and she wouldn't bat an eyelash," I offered back. I was in self-preservation mode, pleading my case like we were already in court. "She set all this in motion by being sloppy in the first place, and believe me, if I could have the first time we had sex on tape, I'd use that, too."

"It's funny you should mention that," Coach Bolden snapped his fingers as his memory was jogged. "Campus police checked into a few things at that party, and they found something rather interesting. First, a couple of officers said they did see you with Ms. Parsons that night, and it definitely didn't look like a rape to them."

"And second?" I inquired.

"They caught another student videotaping another engagement that night and charged him with peeping charges, since the parties involved with the sex did not consent," Coach stated. "Come to find out, he had been taping a lot of stuff from outside of his window, including when you 'handled business,' as you said."

I felt like the heavens were opening and I would be free to roam again. She didn't have a leg to stand on, and once the university administration got wind of this, they would have to play damage control. "Okay, so, you have the proof that I didn't rape her, so why are we even talking about this?"

"Because we need to have a man-to-man meeting of the minds, Kee." Coach leaned back in his seat. "When I sat in the living room in front of your parents, what was the first thing I said to them?"

I didn't have to flinch or struggle to remember those words. "You said, 'I'll make your son into a man before I make him into a superstar.'"

"Good memory, Keenan, I'm glad you listened then, because I need you to listen now." The way he leaned forward in the chair, I remembered the reason I needed to fear him. Yes, I loved him like I did my father, and like my father, that "look" froze me in my tracks and damn near turned me into that fourteen-year-old again. "This is the first and last time that I will cover for you. You need to man up and get your house in order, or if you're going to do dirt, you need to be a hell of a lot less messy than you were in this case. Do we have an understanding?"

"Yes, sir, we have an understanding." I was a little irritated that he would call me out like that. I knew once I calmed down from my anger I would see things Coach Bolden's way. This was bigger than me; this was about the program. I stood and shook his hand, maintaining eye contact the entire time. "I won't embarrass you again, sir."

"See that you don't, Keenan. The last thing I want to do is have to do is start Evan ahead of you, especially when you've been on a roll lately." Coach finally smiled for the first time in our conversation. "Now, get to class, I'll see you at practice in a few hours."

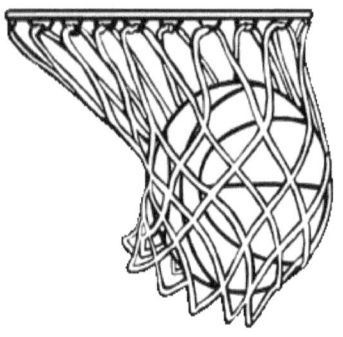

CHAPTER EIGHT

"You had a really good game the other night, youngster. You might be ready for the big time. Another forty-point game? Wow!"

Hearing that from one of the long-time staples of the Temp-State campus was high praise, to say the least. Sometimes hearing compliments helped more than most people realized, considering the brutal practices I endured until the allegations against me were dropped. I couldn't get into any type of rhythm, and it frustrated me to no end. I promised myself I would never do anything to cause this type of distraction again.

Evan took advantage, giving me the business with each missed shot, hounding me about having to give up "his" spot to a wannabe baller to anyone who would listen. He brought up my recent troubles every chance he got, in an attempt to continue to rattle me. I still had the upper hand, though; one glare in his direction shut him down, as he remembered our little "talk" earlier in the month.

After practice, we hung out at a sports bar right off campus called Ballers. The seniors rolled through for a bite to eat and a brew or something harder since they were old enough to drink. The rest of us used it as more of a spot to see and be seen, and since we couldn't drink, the food and the girls were the draw to the place.

Ballers was owned by a former Temp-State football player by the name of Solomon Savage. We affectionately called him "Pops" since he always acted like a father-figure to a lot of us. He was a big man, and he reminded me of one of those old school ballers like "Deacon" Jones or "Mean Joe" Greene. He didn't take no mess off anyone, but we appreciated him for that. He walked with a slight limp, no doubt from the years on the field, doing damage to opposing offensive players. I heard he was a beast back in the day, too, until he tore his ACL his fourth year in the pros, which was a death sentence back then.

He never played ball again. He did, however, pick up enough money on the signing bonus to open the place up on campus. He'd been here ever since.

I walked in and saw the eyes watching me. When I turned toward where I felt the stares coming from, I noticed Evan and the rest of the seniors having a conversation, looking at me as they were talking. I wasn't about to worry too much about them, though; they hung out on their own without worrying about whether we were with them or not, so we stuck to ourselves, too. How's that for team chemistry?

I sat at the bar and gave Pops pound, trying my best to keep the smile off my face. "You really think so, Pops?"

"Kid, I've seen a lot of ballers come through here over the years, and there's something special about you." Pops stroked his chin as he continued pondering. "I notice it every time you come in here with your teammates. The whole bar takes notice."

"Come on, Pops, quit gassing me up, I'm already high as it is," I laughed to shake off the nerves I felt. I had good reason, too; Coach made me the permanent starter after practice today after I made up for the lackluster practice and blitzed Evan in a simulated scrimmage. "But I ain't gonna flex; I think I'm ready to show the country how good my game really is."

"Yeah, just don't get the big head quite yet, you have a lot of history to make it through before you can start calling yourself anything," Pops explained. "Outside of UCLA and Kentucky, no one has won more titles than Tempest State. You gotta get the ring first, or it's a failure on the season."

He had a point, and the way Evan kept eyeing me, I had a feeling this year would be a little harder than I thought. I thought we'd squashed all that beef, but I guess I was wrong. In my mind, I felt like I should have given him more to fear when we were alone, but the problem with that was that mysterious voice that popped up and kept me from finishing the job.

Pops noticed it, too. "Don't worry about Evan, Kee. He came in with a lot of dreams, too. The problem was he didn't have the skill set or the talent to back it up. You do, and that's what's got him steaming. But I've also been around long enough to know you need to watch your back, too. Too many people want to knock the big dog off his porch."

I took his words to heart. Pops had always looked out for people that he thought were worth looking out for. That was the word on campus when I got here freshman year. I saw him do it with a few players that went pro last year, so I realized his words carried major weight.

"I got you, Pops, and I will try to do that. I didn't think I would have to deal with all that from my teammate, though."

"Well, when you're the man at the top of the stairs, everyone wants to get at you," Pops smiled. "You're the man at the top of the stairs now."

"Yo, Kee, that dude Leggett from Trent State is calling you out, bro," Rome shouted at me from across the bar. They were all in front of the radio listening to the College Basketball segment. I walked over with Pops to figure out what he was shouting about.

"Yeah, I heard they got a new cat at the shooting guard that's starting for Temp-State now, Keenan Ellis. I ain't worried about him or the rest of that squad."

"Do you hear this dude?" Rome commented.

I asked the bartender to turn up the volume so we could hear what this dude had to say. I remembered him from last year when he made Evan look silly all night. I was backing up Tony at the point last year, so there wasn't much I could do about it.

"He's supposed to be a pretty good player after he took over during the latter half of his freshman campaign. Do you think he'll give you any trouble, Javon?"

"Trouble? I made his teammate look silly last year and I'll make him look silly this year, too."

"I don't know, Javon, I hear he's got some serious vertical and he can stroke the jumper pretty smooth."

"He won't get his shot off on me, and as far as his vertical is concerned, I have no problems revoking his flight privileges if the occasion calls for it."

"That won't happen." I spat as I grabbed my cellphone to call the radio station. "Yeah, this is Keenan Ellis. Yeah, I'll hold."

"Don't say anything stupid, Kee," Javi cautioned. "He wants you to get into it with him, don't let him roll you like that. Nobody can tell who the fool is when they see two people arguing from a distance."

"I'm not about to let him try me without a response, either, Javi," I shot back, walking away from the radio to keep from hearing the feedback. I wanted Javon Leggett to hear every word I was about to say without any hesitation.

"Well, Javon, it looks like your words got back quickly. I have Keenan Ellis on the phone live with us now in the studio. What do you have to say to what Javon is spitting in the studio?"

"You tell your boy in the studio there that he can jaw

all he wants. I definitely got something for him come Saturday." I tried to sound cool, but underneath I was livid. I gritted my teeth so hard my jaws hurt. I wasn't trying to get into a war of words after only two games, but I wasn't about to let anyone try to punk me, either. "He better hope he can catch me on the third floor before I drop him off on the fourth and make a poster out of him."

"Dude, you need to get a few more games under your belt before you start barking with the big dogs." I heard Javon's voice coming through the earpiece of the phone. *"You scored big against a couple of garbage teams, and you know it. You won't get off on me, partna. You're too pretty to get dirty, anyway."*

Too pretty? Who was he kidding? I was really getting tired of that. "And you need to know the difference between barking and biting. Dogs bark when they sense a threat. Are you scared that I'm coming for you, Javon? I promise I won't make you look too bad out there. Maybe you need to see what a 'pretty boy' can do, so you can see how pretty my game is, up close and personal."

That seemed to get him riled up, which was what I wanted from him. *"What? You better hope you can walk off the floor by the time I get done with you. You got two 40-point games and now you acting like you're the baddest on the planet?"*

"I guess we'll find out Saturday, huh, bro?" I snapped back. "I don't have time to argue with scared little boys, let your game do the talking, partner. I'll make you famous."

"Wow, it sounds like Saturday is going to be crazy, folks! You might wanna get there early, there's no telling what you'll miss!"

I hung up the phone and heard applause and screams when I walked back out into the bar. Everyone must have listened in the whole time while I was in the other room. The only ones who seemed not to be so impressed were the seniors on the squad. I looked over at Evan, and he shook his head, seriously pissing me off.

I didn't care what they thought, that dude needed to be dealt with. Besides, he wouldn't do anything to jeopardize his playing career any more than I would mine.

"Yeah, this should be an interesting game to say the least!" Rome was already pumped after hearing the exchange between us. "What do you think Coach is going to say about it?"

I was already too far gone and still on a severe adrenaline rush to even care at the moment. Pops clapped his hand on my shoulder to bring me back to earth. "Look, I got a vibe with Bolden, I'll let him know you finished this mess. But you better make sure you make that dude eat his words in a couple of days."

By Friday, the world was tuned in.

Every sports media outlet that could pick up the broadcast had it running at least once during the day on their different shows.

The campus radio hosts were uber hyper, breaking down the heated exchange between us, telling listeners how tomorrow night's game would play out, focusing on my matchup with Leggett as the one to watch out for. My cell phone wouldn't stop ringing with all the media requests to talk to me. This wasn't how I planned on getting noticed on the national stage, but there was no turning back now.

I went to class as usual, trying my best to ignore the madness that swirled around me, but the pressure to go off during the game mounted with each passing hour. I resolved to meet the pressure head-on, to give folks a reason to say my name, and not simply because I got into a beef with a player from a rival school. There was no way I wouldn't shine. I worked too hard not to get to this point.

"Yo, we just got word that ESPN is broadcasting down here live on campus!" Rome's eyes lit up as he tried to keep it quiet in class. "The Quad is going to be bananas!"

"Shhh, come on, bro, we can rock with that after class." I tried to shut him down a notch. The last thing I wanted him to do was get all Hollywood on me. "Keep it on the low until we get out of here at least, all right?"

Rome rolled his eyes, but he wouldn't let up. "Yeah, yeah, superstar, you got us into this mess, I hope you can ball out so we can get on with the rest of the season."

"I'll handle my end of things, believe that."

"I hope you plan to handle your end of things, Mr. Ellis and Mr. Dantley," the professor interrupted us as he overheard some of the conversation. "Mr. Ellis, we're hoping you put your money where your mouth is tomorrow night. Trent State has no business being in the same gym with you tomorrow."

Damn, even the professors were in on the hype?

"Yes, sir, I'm planning to do some damage tomorrow," I answered back, waiting for the yelling to die down before I continued. "I haven't backed down from a challenge yet, and I'm not about to start now."

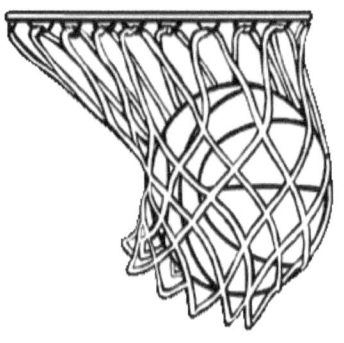

Chapter Nine

"I'm here to deliver this to Keenan Ellis. Is he here?"

Rome and Javi did their best to keep me from taking a look at the stunning woman standing outside of our dorm room with an envelope with my name on it. By the time I was able to get around them to acknowledge my presence, I couldn't take my eyes off her. Her hair was tightly coifed in a bun, and the attire was definitely corporate, like she was from the legal department of wherever it was she came from.

For a moment, I didn't know if I was in trouble or not. After that business with Kira, I damn near thought I was being served a summons or something. "I'm Keenan Ellis."

"Mr. Ellis, this package is for your eyes only. I was given explicit instructions to ensure that you were the only person to see the information inside." She was definitely all business, ignoring the appreciative stares from my shotgun partners, focusing only on her connection with me. I wasn't sure if that was a good or a bad thing. "If you would prefer, I can be present while you view the contents of the package."

I kept getting elbows into my ribs from Rome, who made it obvious he wanted to see about this beautiful woman. He didn't have the juice to keep her attention. Javi wasn't so shy about approaching, and he made sure he wanted to see about her before she left.

"If you don't mind, I would love to holla at you once you're done with the business you have with my boy. I can't let you get away from me without at least finding out if we can at least have dinner or something." Javi slipped in front of me to take her hand and kiss across her fingers. "May I at least know your name?"

"My name is Ms. London, Mr. Sanchez, and that is about all that you're going to be able to get from me, sir." She shot a look in my direction, her eyes locked in to make sure that they knew that she only had business with me. They way her eyes danced, I wondered if that was all she was there for. "As I stated before, I'm here to ensure that the package is viewed by Mr. Ellis—and only Mr. Ellis. If you would be so kind as to find something to do for the next hour away from the apartment, it would be greatly appreciated."

Javi's shoulders slumped, disappointed by the brush off to what he thought worked the majority of the time with the other girls on campus. The problem was, she wasn't like the girls on campus; the way she carried herself let me know to keep it on the level. Rome didn't even bother to speak at that point, realizing that whatever he was going to say would be met with the same stone-cold reaction.

"I'll holla at y'all at the pregame shoot around. We don't want to keep this woman from executing the directions she was given." I did my best to let them both down as easy as I could. Truth be told, if it was this serious, I would rather that they be there. After all, they are my closest friends. "If it's anything earth-shattering, you know y'all will be the first to know."

"All right, bro, we'll get at you." Rome tapped pound, leaving out with Javi and heading out the door.

The moment they left, Ms. London turned to me, letting her hair down and unbuttoning her blazer. "Whew, I thought they would never leave. Now, about the package and the surprise that the interested party wanted you—and only you—to see."

Now, I might not have been around as much as the older players that were friends of my father and my uncle, but I listened long enough to realize why she wanted Rome and Javi gone. I smelled a setup, and I closed her blazer seconds, trying my best to ignore the bra that was underneath the fabric. "I'd rather see the package—and only the package—Ms. London."

She smirked, realizing that she hadn't run into another horny teenager who might have had MILF fantasies to fulfill. She handed the package over to me, sitting on the couch to make herself comfortable while I read its contents. "Suit yourself, Mr. Ellis."

I sat down in a chair, making sure to keep my distance from her. The moment I opened the package, a tightly-packed stack of hundreds fell onto the table. From simply eyeballing the stack, I guessed it was a ten-thousand-dollar wad sitting in front of me.

My nerves were on edge. "What is this about?"

Ms. London didn't acknowledge my apprehension, she was too busy wrapping her hair back into the bun she displayed before. "Read on, Mr. Ellis."

I pulled out the hand-crafted letter, addressed to me, and read it in its entirety:

Keenan,

I have been keeping an eye on you for some time now, ever since your freshman year when you began to show the promise that I like in potential superstars. I thought it might be in our mutual interests to meet up after the game tonight, talk things over, and maybe discuss your future.

I see you balling in the League one day, and I know that you want to take care of your family as soon as possible, so I included this small amount to, shall we say, take your mind off the pressure for a while. Consider it an investment, and if you should decide to want to have that conversation, I'll be waiting.

Regards,
A friend of the program

This dude was starting to get on my nerves already. It was one thing to slip me a few hundred here and there; I could get up with that, no problem. It was an entirely different matter to think that I could be bought. What was he, a freaking agent or something?

I put the money back in the package, sealed it, and got up from my seat to give it to Ms. London. "I'm sorry, dude got me fucked up to think I would jeopardize my eligibility. Coach Bolden has taken very good care of me, and I'll be damned if I betray all that for money I know I'll be making in the pros without his influence."

Ms. London frowned, disappointed as she received the package and placed it in her lap. "You're making a mistake, Mr. Ellis. He's not the type of man you say no to."

Now I was pissed. When people started talking like that, there were other illegal attachments that came along with it. Nope, I was not about to get hemmed up. "Well, I'm saying no. This has the potential to blow up in my face the minute I do something that he doesn't like or whatever. I'm no one's puppet. I'm sorry to have wasted your time, and I assume you came over for your own motives, too, but I'm good, thank you."

"I'm sorry you feel that way. Good day, Mr. Ellis."

She left without another word, closing the door behind her, leaving me alone in the dorm room, confused over where in the world this dude had the gall to even come at me like that.

I shook the image of the money out of my head as best

I could, but I couldn't help wondering if that money could have helped my family in the immediate future, at least until I figured out what I wanted to do after my sophomore season. I would be able to declare my eligibility for the draft if I had a strong showing in the tournament to raise my draft stock and get into the lottery.

Maybe I should have taken the money; it's not like anyone would have known about it.

My thoughts were interrupted by my cell phone ringing. I saw Javi's name pop up, triggering my need to look at the clock and realize that I was almost late for the shoot around. "Yo, I'm on my way now, I'll be there in no time, bro."

"Kee, you better hurry up. They've been looking for you. The ESPN broadcast wants a live quote from you ASAP."

I hung up the phone, racing out the door to get to the stadium, thankful that the dorms weren't that far from where I needed to be. It was time to shine, and I planned on humbling a certain guard at Trent State who honestly had no business being on the court with me.

I knew it, and soon, the rest of the country would know it, too.

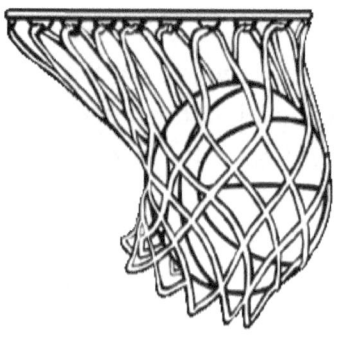

CHAPTER TEN

"I hope I'm not disturbing you, pretty boy."

"If I could stop time so you could have my full attention, I would. To what do I owe this unexpected pleasure?"

"I wanted to wish you good luck before the game gets started, to let you know I'll be cheering in the stands while you take care of Trent."

Ariel looked so damn good in her uniform that I almost forgot that I needed to go through my usual pregame ritual before heading to the arena. I was a creature of habit, on the borderline of superstitious, and if she wasn't inside my head so deep, I would have agreed to see her after the game without exception. I didn't want to tell her no, and I wasn't about to put myself in a position to where I would have to.

"Oh, after seeing you like this, I'll want to get this game

wrapped up so quick that all I'll need to do is get to stare at you during the second half."

Ariel giggled, blushing as she watched my eyes roam all over her. "You know it's going to be a dog fight all game long, baby."

I nodded, pulling her into my lap long enough to receive a small series of kisses. "I'm doing my best to turn this into a blowout. I need to rest a bit, my knee has been killing me the past few games, and I want to rest it before we get through the bulk of the schedule."

"I could always give you a good rubdown to help heal you," she replied as she took her finger and rubbed it against my ear. The sudden current that rushed through me caused such warmth that my knee no longer hurt. "I can't have my potential conquest limping, now, can I?"

That last part wasn't lost on me, but I couldn't say anything about it in that moment. She lifted from my lap and headed out the door, blowing a kiss before leaving me to stew over the possible reality that we could be together. I wanted to wipe the smile off my face, but I didn't want to wipe the smile off my face. The way I felt, I might be able to physically jump out of the gym.

"Seal off the baseline, J!"

The game with Trent was intense, and it was obvious they came to play.

I drew Leggett on the defensive assignment and was left

to handle him, whether we were in zone or man-to-man. I knew his jumper was weak, so his only avenue was to try and break me down off the dribble every chance he could get. I didn't want to fight through screens all night, so I did what I could to shadow him whether he had the ball or not.

Coach Bolden avoided using any type of exotic traps because he knew to trust us to stick to our assignments. I tried to keep from wearing down while sticking to Leggett on D, but I made him pay for it on the offensive end, running him through as many screens as I could.

I penetrated into the paint every chance I got during the first half because Trent left the middle soft for Jarmon to do his thing. It was lob central; every time they collapsed on me, they left him wide for the dunk.

It was a highlight reel I had no problems contributing to; in my mind, it made me more of a combo guard, able to run the point and play off the ball. At this rate, I would have double-digit points and assists, and I had a chance to flirt with a triple-double.

Trent's coach wanted me to rely on shooting over the top of the defense and hope my big men would be able to get a lot of offensive rebounds, but I took it as a diss on my jumper and decided to light it up.

Leggett tried to yap in my ear the whole time that he had me shut down, and every time down I shot from insane distances, hitting nothing but net. We were already up by about nine points, so all I did was point at the scoreboard while I continued to shut him down.

He tried a few times to get away with some dirty plays,

and I almost lost my cool toward the end of the half, but Coach Bolden had taken me out to let Evan finish the half.

"What's the matter, superstar? You can't finish what you started?" Leggett kept yapping as I walked off the floor. I couldn't figure out what he was trying to run his mouth about, I had twenty points in the half, and I was a second-half type of player.

"Do yourself a favor and hope that your coach can come up with a way to stop me," I yelled back as he narrowed his eyes, trying to stare me down. "What? I already dropped twenty on you this half, do you want me to drop forty in the second to prove you can't guard me?"

I guess that was the straw that broke the camel's back. The next thing I knew, Leggett's all up in my face, nearly inciting both benches to clear.

Rome yelled from the bench while trying to keep the others from getting into it. He knew if anyone left, it would mean suspensions. "Come on, ref, get him off my man!"

The referees managed to break us up so that the rest of the half could play out. I was a little worried that Coach would let Evan start the second half and let me cool off before putting me back in the game, but when we were in the locker room during the half, it was a whole different tone that Coach came at us with.

"Tony, Jarmon, I want you to run with the youngsters," Coach said, speaking about me, Rome, and Javi. "We're going to take advantage of our size advantage and pound them in the paint. Thanks to Keenan, they have no choice but to come out of that zone."

He looked at me for a moment. "Kee, cut the jawing with Leggett, we have them where we want them. We don't need anything to screw with the momentum, are we clear?"

"Yes, sir," I replied. I was pretty much bored with Leggett anyway. There was no point in pouring salt in the wound, no matter how much fun it would be. "I'll just keep burning him on the perimeter and make him wish he hadn't called me out."

At the beginning of the second half, Trent coach saw what Coach Bolden put on the floor and I could see it in his eyes. With me at six-foot-eight in the backcourt with Tony, who was at six-foot-four, he was already at a dis-advantage. He really knew he was in trouble with two seven-footers in Javi and Jarmon on the floor and his tallest player was six-foot-nine.

Leggett saw what was up, too, but it didn't stop him from jawing some more. "Man, get these bigs off the floor and take me to school, if you think you can hang."

I wanted to say something back, but I wanted to keep my word to Coach Bolden, so I kept silent as I passed the ball off to Tony to set the play.

I saw Javi sealed down on the block and his man was completely helpless to stop him, so I dropped the ball in to him and let him go to work. A few seconds later, he dunked over his man and the rout was on!

I jogged back down on defense to get ready for Leggett. Sure enough, he came down jawing again, "You think you bad, huh? Well, what do you think of this?"

He attempted a three-pointer that hit the side of the rim badly. I couldn't resist. "I think you need to work on that stroke, that's what I think!"

I felt like it was time to work him over a little more, and now I had my boys on the floor with me. I yelled over to Tony and held up four fingers, which silently signaled to him that I wanted the lob.

Tony nodded and smiled. He wanted in on the highlight reel, too. "Cali!"

Rome had a slick smile on his face; he also knew what it meant. He immediately hit the top of the right elbow and was ready to seal Leggett off so I could get free for the lob.

I slipped over the top of Rome while Leggett ran into him, stopping him only for a second, but it was the opening I needed to do what I do.

"Flight 2-0, ready for takeoff!" Rome yelled out, catching the cameramen's attention. He turned around to watch everything happen in front of him, letting Leggett trail after me on the play.

I was already airborne, eyeing the ball as it left Tony's hands. I was about to grab the ball when I felt something brush against my legs.

The average fan had probably never been on the court before, they could never really understand what happens right before a big play was executed. Everything feels like it's happening in slow motion. The only thing I had left to do was to catch the ball and throw it down through the hoop.

Leggett couldn't rise with me, but I wanted to give the

folks at home and in the stands the show they came to see.

I guess Leggett didn't want that show to take place.

I crashed to the floor, subconsciously putting my hands out to try and brace myself for the inevitable. That proved futile. Everything went black the moment my head hit the floor.

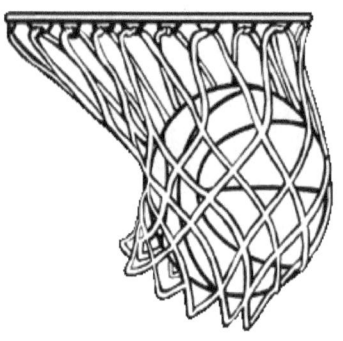

CHAPTER ELEVEN

"Keenan Ellis, you have had a rather unfortunate series of events."

The first thing I noticed about the man standing in my hospital room was the Temp-State t-shirt that he wore. I wasn't sure what to think of him at first glance. Laying here in this bed, I didn't want to think of anything except how to figure out the best way to get back on the floor.

"Who in the world are you, and where did you come from?"

"Lucius B. Prince, but you can call me L.B."

"And you still didn't answer my question: who exactly are you supposed to be? No one is supposed to have access to my room but family and selected friends." I didn't exactly get a bad feel for this dude, but I wasn't sure I wanted him there, either. "In fact, I was waiting for a special friend to show up a little later to help take my mind off things a bit."

"I am a friend, Keenan," L.B. smiled as he walked closer to my bed. "I'm a friend of the program."

That got my attention. "So, you're the one that sent the note and the money after my game a few weeks ago?"

"You catch on fast, kid."

"Yeah, and you were also the one who sent me that wannabe proposal and the care package wrapped up in that trick who wanted to, how did she put it? Oh, yeah, make sure I got your surprise, along with the care package, right?"

"Well, Ms. London does like to take certain liberties with the instructions that I give to her, especially if the person of interest strikes her as attractive." L.B. sat down in the chair next to my bed. "I assure you, Keenan, my proposals are legitimate. The extra slice of heaven she wanted to offer was of her own volition."

"Is that right? And what exactly is this proposal of yours?"

"Oh, come now, we could at least relax a bit before we get to the particulars." L.B. leaned back in the chair like he didn't have anywhere to be at all. "Tell me about this special friend of yours. Is she one of the girls that was in your rotation?"

"I'm not in the mood for pleasantries, Mr. Prince, and that bit of information is none of your concern. Say what you need to say and let's get this over with." The fact that he even wanted to get into the more intimate details of my life with regard to Ariel let me know I need to be wary of his real motives.

"Okay, since you want to cut right to it, let's cut right to it. How badly do you want to prove all of them wrong?" L.B.'s face turned serious. "Your coaches? Your family? Your teammates? How badly do you want to show them, and the world, what you can do? What you can *really* do?"

"I'm waiting for the part where you're proposing something." I was in no mood to bother with riddles. "Get on with it, bro. I hate having to repeat myself. What's the deal, and what's the catch?"

"See, that's what I like, a man that knows what he needs to do to get where he wants to go." L.B. gripped my knee, causing me to flinch and nearly punch him in his mouth. "The only problem is you're not going to be able to go very far on that knee. We need to do something about that."

I wanted to kill him the minute he touched me. The pain was unbearable, and I didn't want anyone touching me anymore. I glared at him, my fists clenched, wanting to do whatever it took to get him off me. "What do you know about it? It's not like you can do anything, anyway, so raise up and be ghost, playa."

"But we're getting to the best part, playa." He squeezed my knee again, and the pain was as intense as the first time he grabbed it, but then the strangest thing happened.

The pain began to subside. It was gone within minutes, and when I bent it, there was no pain, absolutely none at all. There was no way this could be happening.

Shock was written all over my face. "What in the—?"

L.B. was undeterred, almost dogged in his insistence. "Now that I have your attention, answer my question: are you willing to give anything, Keenan Ellis? Will you do anything it takes to get back on top?"

There was no hesitation in my voice whatsoever. This was my ticket back into the fast lane. "Anything, whatever it takes."

"I'll expect you to remember that when the time comes to settle up, Keenan," L.B. grabbed my knee again and closed his eyes. My knee began to glow bright red under his fingers, and I heard the crunch of the bones and felt the tendons as they mended. After a few minutes, the glow faded and L.B. opened his eyes and released his grip from my knee. "You will remember your promise to me."

He faded to black almost as mysteriously as he arrived, and I found myself exhausted from the entire ordeal. I didn't want to make any sense of what had occurred; I was happy my knee no longer hurt as badly as it did earlier in the evening.

Sleep took me again, this time it came quicker than I expected. I couldn't remember the last time I'd been so deep in slumber; it felt like I'd gone through practice, a workout session, and some extracurricular "fun" all in one day.

This was a dream, none of that was real, I thought to myself as I closed my eyes. *Get it together, Kee, you have rehab to start thinking about in the morning.*

97

"Good morning, sleepy head."

Her voice called to me from the darkness I'd wanted to stay wrapped in. It was so enchanting, I couldn't help opening my eyes to find out who the voice belonged to. I thought I was still dreaming.

Her eyes were the first things to capture and take me prisoner, making me forget anything I had planned to do this morning. They wouldn't be the only things to keep me entranced. Her body was to die for, almost like it was created to do sinful things. She had some serious sway in those hips, and her uniform seemed to hug every curve like it was painted on her body. She kept smiling at me every time I looked in her direction, teasing me with every lick of her lips.

All of a sudden, being in the hospital didn't seem like such a burden.

"Good morning to you. How are *you* doing?" I didn't hide my interest as my eyes did the once-over, and then grabbed a second glance for good measure. "Can a brotha know your name?"

"You can, but I don't know if I want to let you know my name yet," she grinned.

"Oh, so you wanna play hard to get, hmm?"

"Maybe I do, maybe I don't. Maybe you might want to try and find out. See if it's worth the trouble?"

Yeah, I was going to have a hard time leaving this hospital.

She went to check my knee, and I flinched a little, but I didn't feel the pain I felt yesterday. There was a dull ache for the most part, but I could bend it without sounding like a baby. Could last night have really happened and L.B. actually did fix my knee?

"Wow, you must be a fast healer," the cute nurse mentioned. "From all the commotion and fuss over you yesterday, it sounded like it was something serious."

"I'm not exactly a fast healer, but I guess I had a little help last night," I replied, not sure if I wanted to say anything further for fear of sounding insane.

"Well, whatever it was, it looks to me like you might be out of here a little sooner than anyone thought."

"Okay, so if I'm not going to be here that long, that means I need to get to know you before I get out of here, right?" I pushed the issue because I simply had to have her. "May I know your name, please?"

"Mmmm, you are a cutie, too. Maybe I should put you out of your misery? After all, you might have a girlfriend or something like that."

Before I could form an answer that referred to Ariel and the fact that I needed to call her to bring her up to speed so she could come see me, the young woman's eyes caught my attention. I didn't know what came over me in that instant, but I couldn't resist falling inside them. Everything else faded away, no matter how hard I wanted to remember. All that mattered was having her.

"Maybe you should put me out of my misery before I put you out of yours. Besides, I have a girlfriend, but for some reason, I can't figure out why she isn't here right now." I shook my head, trying to figure out the images that were being placed inside. The more I tried to remember Ariel, the further away she drifted from my psyche. I kept fighting, but it was no use anymore. Before long, all I wanted was the woman in front of me. "Maybe you should take her place, so you can handle some of what I got going on."

"You'd be amazed at what I can handle, sexy. But your knee isn't completely healed, so you might want to be careful what you say if you can't back it up."

"Only one way to find out." I smiled wide, realizing I had her ready to give in. "What's your name?"

"Eldora, but my friends call me Ella."

"That's a beautiful name, Ella. My name is Keenan."

"I can see that from the patient notes, silly."

"What else can you see, since you think you can see so much?"

"I can see you're a lost cause, but I guess that's a good thing. I have a weakness for lost causes." Ella smirked, trying to give me more of a hard time.

"Oh really?"

"Yes, really. I'm Catholic, and my favorite Saint is St. Jude. He's the Patron Saint of lost causes."

"What makes you think I'm such a lost cause?" I wanted to satisfy my curiosity no matter what. "I don't think I am."

"You must have been for my uncle to come by and see you last night."

She really had my attention now. "Your uncle is L.B.?"

"Yes, and it wasn't a coincidence that you were taken

to this hospital, either, cutie," Ella caressed my cheek. "There's a reason we were placed together like this, and I think I was meant to take care of you. I don't believe in coincidences, only fate."

I didn't care what she said, no matter how crazy it sounded. I was willing to believe anything she told me, as long as she kept touching me. Her skin felt as smooth as silk, and I wanted to find out if her whole body felt that way wrapped around mine. I know she said she was Catholic, but I knew how Catholic girls were. At least, what they pretended to be, anyway. All I had to do was convince her that I would belong to her forever and I would find out everything carnally that I wanted to know, for as often and as long as I wanted to.

"Penny for your thoughts?" Ella inquired, tilting my head in her direction.

"What would I have to give for a kiss?"

She leaned in close enough to whisper her answer, her perfume as intoxicating as her voice. I was close enough to press my lips against hers when she moved to my ear and told me what it would take to open the lock to all that she had and was.

"Your heart."

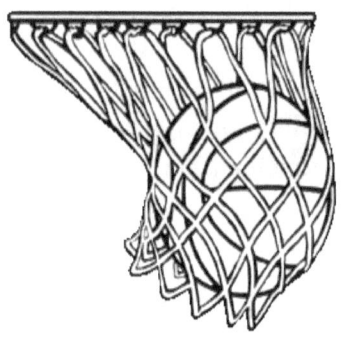

CHAPTER TWELVE – JUNIOR YEAR

"National Champions baby! Yeah!"

Cutting down the nets was unlike anything on the planet! Being on top of the basketball world, having the camera in your face everywhere you turned, everyone chanting your name at every possible moment, being a god on campus. It did NOT get any better than this!

I watched as every one of my teammates got up on that ladder and cut their piece of the net, waiting my turn as the tournament MVP to cut the last piece and put the net around my neck.

I searched the stands and saw my parents, looking as proud as I had ever seen them; watching Tyler, with my jersey on, yelling and screaming, too. He was finishing his sophomore year in high school now, and he was getting as many offers—actually, he was getting more than I did—

from every program in the country.

This was the pinnacle achievement. This was the reason I came to Temp-State with the rest of the recruiting class that came with me.

There were three of us: Javier Sanchez, who was the centerpiece of the class as the top-rated player in the country and the top center. At seven-foot-one, it wasn't hard for him to dominate the paint. He was a rare combination of size and speed and could handle the rock like I could.

The other piece of the "Big Three," Jerome Dantley, was the great nephew of an NBA baller back in the eighties. The old heads recognized the last name and knew who he was the minute he began to get some press. He preferred to be called Rome, so that's what we called him the minute we met.

Rome was the top-rated power forward and one of the top five players in the country overall. He was a few inches taller than I was at six-foot-eleven, but he could do some damage on the boards and then some since he was built like a brick wall.

Now, I might be arrogant, but I had to admit that while I wasn't as highly rated as Javi and Rome, I wasn't a slouch, either. I was still one of the top twenty players—and the top-rated shooting guard—in the country. At six-foot-seven, I felt short standing next to my big men.

The moment we stepped on campus, I was determined to change the perceptions of not being as highly-touted as my teammates and shine brighter than anyone would have ever thought. By our junior year, even if the basketball world didn't pay attention, we would make them pay attention.

And here we were...NATIONAL CHAMPS!

I rose up the ladder to cut the last of the netting down, giving the cameras something to show off the next morning when the papers across the country roll off the presses.

I was ready for the spotlight. But with that spotlight came pressure. That pressure would come the minute we got into the press room to answer questions, and there would be one that would come up above all the others, especially after a night like tonight.

Would I go pro? I would have to give an answer one way or another, but tonight, I was going to celebrate with my teammates. The questions could wait...or could they?

"Man, I can't believe you said you were coming back for senior year." Rome sat in the locker room, shaking his head in complete bewilderment. "If I had your draft stock, I would have been on the plane this morning!"

Javi chimed in, echoing Rome's sentiments. "Kee, seriously, you need to go pro. This is what you wanted. It was all you talked about since freshman year, especially since you came back from your knee injury. Take the money!"

I laughed; technically they were right. This was what I wanted, but there were things that were on my personal to-do list that hadn't been handled yet. Everyone was shocked and confused by my decision. Coach Bolden admitted when he was interviewed he thought I would skip my senior season. Even Jay Bilas said during an ESPN broadcast he couldn't understand it, but he was happy since he got to call some more of my games next year.

"Look, man, I'm not ready to leave yet, all right? I'm having too much fun winning titles with you two."

"Aww, we love you, too, Kee, but we just won the title and we can still repeat without you," Javi tried to push me out the door against my will, figuratively speaking. "Besides, how else are me and Rome gonna be able to join you in the pros if we can't shine?"

"Okay, real talk, and I mean this, all right?" I leaned in so they could hear me clearly. "If everything goes according to plan, we'll all be lottery bound next year after we win the title."

"See, now you're talking crazy!" Rome shouted. "Do you know how hard it is to repeat?"

I stared in his eyes for a few moments, so he could see how serious I was. There was no hesitation, no apprehension whatsoever, and they knew it. I was used to getting what I wanted, and there was no one who had the talent or the passion to take what I felt belonged to us as newly-minted defending champions.

Rome shot Javi a look of resignation. "Lawd, this boy has turned into LeBron in here!"

"It figured. Keenan's on a mission again, we're just along for the ride." Javi threw his hands up and laughed. "So, you're not leaving until you make us completely miserable, right?"

"Well, well, well," Evan and his clique decided to show up and try and ruin some of the good vibes we had going on. "So, you managed to get Temp-State back on the map, just like you said, right? No help from the rest of us, of course. And now you're talking about repeating? Check this fool out, fellas."

I wasn't trying to make our senior year any more difficult than it already was. Repeating was a one-in-a-million shot, but I wanted to try, and I couldn't think of two better guys to try with. Besides, Evan and the rest of his clique would be gone, thanks to graduation.

We managed to survive all the shade being thrown by last crop of seniors and put together a respectable season after I came back from injury. We would be the upper-classmen, which meant we would be able to set the tone moving forward, instead of constantly in the throes of a power struggle, with Coach in the middle of it all, playing referee. Why on earth would I care if he had two words to say about going back-to-back?

I wanted to ignore him, but this negativity that I kept getting pissed me off on levels that he didn't have a clue about. He'd been fighting me at every corner, trying his best to throw as much salt on my game as he could, and sooner or later, he was gonna catch me in a really bad mood. Actually, he did last season, but he needed to be reminded of who I was. He was coming close to catching a fade and getting dropped like a sack of bricks.

"We just won a national title, you idiot, and you got the nerve to complain about it?" I stood up and moved close enough for him to feel my aggression. "What's the matter? You're pissed because you had to play second-fiddle instead of being the man? Get over yourself, partner, it's really not that serious."

"Oh, but I think it is," Evan barked, pushing me away from him. "What you should do is get the hell on and take the dollars in the NBA while the taking is good. You never know what could happen between now and the end of your senior year, you feel me?"

He hit a sore spot, and he didn't realize it. After everything I did to get back, the things I did to get through "rehab" and get back on the court, and he had the nerve to put the words in the air about possibly getting injured again?

Yeah, he forgot who I was.

He was reminded quickly; the next thing he felt was my hands clamped tightly around his neck, with malice in my heart to squeeze the very life out of him. I needed him out of my universe. He could go pester someone else in the next life.

Javi and Rome tried their best to break my hold on Evan, but their attempts felt like nagging scratches on my skin as my focus was on nothing more than relieving the source of my stress and tension for the last two years.

"Kee, let him go, man! It's not worth it!" Rome yelled as he tried to pry my hands away.

"Keenan, you're killing him, man! Let him go!" Javi yelled as he grabbed my neck to get me to let go.

Feeling the pressure around my throat didn't deter from

107

the darkness in my mind. If he died, he died, but no one was going to dictate what I was going to do—especially this fool.

The truth was I wasn't ready to go. Not yet. The other part of the truth had a lot to do with another decision I made earlier in my sophomore year. A decision that meant I would have to settle up and pay my benefactor—L.B. The problem with that payment was that I never figured out what he wanted from me.

The only thing I did was sign a contract. I even had one of the law students take a look at it—discreetly, of course—to make sure that, if I wanted to, I could get out of the contract without any legal penalties. There were penalties, all right, and even with my due diligence, I neglected to read the fine print. I needed more time, and there was no way anyone would accelerate that conclusion. Anyone who would try would suffer the consequences.

Hearing Rome's and Javi's frantic pleas to let Evan go roared into my ears, cutting through the haze created by my fear. It felt like someone flipped a switch, and in the next instant, I released my grip around his neck.

Evan dropped to the floor, struggling to breathe, flopping around like a fish out of water. The assistant coaches did their best to keep everyone separated, but it was difficult to calm me down. That changed as the room quieted and all eyes turned to the ominous figure who watched the entire scene unfold.

Coach Bolden's surprised look at the aftermath of noticing Evan on the ground gasping for air and my agitated demeanor was enough to sober me even further. The first thought that crossed my mind had everything to do with pleading for mercy and hoping he wouldn't have me arrested.

Evan tried to talk, but his throat was still constricted, and he only managed a few mangled words. "He … tried to … argh …"

Coach managed to adjust to the situation quicker than any of us thought. It made me wonder exactly how long he had been watching things before we noticed him. "Spare me the drama, Evan. Whatever he tried to do, you provoked it. You've been trying Keenan from the moment he stepped on campus, and you finally got your ass whooped for it. If I were you, I'd take the championship ring, graduate in about a month and do whatever it is you plan to do with the rest of your life. Your time here with the program is done."

"Really, Coach? This is how you're gonna spin this?" Evan's shocked look was evident on his face. "You can't be serious about this, can you? He just tried to kill me!"

"And if I really take a closer look at it, I should have suggested that you transferred when you threatened to do it during your junior year, too." Coach's stoic expression spoke volumes. "You're done, move on. I'll even help your draft stock by putting in a few good words with some of the scouts who have been looking at you."

Evan struggled to his feet and cut his eyes at me one last time before walking out of the locker room. He didn't leave without a few parting shots, though. "Your bullshit is going to catch up with you, Ellis, you mark my words! I can't wait to watch it all come crashing down around you, too!"

The locker room was quiet for a few moments, and with the media waiting outside to witness a jubilant championship team, everyone looked at each other with the looming question of, "What do we do now?" and in need of a desperate answer.

I felt the need to explain myself, but Coach beat me to the punch, shutting me down before I could utter a syllable. "Javi, Rome, get him to the press room before something else happens that might become sports radio fodder, all right?"

I still wanted to say something, but Coach turned and headed out the locker room. I saw the camera flashes and the television cameras rolling, and there was nothing more left to do but put on my game face and make myself look presentable.

Rome, Javi, and I had been best friends since freshman year. We'd been through nearly everything together, including the night I tore my knee up.

Rome was with me during the rehab sessions, even though he didn't have to be, and when he wasn't there, Javi was. I really didn't *need* to do the rehab sessions, to be honest, but I had to make it look like I had to get back to one hundred percent despite the fact I felt better than I'd ever felt before.

I had L.B. to thank for that.

I felt a little guilty I had to fake an injury until I got "better" in order to hide from the decision I made. Frankly speaking, it was worth the trouble, especially when it came with some seriously sexy perks. That came in the form of an absolutely beautiful sista who happened to slip into my room after L.B. left that night.

Well, she didn't exactly slip in, per se.

Ella had been there for me since I left the hospital over a year ago; said she had been a fan and her heart went out to me when I was laid up in the hospital. She was also a nursing intern at the hospital. She told me one night while I mended that she had a thing for lost causes, and her "Uncle L.B." needed her to be by my side. I was confused at what she meant until she told me she was Catholic and that St. Jude was her favorite Saint.

St. Jude, I remembered her saying that night, was the Patron Saint of lost causes. She was convinced that God had placed her into my life to help get me on the path back to super-stardom, and I believed every single word of it. I looked at those banging-ass curves and that mocha brown skin—that was my weakness—and it was a rap.

Then I looked into those beautiful hazel-brown eyes the night before I was being released from the hospital and it was love at first sight. At least, I thought it was love at first sight. It didn't matter; I was under her spell. I know it sounded silly, but that's the only way I could explain it. All the other girls that I messed with faded to black almost overnight. Ella made sure of that, and let me tell you, that was no small feat. In some ways, it was almost like she was trying to erase a memory.

I mean, she was on it; she made sure my diet was proper. She became my tutor for school, my personal paramour at night. I even believed her when she said the only reason she was having sex with me was that she would be my wife one day, so why wait? It was against her beliefs as a Catholic, but I wanted her to be mine, no matter what.

I didn't even care that she brought in a girlfriend of hers, Siren, who flew in from out of town after game days to get down for the ménage. I wanted what I wanted, and they both were willing to give it to me. Anything I wanted, anything I needed, she made sure I had it ASAP.

What more could any man ask for?

Being the best college basketball player on the planet had its benefits, and I was going to take advantage of it for as long as I could, even if my conscience threatened to make me pay dearly for my decisions.

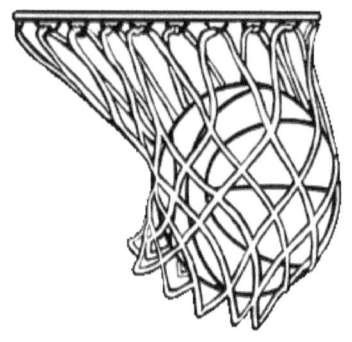

Chapter Thirteen

"Okay, superstar, now what?"

The three of us were sitting in the living room of the apartment that Rome and I called home for the last three years, conversing on the summer plans and where to go from the top of the mountain.

"I want you and Javi to roll with me. I got this summer camp that L.B. wants me to do with another cat that's in the league."

"L.B. got you doing a lot of stuff lately, Kee," Javi mentioned. He gave me a curious look, which made me more nervous than I wanted to let on. "I thought you were heading home for the summer to see the family and unwind?"

"Yeah, bro, I know I'm going to head home and see the folks, veg out on the couch for a few weeks, chill out, anything but work." Rome's grin was evident as he thought about it. "You sound like you're about to go on tour or something. You already said you didn't want to go pro yet, but you're doing the things that pros do. Which is it, are you going pro or not?"

That question caused me to pause. I didn't want to go pro yet, for my own selfish reasons, and I wanted to argue I was doing what I wanted to do, but in reality, was that the actual case?

From the moment I inked the deal with L.B., it was all gravy, I did what I wanted, when I wanted, and I didn't answer to anyone when I did it. All the stuff I did with Ella was done under the pretense that we would be together once I turned pro. It wasn't until about mid-season when I began to notice the obligatory appearances starting to pile up. I was so busy being selfish that I didn't realize that my time was no longer mine.

I pulled out my cell phone and took a look at the calendar that Ella updated for me nightly, and I saw the gauntlet that lay before me. All of the basketball camps, speaking engagements—it was all getting to be a bit much. I was exhausted before I got to June, and it was only April.

Javi noticed my sudden distress and grabbed my phone. "Look, Kee, I know L.B. has been doing all this stuff for you, but what price are you paying for it? Did you ink an agent contract with him or something?"

Rome's ears perked up. "What are you trying to do, fuck up the title we worked our asses off for? Is L.B. an agent?"

"No, he's not an agent." I tried to sound convincing in my denial of what was nothing more than a convenient half-truth. While he wasn't an agent, he was greasing the wheels for me to sign with the agent of the other big-name ballers who were currently in the league.

"I need you to make sure of that, all right?" Rome cautioned. "We don't need to be the next school on the FBI's most wanted list. It's bad enough everything went down with them that caused all kinds of ruckus, but we just won the title."

"Look, I love you guys, I love the program, and I would never do that to Coach Bolden, he's been too good to me … to us."

Javi sat up in the chair he sat in and clasped his hands together. "Look, man, if you say dude is on the level, then he's on the level, we trust you with that. So, how long is this thing you talking about?"

"It's a two-day camp, and it's good exposure, considering it's that dude that's balling out of control up in New York. He's connected with Isaiah Taylor; he's the one hosting the camp."

Javi and Rome raised an eyebrow, which let me know their curiosity piqued. Rome sounded like he was already in before I could get the details out of the way. "Okay, that changes things, I didn't know L.B. was rolling with Isaiah Taylor."

Javi nodded. "It looks like we're rolling with you after all, Keenan. We got time to see family the rest of the summer. This is a once-in-a-lifetime opportunity to raise our profiles."

I was thankful they changed their minds; I needed the familiar faces while we were up there. I couldn't wait to meet Taylor, but at the same time, I wasn't sure I wanted to get caught up in any craziness, either.

To complicate things, I started to come to a crossroads when it came to Ella, and being around an All-Star like Taylor meant that, after camp was over during the day, the groupies would be out in full force. I was already weak for a new piece or two; she had been putting the shackles on me on campus.

"Yeah, this is what we need to keep all eyes on us, fellas," I shook the thoughts out of my head to concentrate on closing the easy sale. "By the time we get back on campus, the basketball world should be talking about all of us. The camp isn't for another couple weeks, so we can go see about family first, and then it's business from there."

"I can't remember the last time we did this."

My entire immediate family was chilling in South Beach for the Fourth of July holiday week. When my parents wanted to do it big, they do it BIG! We were on the concierge level of the South Beach Marriott on Ocean Drive, and what made it even sweeter was when Mom and Dad let me and Tyler have our own rooms on the concierge level!

I didn't care what anybody said, my parents were the

bomb! To make things even better, there was a basketball court nearby for Tyler and me to run during the week to keep sharp. Not to mention the women that would be in next to nothing trying to get their tan on didn't hurt, either. I think that might have been one of the reasons Ella objected so fervently.

I needed the week break, regardless, and I was going to get that break, no matter what she or L.B. said. They both fought me tooth-and-nail to keep me from being with my family, and that was something I couldn't get with. Once my father told me we would be in the 305, I told them both to go…well, I made them change my schedule, and we could leave it at that.

The recharge would do me well; I was beginning to feel overwhelmed from the hectic schedule. It seemed like every other day for the past month, I was in a different city, doing all kinds of nonsensical stuff to keep my image out there for all to see.

Javi was right; if I was going to do all of this, it would have been better for me to turn pro so I could get paid for my appearances. Thanks to the NCAA, I couldn't cash in on any of this madness. L.B. kept trying to tell me it was a taste of what was to come once we got into the NBA season, but I wasn't buying it. He was trying to ride me like a racehorse and I wasn't about to be ridden into the ground, not without a break. I might have been grateful for the exposure and the opportunity, but not at the cost of not seeing my family.

Oh well, at least for a week I could be a son, a brother,

and a young man who didn't have a care in the world before I had to jump back into the grind of school and being Keenan Ellis, All-American and National Player of the Year candidate.

"Yo, Kee, are you gonna be able to make a few more of my games this year?" Tyler asked me as we lounged around by the pool. "Coach Al said I'll be starting this year from the jump instead of being the sixth man last year."

I couldn't stop smiling when I heard that. My old coach and Tyler's current coach, Coach Alexander, was one of the best in the state of Georgia. But he had his system, and it didn't matter how good a player was in his system, they went by his rules of progression.

Freshman year, it was JV ball, period.

Sophomore year, if you were good enough, you got some time on the bench on the Varsity level. But even if you were good enough to run with the Varsity, you still played majority of your minutes on the JV level.

Junior year, it was Varsity ball, whether you were ready or not. If you were good enough to crack the starting five, get yours and get ready. If not, you still got significant minutes since Coach Alexander loved having a deep bench.

It had been a tradition at my alma mater, Lake Grove High, and that tradition had produced so many state titles and tournament runs that parents moved into the district to have their kid play for "Coach Al."

With Tyler as the sixth man, Lake Grove made it to the title game before losing on a stupid call, but I was biased.

I already knew that it was a matter of reloading for this year, and my kid brother would be starting at the two-guard at the start of his junior year. The rest of the state, and the country, was already taking notice.

This week, none of that mattered; that was the primary reason for vacations, after all.

"I'll be there for the first game, Ty, definitely," I replied as I gave him pound. "You know I have to see my little brother do his thing on the court."

"Thanks, Kee, I wouldn't have been able to get to this point without you pushing me," Tyler commented, grinning at the havoc he would be permitted to unleash this season. "I got my first recruitment letters from Temp-State and a couple of other schools last week."

"Well, don't think that I had anything to do with Coach Bolden sending you the letter from Temp-State." I lied through my teeth. Coach couldn't come through the locker room without me yelling about the things my brother did on the court.

"Yeah, I know, I gotta earn my way in, just like high school," Tyler laughed as he dropped his sunglasses to get a better look at one of the Latinas that walked by us. She giggled as she stared at him and wouldn't break eye contact. "Umm, Kee, I think I need to go handle that real quick, brush up on my Spanish, you cool?"

"Do you, little brother, I'll be right here," I stretched in my lounger to relax some more. "Just make sure you're back before dinner with Mom and Dad, all right?"

"That's a bet!" Tyler shouted back as he ran to catch up

with the young lady.

My phone started buzzing, and when I picked it up, I saw Ella's face on the screen. I blew air as I tapped my Bluetooth to answer the call. "What's up, sexy?"

"Hey, baby, how are you enjoying your vacation?" she cooed over the earpiece.

"It's been cool so far, I've been able to recharge a little bit." I tried not to make it sound like I didn't want to hear from her. This was only the second day of the week-long trip, and I wanted a chance to miss her or something. "How are things with the summer gig you're working?"

"It's cool, but I prefer being on the road doing what I do best," she giggled.

I sidestepped that attempt at flirting and continued the conversation. "So, the camp that my boys and I are supposed to be doing with Isaiah Taylor is in a week, right?"

I heard a sigh come through before she answered the question. "Yeah, baby, that's right, and I'm still trying to figure out how to switch the schedule to be there with you."

I wanted to get my hopes up that she wouldn't be able to roll out to the camp, but I learned how to keep my emotions even so it wouldn't show on my face. "Don't worry about it, there's no need in stressing yourself out trying to be in two places at one time."

"Yeah, I know, but I miss you, baby."

"I miss you, too." *Yeah, right, I haven't had enough time to miss you, you twit.*

"If I can't make it out there, I'll check in with you and Uncle L.B. to make sure you got there in one piece, okay?" Ella wrapped up the call. "Bye, baby, and I'll make sure to take care of you when I see you."

I hung up the phone, not too stressed about whether she would follow through over her "promise" or not. To be real, I wasn't holding my breath over it; the whole routine began to bore me.

We'd been together for nearly two years and it was beginning to feel more like a chore to be with her than a joy. There was only so much "togetherness" a man could take. I needed to breathe a little bit. Damn.

I began having second thoughts about what I had been doing with her. Something kept nagging in the back of my mind, and I couldn't figure out why it was bothering me. In my dreams, I kept seeing a face that made me smile, the type of genuine smile that made things easier when she was in my space. For the life of me, I couldn't figure out whether I was making this woman up or if she existed for real. I could feel her touch, I could hear her voice, but I could not remember her name.

My thoughts were interrupted as I watched my parents walked out to the pool area, and I saw the lust in their eyes for each other. Even after twenty-five years of marriage, my father looked at my mom like all he needed to do was say the word and she would be putty in his hands. The passion between them was evident for all to see, even if I was queasy at the thought of my parents being intimate.

Still, I wanted that, and the more I thought about it, the

more I wondered if Ella was the one I would think about like that twenty-five years from now. I didn't think it would be that with her, but I wasn't about to work myself into a frenzy over playing some type of "what if" game.

Only time would tell, but as a thick little beauty waltzed by me with that look in her eye and a sway in her hips that begged for my attention, I wasn't about to act like I'd taken a vow of celibacy, either. I ain't married yet.

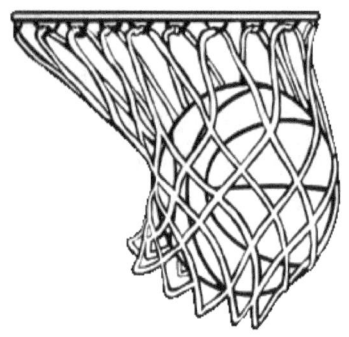

Chapter Fourteen

A week after my vacation, I touched down at JFK.

I was tanned and relaxed, looking forward to the challenges that lay before me at this camp. I briefly thought about the possibility of bringing Tyler along for a little more family bonding between brothers, but I didn't want that to cloud my judgment. I had the chance to see how much his game developed while we were in Miami, and I was proud of his progress—and a slight bit jealous of how gifted he was.

Rome and Javi were already inside the airport awaiting my arrival, sitting in one of the restaurants enjoying some appetizers. They already had a small group of fans who recognized them when I walked into the area. Javi made sure to point me out, almost in a manner that suggested that he needed them to swarm me for a little while so he could catch his breath.

I didn't know what was funnier: the relief on his face or the sheer panic I felt as the group converged on me, nearly over-whelming me with papers and pens, dying for an autograph. My cheeks hurt from smiling for selfies and regular camera phone pictures.

This was the price of fame, and this was a price I was willing to pay.

Rome already had jokes the minute he saw me, standing up with his impersonation of "The Rock" with his greeting. "Finally… White Chocolate … has come back to NEW YORK CITY!"

The crowd around us broke out into laughter upon hearing this loud and boisterous announcement, causing passersby to stop for a moment to see what the commotion was all about. I wanted to shrink from all the added attention, but that small bout of apprehension withered away as I took a seat with my boys to grab a quick bite before our ride was scheduled to pick us up.

Once the crowd disbursed, it made it easier to have a conversation again. "I missed your ugly mugs. What did you guys get into?"

Rome sat back, enjoying the hot wings and downing a glass of water. "Bro, I had to rest up for this thing right here. I don't have your energy levels, superstar."

I let out a nervous laugh. I didn't mention the need to get away for my mental health instead of my physical health. I honestly never felt better. That particular fringe benefit wouldn't help them for obvious reasons, but they didn't need to know that. "Come on, Rome, you know you can rock this and then some. You and Javi have the chance to raise your profiles like we talked about."

"Yeah, yeah, I'm here, remember? You ain't gotta sell me anymore, okay?"

"Listen, I know I've been cryptic about all of this, but this is Zeek Taylor, bro. One word from him about the skills we possess and the NBA scouts will be at damn near every game this season." I looked over at Javi, still in promotion mode. "If he says you have the potential to be better than Anthony Davis or Joel Embiid, you go number one in the draft, even ahead of me. You know how rare big men like you are in the game right now?"

Javi shook his head, laughing so hard he held his stomach like he was in pain. "Man, you need to go into politics when you're done playing ball. You're really trying to sell this thing when we're already here and on board. Let's get this done and have some fun in the process, all right?"

We settled the bill, heading out toward baggage claim, stopping every few minutes to take more pictures and sign more autographs. People thought we were already in the league the way people kept swarming around us.

Championship pedigree really did have its privileges.

The chauffeur was out near the exit, holding up a placard with our names on them. He nodded in my direction, recognizing me before I had the chance to acknowledge him, walking in our path to introduce himself. "I'm Ivan. I'll be taking care of your

SHAKIR RASHAAN

transportation and entertainment for the duration of your stay. Mr. Prince wanted to make sure you got to the location in one piece without any distractions."

Javi and Rome gave me this look, and I held my hands up in mock defense. "I don't know any more than you do, fellas. All I know is that it's an hour from the airport and we were riding in comfort."

That comfort came in the form of a long Escalade limousine sitting in the parking lot.

"Yeah, I think I'm gonna like this star treatment." Javi clapped his hands together as we walked toward the vehicle.

The vehicle was already running, which I felt was a bit odd, but maybe it was more in the lines of it being ninety-four degrees and the dude was trying to make sure we had the first-class service. Even though it was an airport parking lot and there were surveillance cameras everywhere, I couldn't stop giving Dorian the side-eye over leaving our transportation in such a vulnerable state.

Ivan smiled as we approached the car; I sensed another setup, which made me uneasy. He opened the door, revealing a quartet of women, all sitting pretty and oozing sex appeal as they stayed cool in the passenger area.

Rome did a double-take, wanting to believe what he saw in the car, but not quite sure if he should. Javi was in shock; I saw the wheels turning in his head, and I couldn't blame him for what he was thinking. The way the ladies were looking at them, this hour-long ride would be more entertaining than we thought.

While Rome and Javi couldn't stop grinning, I had to do a double take when I noticed the familiar faces of two of the beauties in the car: Ella and Siren.

Ella staked her claim immediately, nearly breaking her neck to hug me. "Hey, baby...surprise!"

Damn. What the hell is she doing here? Why couldn't she have been tied up with the other obligation? I tried my best to make it look like I was happy to see her, but the truth was, I wasn't.

Since classes were done in May, we had been inseparable on the road with the hellacious schedule that she and L.B. had me on. The only time that I got any type of break from her was when I went on vacation with my family. I wanted to treat this trip like it was business, with a side of fun to make the trip worth it, but I saw the latter part of my plan was not going to happen.

Realizing I was the one who Ella was referring to, the other two girls latched on to Javi and Rome like their lives depended on it. Their lives probably did if they so much as looked in my direction, which added to my frustration. I felt trapped in a situation I couldn't find myself being able to get out of, and I wasn't sure how I managed to get into the situation to begin with.

Javi was into the woman that he was with, Lauren, and had become oblivious to any strife I might have been suffering. Rome, on the other hand, "forgot" about his girlfriend, Angela, the minute that his companion for our stay, Shari, whispered something in his ear that put a grin on his face that I guessed wouldn't come off until we got back to JFK.

As fine as they were, all eyes in the parking lot were on Ella and Siren, who wore matching sarongs that left so little to the imagination there was no point in guessing if they were naked underneath.

Ivan couldn't resist enjoying the show, but he also had things to do and places to be. "Okay, ladies and gentlemen, we need to get on the road. I don't like to keep Mr. Taylor waiting."

I already knew that was the case. L.B. was the type of man who ran on a precise time schedule. Ella was no different. She ushered the other two women into the limo and snapped, "C'mon boys, we need to get this show on the road."

Before Ivan could get the limo onto the highway, the women began their assault, finding weaknesses that we didn't realize we had. I ignored what was going on in the other areas of the limo, focusing on the two women who vied for my carnal attention.

Maybe it was wrong of me, but I focused on Siren more than I did Ella as they converged, each trying to gain the upper hand on the other. I needed to find a way to enjoy myself despite my girlfriend on the other side of a carefully planned tryst that I assumed she had set up since we left each other earlier in the month.

Siren curled her body around my hip, straddling my left leg as she whispered into my ear, "Did you miss me, sexy? I've been dreaming about you ever since the last time we were together. I can't wait to feel you inside me again…and this time, you can slide in wherever you want, okay?"

She had me weak, and there was no turning back; I'd reached the point of no return. She turned my head and kissed me, and it no longer mattered what Ella did to me. I was lost inside of the lust I had for Siren, with no desires to leave.

Ella was blind to the connection between Siren and me, and although I felt her between my thighs, Siren's eyes kept me where I wanted to be. Siren cooed in my ear, leaving small kisses on my lips, breaking down every wall I had to try to keep her at bay. "Take me. I'm yours for as long as you want. I promise I won't make you wait so long next time. I have to have you, baby."

I was powerless against the spell she'd cast over me. Nothing else mattered except letting them have their way with me. I did everything I could to stay inside the bubble Siren and I had created, enjoying everything she did to me while doing as much as I could to keep Ella from realizing that her touch no longer had the effect it once did. I had to keep up the façade long enough to figure out what I wanted to do next.

One thing was for certain…it wasn't going to happen during this trip.

Zeek Taylor was waiting for our arrival.

"So, are you digging the spot or what?"

I couldn't flex, his twenty-thousand square foot home was ridiculously huge, especially for a bachelor with no kids. We were chilling on the balcony after doing some work in the gym with the kids at the camp. It wasn't far from the campus that he rented out for the week, but I found out later on that it was his alma mater; they let him have at the campus as a prized alumnus.

He wanted to talk one-on-one and away from Rome and Javi; he said he needed to see where my head was, so to speak. I had other ideas in mind for our conversation. I took in the grounds; there wasn't a neighbor within at least a few hundred yards of the house, and he had the trees block off the property line so I could figure out how much acreage he had. "Yeah, I'm definitely digging the spot."

He gave me a look for a moment, regarding my demeanor before he made his next statement. "Good; this could be you next year, if you ball like you did this past season."

I wasn't trying to think that far ahead, but I did have some questions for him. "Mr. Taylor, are you good with everything that you're doing? I mean, are you happy with the way your life turned out?"

"Yo, call me Zeek, partner, especially if we end up with the same agent," Isaiah responded as he patted my shoulder. "What do you mean by 'am I happy'? Of course, I am."

"I mean, you don't want to be partying and stuff right now?" I asked a different question than the one that was in my mind. "I'm saying, I have been on this grind like I'm at work or something except I'm not getting paid to do it, and it's not like I don't enjoy it, but—"

"But you want to control your schedule, right, kid?"

"Yeah, that's it, exactly. I feel like I'm a puppet on a string or something. I had to fight to spend some time with my family before I came here."

"Look, kid, let me give you the real, all right?" Isaiah sat in the lounge chair and invited me to join him. Once I sat, his demeanor changed to something more business-like. "This thing in the league is still a business, and you're on stage twenty-four hours a day, seven days a week. The more you can look good in front of the cameras, the more worth you are to the league. Yeah, I'd rather be partying and shit like that, but at the end of the day, what money is it making me?"

He had a point, I couldn't deny it.

I listened to him, trying to soak it all in and understand that maybe I was being a bit childish about the whole bit, but there was something else bothering me. "Zeek, how were you able to get back so quickly from your Achilles injury?"

That question froze him. He didn't think I paid such close attention to his career. I paid closer attention that he'd realized, and for good reason; I felt like my career and his were somehow synchronized, and it was like I had a glimpse into my future, watching his career.

About four years into his pro career, Isaiah Taylor ruptured his Achilles tendon, something similar to what happened to Kobe Bryant before he retired from the

Lakers. It took Kobe a year to come back fully from the injury, but some of his explosiveness was gone.

"Zeek" Taylor was back in less than six months.

The sports medicine community called it a miracle recovery, and the doctor that performed the surgery became an instant celebrity and millionaire overnight, as every athlete—regardless of the sport—flocked to him for injury treatments. What had my attention was the fact that no one questioned how he was able to get back so fast when a Hall of Famer couldn't do it in twice the time.

Isaiah paused for a moment, took a sip from his drink, and looked me in the eyes. "I did what I had to do to get back on the court, and L.B. helped make it happen. That's all you need to know."

"I see you two are getting along." L.B. walked out on the balcony with us, noticing the tension between us. He seemed to bypass that, worried more about the immediate question in his mind. "So, what do you think, Zeek? Does this kid have superstar written all over him or what?"

Isaiah's mood changed in a heartbeat. He flashed the megawatt smile that I was so used to in the commercials he was in and on the court. "Man, this dude has what it takes to be the next face of the NBA."

I couldn't help smiling once I heard that comment. I almost forgot about the tension between us, but I still felt like I needed answers. "You really think I've got what it takes? Coming from an All-Star, that's crazy."

He laughed before laying on the compliments. "Look, Keenan, I've seen your game, and I watched you destroy your man in the title game. I was as shocked as everyone else when you decided to stay in school. You're ready now."

"That's what I told him, but he sometimes has a hard time listening to people, even when they have his best interests at heart," L.B. commented, staring down at me as he said it. "I'm sure by the end of his senior year, he'll come around and see things the way they're supposed to be seen."

I bristled at that last statement. What the hell was that supposed to mean? I still had control of my basketball career, I didn't care what L.B. said. But I put on a mask in front of them both and acted like I didn't have a care in the world.

I probably should have cared, but I didn't. All I cared about was getting back on campus and getting ready for the season. L.B. didn't control me.

At least, that's what I led myself to believe.

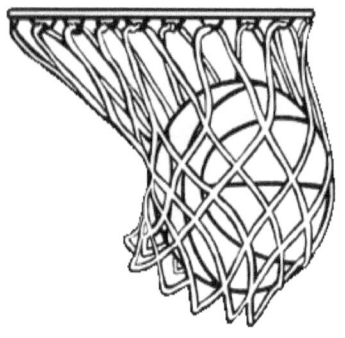

CHAPTER FIFTEEN

"Yo, Kee, let me holla at you."

We were on a flight heading from New York to Chicago, where we would take connecting flights back to our hometowns. I would be heading back home to the A, Javi would fly home to Dallas, and Rome would be flying out west to L.A. I didn't mind flying out of the way, even though the flight straight home to Atlanta would be shorter. I wanted to get some male bonding in before we parted ways for another month.

I kicked back in the seat, looking over at Rome, finding him reclining in his seat, getting ready for the two-hour flight. "What's on your mind, bro?"

"Look, Kee, I wanted to say thanks for making Javi and me roll with you on this trip, all right?" Rome gave me pound, a smile spreading across his face. "I didn't know so many of the NBA scouts would be out there."

"Well, you'll have to keep that on the low, both of you; we weren't there, you feel me?" I tried to make them understand that it would be an NCAA violation if we told anyone about that. "As far as we're concerned, we were there in nothing more than a camp counselor capacity."

"Speaking of keeping things on the low." Rome lowered his voice so none of the other passengers could hear. "Angela knows nothing about the stuff that went on in the limo and in my room while we were here, right?"

Javi chuckled to himself. "I told both of y'all to stay single so you wouldn't have to get your stories straight on the flight home. But fine, Angela ain't heard nothing from me."

"You know me, dawg, I got your back," I concurred with Javi. "Secrets to the grave, you know how we do."

"Man, I got to holla at the scout from the Bulls," Rome beamed. "He said if I put up some decent rebounding numbers to go along with my scoring they will consider taking me in the mid-first round. Guaranteed contract, here I come!"

Javi had his own reasons to smile. "I might be able to go to the Rockets and help them get back to where they were when Hakeem was there. I'm definitely trying to do my thing in my home state."

I stayed away from the scouts on purpose; they would be on campus trying to see what's going on during the season. That brought me to the conversation I wanted to have with them. "That's part of the reason I came back, fellas. In order for me to make it to the next level, I can't do it as a shooting guard. I gotta get my assist numbers up."

"Dude, you averaged almost ten dimes a pop, what are you talking about?" Javi raised an eyebrow. "If it weren't for Coach telling you to let us crash the boards, you would have averaged a potential triple-double last season. What's this really all about?"

I should have known I couldn't pull the wool over their eyes. They knew me as well as my family did, but I couldn't tell everything. I wasn't ready for that, and I wasn't sure I would ever be ready. But I had to tell them something.

"All right, I can't lie to you. I really don't want to go pro yet, regardless of the scouts and agents banging down my door and blowing up my phone." I shook my head as I thought about the times I had to change my number only to have someone get the new number and the cycle started all over again. "I might be ready physically, but I'm not ready mentally, not yet. There's that, and there's the fact that I want to win another ring with my boys so we can go out on top … together."

"Damn, I think I'm gonna cry." Rome even faked a tear for dramatic effect. "Come on, Keenan, we're in this together, all right? It wouldn't be right not having you out on the perimeter doing your thing. I mean, who knows what the future holds for us? He's got the plan and we just need to follow it."

"Who's He?" Javi chirped. I started laughing again

because I knew he was playing, but Rome dug into him anyway.

"Man, quit acting like you ain't got no religion in your life, Javi, you know who HE is."

I laughed as they bantered back and forth for the rest of the flight, even getting some of the other folks in first class involved in some trash talk because an alumnus from our chief rival, Trent State, was there.

This was what I would miss in the pros, and I wasn't ready to leave that yet. I loved my boys to death, and I was deadly serious about making sure they got into the league. I wanted to feel like I at least helped in some way and not made it all about me.

Despite evidence to the contrary, I hoped to redeem myself, if for anything, it might make me feel better about the decision I made.

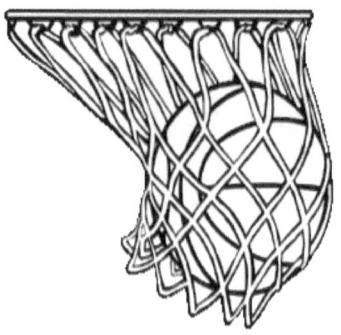

CHAPTER SIXTEEN – SENIOR YEAR

"Yo, Kee, you're on *SportsCenter* again!" I heard Rome shouting from the living room of our off-campus apartment at the latest in the long line of highlights that we'd put up over the past couple of years.

"Man, Rome, do you ever get tired of watching that?" I asked. "You know we'll get to see that shit in film session later in the week, right?"

"Dude, when you're on the highlight reel, *we're* on the highlight reel!" Rome replied. "Don't act like you ain't like the way I blew up the point guard while you slipped behind me to bust that three?"

I took a second look at the play on the DVR, and he was right. While the cameras were watching me blaze the nets for yet another three-pointer, what they missed was Rome flattening the point guard with a forearm shiver on the screen. The hit was so nasty I had to hit the rewind button on the DVR remote to catch it again. I was surprised the refs didn't call a foul on that.

"Damn, Rome, that screen was ferocious!"

"Why, thank you, thank you very much!" Rome stood up to take a bow. "There ain't no one in the country that can open holes like me!"

"Look, you keep them holes open and I'll keep flying through them," I told him. "Besides, we have some more hardware to get before we roll out."

"And where are we rolling out to?" I heard Angela jump in on the conversation. "You know y'all got curfew, even if you are off-campus."

"Lawd, woman, would you ease back off a that, please?" I retorted, a little irritated that she interrupted the vibe. "Did you at least hear the whole damn convo before you decided to jump all in it? Just loud and wrong."

"Aw, Kee, lay off my girl, she ain't mean no harm by it," Rome defended as Angela slid onto his lap. He gave her a soft squeeze before popping it.

"No, I didn't mean nothing by it, baby," she replied as she rolled her eyes at me. That woman had a way of grinding my nerves to the point of no return sometimes, but that was his headache to deal with, not mine.

"Yeah, whatever, I'm about to go hit the books for a bit, these midterms are gonna wreck me if I don't put in some time," I announced while they were in the midst of a heavy make out session. I knew they didn't hear me, so I headed into my room to get it done.

I don't know what happened once I got in my room, but with the plan in my head never got executed. Once my head hit the pillow, exhaustion from the day took over and I was asleep faster than my forty-yard dash time.

Remember your promise to me.

I woke up in a cold sweat with those words echoing in my ears. The nightmares were getting worse by the week, and they were becoming more vivid the closer I got to the beginning of the season. It was coming up on the anniversary of the game when I tore up my knee. That was also the same day that I had the "talk" with L.B.

I had no regrets about doing it, at the time, anyway. I wanted to get back on the court badly. I wanted to show them all that I wasn't done.

My coaches...

My family...

My teammates...

Whatever it took, it didn't matter to me. I never, ever suspected that there might have been consequences to that decision. I mean, why should I? If anything, the side effects were absolutely stunning.

But I didn't even pay attention to the unusual things that were happening around me. Increased stamina and strength, both on the court and off. Speed that would have made Allen Iverson proud. I mean, I was a monster on the court, even more so than I was before the injury.

My coaches were mind-boggled, and so were the scouts during the rest of my junior year, especially considering I'd only missed ten games. The stats were damn near *NBA 2K*-like:

31.3 points per game; 9.3 rebounds; 14.2 assists...

I even blocked about three shots a game for good measure. I did it all.

I played a little point guard in high school, and I almost convinced the coaches to let me play both positions. That was how good I felt some games, like nothing and no one could stop me on the court. Maybe that should have been my first clue, but I was having too much fun to care.

I never saw L.B. much for a while, except for the nightmares that popped up every so often. I shrugged them off as more side effects that I would have to get used to, like headaches that I had to live with. After all, it was my senior year, and I couldn't lose, not this year.

I couldn't forget my home boy, Rome, or Javi for that matter. Those were my boys. There was nothing I wouldn't do for them. Rome was the forward that paved the way for me to get the stats I had the last two years. He was the Robin to my Batman, the Pippen to my Jordan. With Javi at center, we would be a force to be reckoned with, and no one could touch us. We came in together in the same recruiting class and had been close ever since. Brothers, on and off the court.

Ella made sure they were taken care of, too. In fact,

thanks to her connections, Rome was already set to be a high-first rounder, which meant guaranteed money on the rookie contract, and Javi was a lock for the lottery like I was.

It was too bad that Angela and Ella didn't get along, though; that was the only downer in this whole thing. Angela said she never did trust Ella as far as she could throw her, and I always chalked it up to women being catty or some shit like that. I did my best to try to convince them to have a conversation, for our sakes, but it never happened. Angela was convinced, and nothing would change that, no matter what Rome and I tried.

Javi stayed out of it; he was the confirmed bachelor until he got in the league, going through women the way most people went through underwear.

Oh well, no skin off my back, they didn't have to see each other, for all I cared. There was no guarantee that we would be on the same team in the pros, anyway.

As the season finally approached, the nightmares were getting bizarre. This last one was crazy. I dreamed that I broke my neck in that fall two years ago on the alley-oop attempt and that it was L.B. that brought me back from the dead. I heard my mom screaming before everything went black and I woke up damn near screaming myself.

"Baby, are you okay? Was it the nightmares again?" I heard Ella's sultry-smooth voice calling for me in the darkness. I always marveled at how a couple of words out of her mouth calmed me down. "Come here and let me kiss away the bad dreams."

I didn't know when she'd gotten in my room, but considering that she was naked, I had to guess that she'd been here for a little while. Even while half-asleep, I felt like I was under her spell.

I sat up in bed for a moment, wanting to shake the images out of my head before they drove me insane. It was getting to the point to where a week didn't go by without having a nightmare at least once. If I wasn't careful, I'd be no good to anyone, regardless of the fact that I felt as good as I did during the day. I couldn't live like this forever.

I looked into Ella's eyes and I got lost in seconds. She had the type of eyes and stare that made a man think he wanted to remain hostage even if he wanted to find the first escape route possible. Her body was to die for, and I enjoyed dying every time we were intimate.

Lately, even her beauty and feminine charms weren't having their desired effect. In fact, it was almost boring me. That's how I knew I was in trouble. No matter how much I wanted her, every time I looked at her I saw slivers of the nightmares playing like a movie in my head, taunting me.

The thing that threw me for a loop was, once in a while, I would see the vision of the mystery woman who'd still managed to enter my dream state. I still couldn't remember her name, but she was there, reaching for me, like she was trying to pull me from my nightmares. I felt guilty sometimes for wanting her to exist, to be a real person, but I put it out of my mind as best I could. I wanted out of this situation with L.B. so much that I conjured up people to help me.

"They're getting crazier by the week, babe," I told her, feeling on her hips and thighs as she nibbled and kissed on my neck. "I think I need to get something for them to keep them from popping up."

Ella placed her finger to my lips to quiet me, brushing her soft lips against my eyelids. That move seemed to do the trick as my eyelids felt heavy and my body felt like I weighed at least half a ton. She kept the eye contact with me as her hands moved across my shoulders, my stomach, and over my thighs.

I wanted to move but I was at her mercy. I didn't mind it all that much when I was in the mood, but my mind screamed for my release. The only problem was my mouth never opened to convey the thought. I tried to mouth to her to let me get up so I could at least be an active participant in this interlude, but Ella was having none of it.

I tried with everything I had to at least make it look like I could fight her off, but she only laughed in the darkness, her eyes looking through me, reducing me to nothing more than a toy to be played with.

What freaked me out was my body betraying me, responding to everything she did to me. Every touch … every kiss … every stroke against my crotch seemed to awaken my body to her unspoken commands. I felt paralyzed, but I wasn't paralyzed, and it terrified me beyond explanation.

As my body continued to dance with hers, I felt a strange sense of dread come over me. I felt like my body was no longer mine; that I was a prisoner trapped in the psych ward with a strait jacket wound tight around me with no escape until the nurses came to untie me. My eyes pleaded with her to release me from this torture. She had never done this to me before, and that included the nights where she wanted to get a little "kinky."

"Shhh, relax, baby, you don't need anything, I'll make it all go away." Ella cooed in my ears, flashing her eyes at me as she climbed on top, straddling my hips. "All you need is me. All you'll ever need is me."

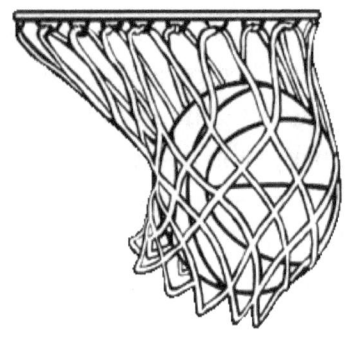

CHAPTER SEVENTEEN

"Yo, Rome, check the four coming on the switch!"

We were popping off in practice as usual before the first game against Kent, the second-ranked team in the country, and it felt like old times between us. I couldn't wait for the season to begin!

We were doing a live scrimmage against the second unit, and we were running them out of the gym. The assistant coach was mad as hell because he couldn't stop me. Whether we ran the pick and roll, dropped me on the post in a version of Phil Jackson's famous "Triangle" offense, or simply freestyled like hell on an isolation setup for me, he figured out whether his defense was coming or going.

It was all in good fun, though; we had to keep them boys on the second unit hungry. Whether we liked it or not,

Coach Bolden's words always rang true: *Offense wins games, but defense wins championships.*

I already found that out one time, but I was greedy for more jewelry.

I wasn't about to beat them down to the point where they couldn't do no damage against the real opponents geared up to take down the top dog. We would need a blow from time to time, and they needed to be on their game.

"I got him, just do what you do." Rome yelled out as the point guard ran the play.

I took the ball with the backup guard on me, a freshman by the name of Arian Lopez, who came in as a Parade All-American, and he had the nerve to try to get in my shirt on defense. I saw Rome setting up for a pick and roll with the forward I told him about before the play started and turned inside with a screen that took Arian out and left the power forward on a switch so that he had to try and stop me.

Notice I said try?

He caught a whiff of a spin move before he knew what hit him, and I was already at the front of the rim when Javi tried to rotate over to get in my way.

Javi was playing with the second unit on that particular half-court set to show the backup how it was done. He stared me down and measured for the block, taking my shot into about the third row of the bleachers. Lucky play, but he was one of the best big men in the country, so I didn't take the block too personally.

"Whoooa!" I shouted as I picked up the ball up and clapped Javi's shoulder. "Good play, Javi! Tell Arian to fight under the screen next time. He could have kept me on the perimeter to settle for a jumper."

Javi popped my back, still high from the block. "You need to see me in the paint and quit picking on the youngsters!"

I laughed; he wasn't talking all that during the drills where we went head up and I put him on his butt. But that's okay, I'd let him have his talk. At the end of the day, I could easily break his ankles without breaking a sweat.

I slapped hands with Rome, who was gloating over the screen that he put on his man that sprung me. "Man, all day, do you hear me?!?! I can do this all day!"

"Yo, Rome, you need to calm all that noise down. It's just practice, damn," Javi continued. "Save that for when the games count, all right?"

I could always rely on Javi to try to be the voice of reason. Outside of Rome, he was the only one who could shut me down if I was real about it.

"All right, old man, don't get so puffed up about it," I replied as I jogged back to half-court for the next play. "Besides, if you ain't ready for what I'm bringing, the rest of the conference won't be, either."

"All right, boys, enough with the chatter," Coach Bolden cut in to get us to focus. "Run it again, this time, second unit, give me a Diamond-and-one. GO!"

I needed some time to unwind before I headed home to

hit the books, and the eye candy at Ballers was a nice surprise for a Tuesday evening. Some of the women were coming from work, while others looked like they were going to head in to work soon.

Pops kept giving me these glances every so often, which had me confused to say the least. I hadn't started coming on the regular until the latter half of my sophomore year, and I never drank until my junior year when I was legal. We were on good terms back then, but nowadays all he did was stare at me like I had done something to his daughter.

Rome saw it, too. "Yo, what you do to Pops?"

"I ain't done nothing to Pops, man," I replied, flexing my fingers to stave off the irritation that rose in my stomach. "He's been on me like that since last year, and I ain't done nothing."

"Well, you must have done something. If looks could kill, you'd be waiting to be carried by six right now."

"Man, whatever, I'm not even worried about that anymore." I stared in Pops' direction as I felt his icy stare on me again. "I'm gonna see what this is about right now."

I got up from my seat and was on my way to have a chat with Pops when this girl caught my attention. She did more than catch my attention, she possessed it. I'd forgotten all about Pops in that moment, there was something about her that I needed to see about.

She wasn't all glammed up or anything like that, but she had this vibe that grabbed me, whether I wanted her to or not. Her reddish-brown hair was pulled up in a ponytail and she wore jeans and a tank top with some tennis shoes, and she had this caramel brown complexion that shined against the dim lights of the bar.

I kept studying her features, trying to figure out why she'd commanded my attention, beckoning me to kill my curiosity. The minute she turned her head and I got a chance to see her face, even from that distance, I felt a jolt to my system. This eerie feeling that washed over my body as my mind began to connect the dots. The visions I'd been having were about her!

How was this possible? I thought she was a figment of my imagination for the past two years, and yet, here she was. I was beside myself with relief, thankful that I wasn't losing my mind. Now that I knew she was real, I needed to know what her name was, so I could close the loop.

I was in mid-stride, heading in her direction, when I stopped in my tracks. She walked over to Pops and gave him a hug and a kiss on the cheek. I saw Pops stare at me again like I stole something from him and he was ready to collect, but baby girl had me subdued when she turned back to see why Pops was so grumpy.

Our eyes connected, and something clicked. Everything came rushing back in bits and pieces, but not enough for me to figure out the whole picture. It frustrated me on levels that I didn't want to deal with, but I had to know, for my own sake and sanity.

She smiled before she turned back to Pops and grabbed an apron to get behind the bar.

"Man, you might wanna leave her alone," Javi

mentioned to me. "That's Pops' niece, Ariel."

"Now, why would I want to leave her alone?" Hearing her name sparked something, but I still couldn't figure out what it was. It was like it was knocking on the door, taunting me. All I had to do was take one more step to find out the answers that had been dogging me.

"Because you know Pops will kick your ass if you don't," Rome chimed in. "And if he doesn't, your girl will. You know, Ella; remember her?"

"Man, get on with that," I shrugged off the salt they were trying to throw in my game. "Besides, what Ella don't know won't hurt her."

I needed to at least talk to her, get to know her or something. I couldn't leave the bar without at least knowing what her real connection to Pops was. Ella pulled that "uncle" card on me before with L.B., and I didn't believe her all that much; the way he always stared at her when they came to visit me in the hospital gave me pause. Uncles were not supposed to stare at their nieces like *that*.

I walked up to the bar while she was mixing a drink, taking in the exquisite view. "So, what drink would you recommend that a bruh sends over to you when he wants to get to know you?"

"Are you sure you want to go down this road, Kee?" She never looked up in my direction, never missing a beat on the drink she was mixing. "Word on campus is your girlfriend is a real piece of work. I don't think talking to you would be a good thing for any woman right now."

"Wait a minute, you know me?"

"Who doesn't know you, Keenan Ellis?"

"There's a difference between know and *know*, sexy…and speaking of know, can I know your name?"

"I'm sure Javi already told you my name, Keenan." She giggled to herself before she looked up and met my gaze. There was this familiarity in her stare, like we had done this before. "Just like I know he told you that Pops is my uncle, which is why I'm wondering what made you get up the nerve to walk over here and talk to me. You must be brave…or stupid."

"Aww, come on, girl, your uncle can't be that bad?"

"The real question is, do you really want to find out?" Ariel winked at me as she finished the drink for the other customer and handed it to him. "Hence the reason for my original question: do you really want to go down this road?"

"Yeah, I think I might. Nothing ventured, nothing gained, right?"

Ariel shifted her body toward me, studying my face for a few moments. A smile spread across her lips as she wrote something down on a napkin. She slipped it in my hand in a deft move that no one else saw. "Sorry, White Chocolate, but I'm not off until after your curfew. It looks like you'll have to crash and burn with the rest of your teammates who have tried and failed."

I put the napkin in my pocket as I turned to head back to the table where my teammates were sitting. I already knew I was gonna get it; Rome was already on his feet, motioning over to give me a consoling hug. The rest of the table was in the throes of hysterical laughter.

"I told you to quit while you were ahead, superstar!" Javi shouted loud enough for the whole bar to hear. "That's what you get!"

"Yeah, man, whatever, Javi," I snapped as Rome kept up the mock hugs and consoling. I brushed him off me. "Rome, kill that noise, man, it's time to roll out."

"Aww, dude, don't flex because you got your feelings hurt," Rome countered, motioning for the rest of the group to calm the laughter. "Nobody—and I mean nobody—bats a thousand, bro, not even the golden child."

"All right, all right, you've had your fun, now can we go, please?" I insisted, grabbing my drink to down it in one gulp.

"All right, man, don't get your panties in a knot, damn." Rome dropped a twenty on the table near the check before we headed out to the car. "It's not my fault you aimed too damn high and fell on your ass."

As I walked by the bar, Ariel winked at me again. I was confused by the flirtatious gesture, until I remembered that she wrote something on the napkin and slipped it to me before she gave me the brush off.

I pulled the napkin out of my pocket and read the note written on it. *Meet me in the Quad, three o'clock tomorrow... I'll be waiting. We have a lot to talk about.*

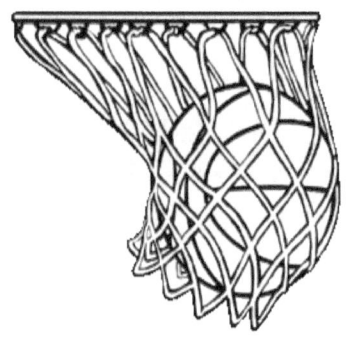

Chapter Eighteen

"I'm glad you came. I wasn't sure if you would."

The smile on Ariel's face was more than worth the risk I was taking in that moment.

Being seen in the Quad, which was located in the center of campus, was definitely a risk, since I wasn't supposed to be there with her in the first place. I mean, Ella was my girl and all, and most of the women on campus got word to steer clear of me or deal with her wrath. I resented that; most of them only wanted to befriend me, but they didn't want to deal with the drama that came with her.

There was something about Ariel that drew me to her. Like a moth to a flame…

I was playing with fire, but I didn't care anymore. Ariel had my attention and I needed to see how this would play out. The problem was, Ariel knew it, too. I wasn't sure if I like the power she had over me and we hadn't even gone out on a date yet. The way she looked at me—it caused my whole body to emit a radiance that I was almost sure people noticed as they passed by.

I mean, don't get me wrong; Ella helped pull me out of a very dark place. She helped me rehab, helped with school as my tutor, and it wasn't like she was slacking in her sex game. Any man would die to have her by his side.

Maybe that was my problem; she was *always* by my side.

Ella took on my major so she could be in almost every class with me. She was at the apartment almost from the moment I got home from class and didn't leave until I was drained and comatose. She even did the grocery shopping for me and Rome, hiding behind the excuse that she wanted to stay on top of our diets. She said the coaching staff was good with it, and as long as we were winning, of course it wouldn't matter to them.

It felt like I was her entire reason for existing, like she was more my keeper than my girlfriend. I wasn't feeling that anymore after the stunt she pulled the other night while she was trying to "help" me sleep. That was worse than any nightmare I'd had before or since. What upset me was when I woke up the next morning, I had no ill effects from the events of night before, when I knew I should have been dragging on only three hours' sleep.

My God…what the hell had L.B. done to me?

Yeah, maybe I was a hypocrite for leading her on these last couple of years. When you're used to people catering to you, you tended to have a skewed perspective on things. After Ella spoiled me all this time, I wasn't ready to give all that up. I didn't have a safety net or a parachute to brace for the free-fall—or maybe I was and I didn't know it yet.

Ariel was the first person since all this madness began who made me work to keep her attention. Not Coach Bolden, or the rest of the coaching staff, not Ella, not any of these other women on campus. She saw me—like she peered inside and saw the real me—and never blinked an eyelash.

"So, why are you glad I came?"

"My uncle's bar was not the right time and place to have a conversation … and we definitely need to have a conversation."

I raised my eyebrow, trying to get a read on her. "Oh, so is that the reason why you gave me such a hard time last night?"

"No, that wasn't the reason I gave you a hard time last night. You're an arrogant superstar and you needed to be knocked down a notch or two. That was the real reason." Ariel grinned, sliding closer to me to keep the conversation private.

I clutched my chest over my heart with my hand and leaned back to feign having my feelings hurt. "Wow, arrogant? Did I come off like that to you?"

"You did to Uncle Solomon," she replied. "That's another reason I gave you a hard time. He doesn't like you very much right now, so I had to make it look like I wasn't interested in you to keep him from suspecting anything"

"What did I ever do to … Uncle Solomon?" I was in a state of confusion; he and I never had a single conversation for him to form that opinion. "He was always in my corner, and then one day, he simply … I don't know, he stopped. I never figured out why. It kinda hurt; I like the old man."

Ariel exhaled for a moment, placing her hand over mine, leaning in closer like she was in the midst of revealing the big secret. "Pops said that you reminded him of someone, but he couldn't figure out whom. It was someone from his past, someone who had the same type of potential that you have. He said there was this aura surrounding you one day after you were injured a couple of years ago. Ever since, he said he's kept an eye on you, unsure of what to make of what you were becoming."

I was taken aback by the mention of aura surrounding me. I mean, I remembered my aunt, who was into chakras and all that, talking about people having energy auras around them and that different people who had the "gift" could see them and knew how to deal with them before that person ever said hello.

My mind clicked on something else she said before the aura part. "You had to make it look like you weren't interested in me? Wait a minute—"

Ariel blushed for a moment, rubbing her hands over her face to compose herself. "Yes, Mr. Ellis, I might be feeling you a little bit, but you weren't supposed to pick up on that yet. You're a little more perceptive than I gave you credit for. I shouldn't be feeling you, though, after you all but forgot about me the night you got injured. You almost broke my heart."

I froze. With that one phrase, she'd unlocked everything that happened that night—including the fact that we were getting closer. I was supposed to call her after I'd talked to the doctor about my knee.

"Oh my God, Ariel? It's all coming back to me now. I was supposed to call ... I'm so sorry, I—"

She placed her finger over my lips to stop me from talking. "A lot of things happened that night that conspired against us. I waited for you to call me back, but I received another important call before you could call me back. When I tried to call you back, the nurse answered your cell phone and told me you were being transferred to a hospital closer to home, so I didn't get the chance to tell you that I needed to transfer schools to handle the emergency I needed to deal with."

I cursed under my breath. Ella. "So, why didn't you call me another time to tell me what happened?"

"I did, Kee, but you didn't recognize my voice," she replied. She wiped a tear away for a moment. "It didn't make sense. It was like I had been erased from your memory or something."

I couldn't find the words to explain to her that I'd been having visions of her the whole time. I was scared she'd think I was crazy. "Ariel, I wish I could make you understand that I'd been dreaming about you, convinced you weren't real, but something told me you were. I know it sounds crazy as hell, but it's the truth. The pieces wouldn't fit, no matter how hard I tried."

"Kee, listen to me, the pieces are beginning to fit now, and that's all that matters to me." Ariel caressed my cheek. "I just have to figure out how to convince Uncle Solomon that you're not the bad influence he thinks you are."

"Ariel, after everything that has happened, why are you defying your uncle? He doesn't strike me as the type to convince of anything, much less that I'm not a bad influence."

"There was something—I'm not sure what that is yet—that was placed over you, that shrouded your perception of reality. You didn't sound like the Kee I was starting to fall for when I called to check on you," Ariel commented. "Uncle Solomon said when I was growing up that I had this ability to see what people didn't want me to see, even when they weren't sure they wanted me to see it."

"So, how does that work? I mean, you're not into voodoo or anything like that?" My nerves were on edge. I wasn't sure what I was signing up for in that moment. "Because if you are, I might need to really leave you alone before you put roots on me or something."

Ariel placed her hand on top of mine and I felt this surge of energy run through me. It spread over me like a warm blanket, keeping me from anything cold and callous. I didn't want her to let me go; everything I'd been dealing with began to melt away, and I felt as close to my old self as I had in a long time.

"Are you sure you want to go down this road?" Ariel asked me, a warm smile spreading across her lips. She looked like she could walk on air, and her body language was wide open to me. "I'm ready, but I want to be sure you're ready."

"I wouldn't have come here if I wasn't sure I wanted to go down this road," I scoffed, a little put off that she would try to gut-check me. "I need to see what happened, why I couldn't remember you."

"Well, I don't want to do anything that your girlfriend might notice later." Ariel bat her eyelashes, breaking down my walls and increasing my comfort level with her with each passing second. "Not that I'd care what she thought if she did. I have a feeling she had a hand in keeping you from me all this time."

"Don't worry about her, she doesn't have papers on me, and I haven't put a ring on it, so, not to worry."

"Okay, it's your funeral." Ariel turned her body toward me, giving me a full-frontal view of her curves. My body reacted as my eyes roamed from head to toe, licking my lips and making my more libidinous intentions known.

The next moment, there was an involuntary shift as my body tensed up. I couldn't figure out why I was resisting; my mind was fighting between opening to her advances and putting up the defenses to keep her out.

"Relax and let me see," Ariel whispered in my ear as she took my hand in hers and squeezed.

I couldn't break the hold she had over me, but I didn't want her to let me go. She scanned my face, looking for some weakness, some crack in the mask. I continued to struggle with breaking the connection between us or opening myself more to what she wanted to see.

She caressed my face, helping me to feel at ease with her probing. *Don't be afraid, I won't hurt you, baby.* I swore I heard her voice ringing in my ears, but she never opened her mouth to speak a word. Her eyes kept me captive the entire time. *Give it to me, let me see.*

I closed my eyes and forced myself to lower my defenses to her. I was scared to let her in, and I realized why I was fighting: I didn't want her to see the day I made the deal with L.B. I didn't want anyone to know what I'd done, including Ariel. As much relief as I'd felt that I'd put all the pieces together to solve the puzzle when it came to the two of us, I didn't want her to solve the puzzle of why it took two years for us to get back to where we were right now.

Ariel continued to penetrate every door I tried to close with the skill of a locksmith who could pick any lock in front of them. *You're not very good at hiding, handsome,* I heard her as I watched her lips turn up into a half-smile. We were oblivious to anyone who saw us, but I knew someone had to get enough of a glance or pay enough attention to what was happening between us.

Slowly, but surely, she saw everything she wanted to see. I shook with each barrier she decimated, acquiescing the fact she would break me down. She saw my strengths, my weaknesses, my desires, my dreams, everything that I thought my bravado and swagger would keep at bay. She saw what I wanted from her, too. She saw that I made a note on the notepad on the side of the bed to call her the next morning. She saw Ella take that note and rip it to shreds before tossing it in the trash. Most of all, she saw I didn't want Ella anymore.

I broke the connection without warning. I had to tear myself away from her, even though I didn't want to. I needed to regain control, if only for a moment or two. I never released the grip I had on her hands, though. I wasn't ready for her to see it all yet.

"Why did you stop me, Kee?" Ariel queried. "What are you afraid of?"

"I'm not afraid," I lied. I was completely disoriented and it took a minute to regain my balance. "How did you do that?"

"I told you, people show me things, even if they don't want me to see them," Ariel repeated. "There's something you're hiding, something that you're ashamed of. Does that have anything to do with why my uncle doesn't like you?"

"Leave it alone, Ariel," I protested, trying my best to detour the conversation. "I'm not ready to go there with you yet. It's not a pretty sight. If you see, it will change how you feel about me. I'm not ready for that. I couldn't take it if you rejected me after you see what I've done."

"No, that's not an option, especially after you showed me how you feel about me," Ariel persisted. "I know you want me, I know you're in love with me, you couldn't hide that from me."

A sharp tap on my shoulder intercepted my potential reply. I didn't need to know who was behind me, I already knew who it was. It was going to make a complicated situation damn near untenable, but this was a long time coming, and it was time that all the things that were done in the dark find its way into the light.

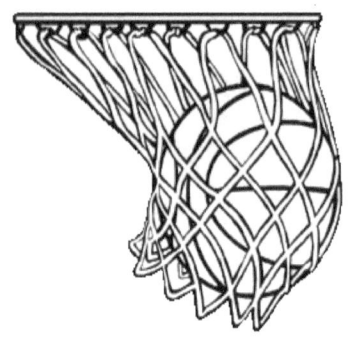

Chapter Nineteen

"Excuse me, but could you explain to me what you're doing out here with my man?" Ella showed up out of nowhere, but if I'd paid close enough attention instead of getting caught in my own fantasy, I would have realized someone gave her the head's up.

"We were having a friendly conversation," Ariel replied, unfazed by Ella's anger. "Until you interrupted, of course. We both know this isn't the first time you'd managed that, though, right?"

"And what is that supposed to mean?" Ella's eyes flashed like they'd caught fire. "Everyone on this campus knows he's with me, so I guess you need to get caught up on the memo."

Ariel stood and took a step toward her, ready for a fight. That move surprised me; I wasn't sure she was ready to claim me like that again. Her eyes narrowed and the grin disappeared as her hands balled into fists. Ella had the same menacing look on her face, her stance stiffening, unwilling to give an inch to her opponent.

I would have stepped in, but my body was weak from the connection Ariel and I went through. Instead, I moved my hand toward Ella and tried to grab her wrist. "Ella, relax, we really were only talking, okay?"

"Don't tell me to relax, Keenan, this bitch needs to be taught a lesson," Ella spat, twisting her wrist from my grip. "She's not the first, and she won't be the last."

Ariel took a closer look at Ella, studying her face with great interest after Ella's last statement. She frowned with disgust as she recognized why she looked so familiar to her. "I should have known you were back on the scene. Some bitches just can't be put down. Where's your handler, huh? I know you have a long leash, but he's usually around somewhere."

A crowd had already formed around the scene, and I noticed thunder in the distance that seemed to move closer by the moment. That was weird; there was not a storm cloud in sight before Ella showed up.

Rome and Javi were in the group of onlookers, too. It wasn't hard to spot them; they stuck out like the trees they were in the midst of the bushes and shrubs around them. I saw Rome attempt to say something when he saw Ariel and Ella standing toe-to-toe looking like Holly Holm and Ronda Rousey, and we all remembered how that turned out, right?

Javi just shook his head, looking in my direction like I'd run head first into a brick wall after he told me not to. *I told you to leave her alone*, he mouthed.

I shrugged him off to concentrate on the mess in front of me.

Ariel laughed and took a step toward Ella. "Didn't you get enough the last time around? Don't you ever learn?"

Ella huffed at those statements until she got a good look at Ariel. Her eyes widened as she took a couple of steps back without another word. "Stay away from me!"

Ariel turned to me and shook her head. "You're lucky you're cute, Kee, but you have a peculiar taste in women."

"This isn't happening! Stay away from my man, bitch!" Ella yelled as she tried to snatch my hand and pull me with her.

I pulled away from Ella and scowled at her. "What the hell do you think you're doing? I'm not some lap dog, do you know who I am?"

Ella's eyes welled up as she stared me down. "I expect to see you back at your apartment. We need to talk."

The laughter from the crowd drowned my reply as Ella walked off in a huff. The crowd disbursed once the fireworks were over, leaving Ariel and me back where we started, alone. Ariel touched my arm to bring the focus back to her.

"I need to handle that, I guess," I uttered. My sheepish demeanor was due to being stripped naked under her touch, and I was embarrassed that I did not play a more active role in diffusing the situation. "I'm sorry you had to go through all of that. I didn't realize how much people feared her on campus. I feel like I'm stuck in a bubble and no one can get in."

I turned to walk in the direction of where Ella had gone when Ariel surprised me with a kiss. I didn't expect her to do that in light of what happened, but her reassuring smile put me at ease. "There's a lot more going on than you realize, baby. Her hold on you is not as strong as she thought it was, and it's going to make someone she answers to very unhappy."

"But she's done so much for me, Ariel," I replied, feeling the need to confess everything. Well, almost everything. "I feel like I'm betraying her after the loyalty that she's shown to me all this time. No one wants to get close; they're afraid of what she might do. Hell, I'm afraid of what she might do."

"I'm not afraid of her, and neither should you," Ariel squeezed my hand to make her point. "You're stronger than you think, Kee. I know you are. I don't fall for weak men."

I wasn't sure what she meant by that, but I wasn't in the mood to argue in that moment. If anything, I needed to try to find a way to work out the issues that somehow found their way to my doorstep. "I don't know how strong I am anymore. I'm not sure of anything right now."

"There's only one way to find out, cuteness." Ariel winked at me as she headed off. "I'm sure you'll find out sooner than later."

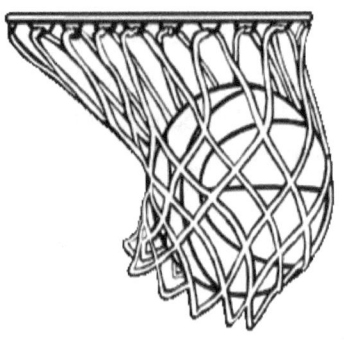

CHAPTER TWENTY

"Lawd, dude, you had to play with fire, huh?"

I could always depend on Javi to try to be the voice of reason from time to time. This was one of those times where I didn't need him to be that. He shot me a look while we were in the living room breaking down film. Usually, it's the three of us, including Rome, but he had to handle a tutoring session, so that left me and Javi to break things down.

It also gave him time to break me down over the craziness from earlier. "So, what's the deal with Ariel, bro? It looked like she was ready to go toe-to-toe with Ella over you."

Javi's personality was more subdued than Rome's tended to be, and he had this thing about being the diplomat. Considering he was a political science major and had ambitions of going into politics after he was done with his playing career, it wasn't too far from his authentic self.

He always had this thing about being on the straight and narrow, and he tried to avoid drama like it was the plague. It wasn't like he hadn't seen me do my share of dirt over the years, but it's not like he hadn't been a little messy himself since freshman year, either. I'd seen him do his dirt, too, and he ain't no Boy Scout, as much as he liked to pretend he was.

"Look, it was a harmless conversation, all right?" I tried to defend myself the best way I could, but even I knew it was paper-thin. "Besides, she left the note in my hand before she made it look like she dismissed me. That whole mess that you and Rome walked in on was Ella's doing. That chick is flying off the handle every time a female gets within breathing distance."

Javi chuckled at the visual. "Yeah, bro, I don't know how you do it, that girl is a real piece of work."

"It doesn't matter, seriously. She's wearing on my nerves, and I might need to cut her loose." The finality of that statement hit me harder than I cared to admit. I said what I was thinking out loud, but I wasn't sure I wanted to believe I had what it took to follow up on that thought.

Javi got silent once I said that, and he rubbed his hand over his face like he was preparing to say something profound. "All right, I don't want you to take this the wrong way, okay?"

"Say what's on your mind, Javi, you know it ain't that deep."

"I know Ella's a handful and all, but do you really want to drop her like a bad habit now?"

"What are you talking about, Javi?"

"Okay, so, follow my lead on this logic," Javi started bringing out the diplomacy and logical deductions again. "This is senior year, and you're gonna have a lot of NBA scouts coming to see about you during the season. Ella's bound to see all that, and she's gonna be pissed if you start rolling with Ariel, even if you try to make her think she's a friend."

"Come on, Javi, we only had one conversation—"

"Yeah, and it was only one conversation with Kira Parsons sophomore year, and look how that ended," Javi reminded me, shutting me down. He studied my face for a moment. "Yeah, I thought you might remember that shit."

Kira Parsons was a mistake that should have derailed my basketball career a couple of years ago. If it weren't for some pervert who happened to have a motion camera in his room—which got him booted off campus for his own illegal conduct—there was no telling what might have happened to me.

It didn't stop me from doing my thing, though, but it taught me to be a little more careful of groupies and their shady behavior. Hell, Ella got rid of them for me once she came into the picture, and I hadn't worried about women with bad intentions since. But what Javi tried to get me to understand was beginning to hit home, I couldn't deny that.

"Look, Kee, I'm not saying that Ariel would turn out to

be another Kira Parsons, but you better make sure."

"All right, Javi, I'm feeling where you're coming from, but you don't understand what type of program Ella's been on since we got back to school, though." I tried to reason with him, the frustration mounting with each word I spoke. "It's like she's everywhere all of a sudden and I can't breathe without her being damn near in my hip pocket."

Javi rubbed his chin as I tried to explain about the incident a few nights ago. When I got that off my chest, he leaned forward to turn off the game film. That was a bad sign.

"Let me give you a hypothetical to rock with," he began. "Say you drop Ella before the season begins, and you and Ariel get together after the season ends as you prepare for the draft. Ella's all up in her feelings because Ariel reaped the fruit that she sowed the last couple of years trying to get you back on the mend."

"Javi, seriously—"

Javi continued, ignoring me as I tried to cut him off. "And say that Ella drops a bomb out of the blue that she's pregnant with your child right before the draft because she managed to keep some of your seed frozen for just such a contingency plan. Ariel's pissed at you because you got baby mama drama on your hands, and Ella squeezes Ariel out of the picture because there wasn't enough to keep you two together to weather that storm."

"Okay, that has got to be the wildest story I've ever heard, bro. I mean, come on, man, do you really think Ella would be that crazy?" I didn't want to believe the lunacy coming out of his mouth. Ella's not that stupid. Was she?

Javi shook his head. "Do I need to remind you of the BS that D-Wade went through, or what about the rumors that floated around about LeBron and the outside relationship with the chick that was a sports reporter in Cleveland who just happened to get a gig down in Miami while he was playing down there? Do you want to sit here and say no one is capable of the unthinkable?"

I froze in my tracks when I thought back to the mess that D-Wade was going through with Gabrielle Union and his ex-wife. People were already saying he was stepping out on the wife with Gabrielle even though he swore they were nothing but friends and didn't start dating until after he divorced his wife. He managed to survive that turmoil and marry Gabrielle later, but the damage to his reputation was crazy.

I had to look at the man in the mirror to figure out if I was being a hypocrite or not.

"All I'm saying is now that you're about to hit the big stage, you need to figure out where things stand, and you need to keep it real with Ella before she does turn into D-Wade's ex-wife." Javi leveled with me. "She could make your life hell, if she hasn't already."

My phone sounded off, and from the ringtone I already knew it was Ella. Her ears must have been burning or something. Javi noticed the disgusted look on my face as I let the call go to voicemail. "Either keep her or drop her, Kee, the choice is yours to make. I'm your boy regardless, ain't nothing about to change all that. But the less messy, the better, you feel me?"

"Yeah, I feel you, bro. Now, I need to get home so I can handle this nonsense before she blows my phone up." I gave him pound and headed out the door. "We can do the film session tomorrow."

"What were you doing with her?!?!"

"The last time I checked, I could hang out with who I wanted to hang out with! What is wrong with you?!?"

"I told you all you needed was me! No one can do for you what I do for you!"

We were at it for at least an hour, and I know the folks under us could hear every single word of what was going on. The walls were thin, so it wouldn't be the first time they'd heard anything going on in my bedroom.

Rome and Angela even tried to break us apart to cool off a bit before something was said that we would both regret. They soon gave up; they saw what was happening and there was nothing either of them could do to stop it.

Ella showed me a different side to her that I didn't like or want in my life: jealous, irrational, possessive. It wasn't what I signed up for, and I wasn't about to condone it, either. It was time to drop the hammer on all this now.

"I honestly don't want to hear all that right now, Ella," I snapped as I slumped on the bed. "Every single time a woman smiles in my direction, you completely go nuclear, ready to erase them from existence for just looking at me."

"I don't want you throwing away your future in the pros over some chick that could be a groupie catching you at your highest point," Ella responded, standing over me like a parent scolding a child.

"I had a good handle on things until you decided to make a scene," I reminded her. "For once, I could actually relax and have a friendly conversation without having to be Keenan Ellis."

"You could do that with me, you still can." Ella frowned, disappointed in the way the conversation was heading. "You don't need them bitches out there trying to gas you up or sweet-talk you into being their friend."

"Look, Ariel was harmless, and for your information, she wasn't into me because of that," I shot back, taking offense that I was being reduced to nothing more than a lottery ticket. "Which reminds me, what was all that between you two? You looked at her like you knew her from somewhere, and it wasn't on campus."

That stopped her cold. "That is beyond your understanding, so lay off. But yes, we have a history."

I tripped a nerve, and I didn't realize how badly I tripped that nerve until she started in on me with no hesitation and no remorse. "You know what? Go ahead and fuck with her, since you think she's harmless. She won't think so once she sees you for who you really are."

I stood fast, determined not to turn this into a personal battle. "Ella, in the two years we've been together, I have never once cheated on you. You have been the one woman that has been on my mind this entire time. But you have to give me some space. I am allowed to have friends and acquaintances."

"Those so-called *friends* won't be there for you when the rubber meets the road," Ella continued. "Do I need to remind you of all the *friends* that disappeared when you blew out your knee? Do I need to remind you of how alone you felt in that room before Uncle L.B. and I showed up? No one was there for you while I was there with you during all of the rehab, all of the training to get you back into playing form. Where were those *friends* you're claiming you need now?"

I didn't think she would confirm my suspicions after the fact, but she did. She was the one who kept everyone at bay, including trying to erase Ariel from my life. My anger rose to molten core heat, and it was getting more intense by the second. I had been manipulated from the word go, and I still had no clue over why.

She clapped her hand to her mouth, her eyes expressing the immediate regret that I was sure she might have felt. She stepped back from me as her eyes looked at everything in my room. Anything to keep from meeting the rising rage coloring the glare that she knew would greet her.

"Kee ... I'm sorry—"

"Nah, you said what you meant, no need in taking it back now. You purposely took everything that mattered to me, picking and choosing who stayed and who went. Admit it so I can remove whatever shred of compassion I have left for you right now."

Ella sat next to me, trying her best to caress my face. I

177

moved away from her, still stinging from the ringing endorsement she gave of my choice of friends.

"Get away from me."

"Look, Keenan, all I'm trying to say…you need to be careful of who you trust, okay?" Ella tried to diffuse the situation, but there was no luck there. "You're not just another jock. You're Keenan Ellis, all right? All these bitches on campus—Ariel included—are after you for nothing but the potential millions that you're going to make. If it weren't for me and L.B., you wouldn't be right now. Remember that."

"I need some air," I huffed as I pushed past her. "Don't bother looking for me. It's really not that deep. I'll be home before curfew. I may be a superstar, but I still have rules to follow."

"Kee! Wait!"

I closed the door and walked down the hall. I felt the walls closing in on me, and the more I thought about it, the more I couldn't breathe. For the first time in two years, I began to question what I had gotten myself into.

That night changed everything.

I didn't realize how much it did until this moment.

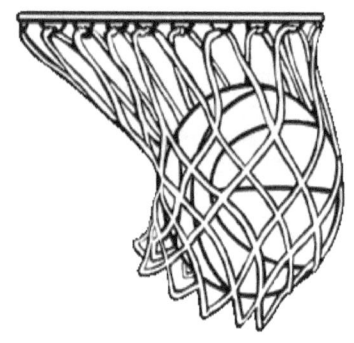

Chapter Twenty-One

I sat on the stairs outside of the arena on campus as memories took me back to the events that unfolded two years ago. I replayed the sequence of events over and over again in my head, trying to figure out what I could have done to avoid getting hurt. The truth was the guard from Trent had it in for me from the opening tip.

Javon Leggett. I would never forget his name. Neither will the rest of the college sports world, not after that play.

If I could take it all back, I swear I would. This was not what I signed up for.

I headed back to my apartment with the hopes that I would be able to go to sleep and pretend this day didn't happen. I wanted to play make-believe for a few more hours, if for anything else, to keep the nightmares at bay. One way or another, if I didn't do something, I wouldn't survive the season, not without losing my mind.

I was powerless to stop whatever was happening to me, and I was scared to find out what would happen if I decided I didn't want to do this anymore.

Maybe that was L.B.'s plan all along.

"If it isn't the National Player of the Year, White Chocolate himself."

"What in the name of all that is holy are you doing here?"

"Well, I figured we needed to have a little chat."

Standing toe to toe with the epicenter of all my troubles put the cherry on top of the mother of mucked up days. I was ready to shred through him with every fiber of my being, but I noticed his clothes, his physical appearance, and I had to take a pause. Something wasn't right. Javon Leggett was standing there, but there was something "off" about him. I couldn't figure out why, but this wasn't the dude on the court I faced two years ago.

I looked in his eyes, and he looked like he wasn't there. He was there in flesh, but he wasn't "there." He looked at me, watching me as I tried to move from his sight, but I was doing it to make sure he wasn't coked out of his mind or something.

"What could you possibly have to chat with me about, considering every inch of me wants to dispatch you to the next world for putting me through everything I'm going through right now."

"If it wasn't for me, you wouldn't be what you are right now," Javon replied. He had a hard time staying upright, which further fueled my suspicions that he was high. "Thanks to L.B., of course."

He had my attention. "What you know about L.B.?"

"I know he convinced me to take you out, promising that he would get me in the League after all the negative press died down." He shook his head, watching my eyes widen over his revelation. "Instead, I got thrown under the bus, kicked off the team, the stench of that one act following me my whole basketball life."

"Wait a minute, you got in the League, though."

"I was there for three years, and I didn't even get drafted, bro. I had to get in as an undrafted rookie, scratching my way in. I was all good, until my rookie contract ran out," he explained. "When it came time to negotiate my new contract, regardless of the fact that I kept my nose clean the whole damn time, my teammates couldn't trust me, felt like I was a dirty player, and they put up with me until my contract was up."

"So, you're telling me it's my fault you did what you did?" I wanted to take a rock and break it off in his skull. "You couldn't take the trash talking, and one word from L.B. and you damn near ended my life?"

"It wasn't supposed to go down like that!" He yelled in frustration. "I tried to get to you, to tell you I was sorry, but they pulled me away before your teammates could retaliate. They wouldn't let me near the hospital, your teammates made sure of that. It doesn't matter anyway. My life is over."

I didn't want to have this conversation anymore, so I

started walking in a different direction to keep him from following me home. I didn't get two steps in before he was in my face again. I tried to take a swing at him, only to connect with nothing but air. I blinked a few times, taking more futile swings at him, only to swipe right through his spectral form.

"I told you, bro, my life is over, and I'm paying for it for all eternity."

I took a few steps back, not understanding what my eyes were witnessing. "You're … you're dead? How on earth are you here?"

"I'm here to warn you—something I didn't have the guts to do in life." Javon stepped toward me, his expressionless face giving no indication of what he was about to say. "You have a way out of this mess, but you have to make a decision. You have the power to make that decision, but you have to be strong enough to make it."

Before I could ask him what he was talking about, he disappeared into the night. The frustration that consumed me was overwhelming. I wanted to scream as I cast my eyes skyward, trying my best to understand what was happening to me. I was starting to see things, and I couldn't trust my eyes to believe what they were seeing.

This was too much, and I needed the first opportunity to find the nearest exit from this—whatever the hell this was. I wasn't sure if I could handle any other paranormal encounters that I wouldn't be able to explain to anyone without them making a phone call to the nearest mental health facility to have me committed. Hell, I wouldn't blame them for doing it, and it would be a welcome reprieve. I might have been able to get a decent night's sleep.

I wasn't in the mood to deal with Ella, either. I'd hoped she'd made herself scarce, considering she was the source of my discontent. I didn't want to be sweet-talked or placed in a carnal coma in an effort to get me to forget what she'd said and meant, whether she said it in the heat of the moment or not. I prayed for peace as I stepped through the door, only to find Rome and Angela snoring on the couch and the Netflix symbol still showing on the big screen.

I smiled as I headed to my bedroom and relieved to see an empty bed. It was the first sliver of normalcy I'd had all day, and for that, I was grateful.

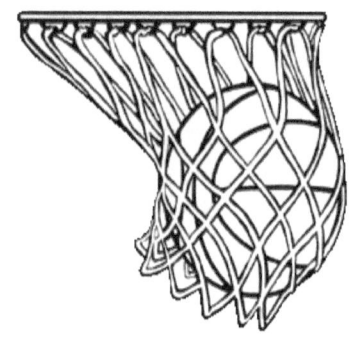

Chapter Twenty-Two

"Hey, Kee, did I wake you?"

My cell phone surprised me at noon, which was crazy. I rarely slept in during the week, unless I didn't have a morning class and I didn't want to put in any shooting time in the gym or weight room work. I tried to keep my voice from sounding groggy, but when I heard her voice over the phone, there was no way I was giving her any reason to get off. "Nah, I'm good, I guess I dozed off for a second or two. What's on your mind, sexy?"

"You are on my mind, cuteness."

If she could see the grin on my face right now, I'd swear I'd be busted. "So, what am I doing, since I'm on your mind?"

"Well, I could tell you, but then my hands would be busy doing something else, and I would have to get off the phone." Ariel let a soft moan escape, teasing me.

"I won't tell if you won't tell," I replied, feeling my body betray me with each passing moment we were connected. I felt a little bold, so I wanted to test her to see how far she would let me go. "Why don't you tell me, and then I can tell you what you're doing. You happen to be on my mind, too."

"I know I am. I can feel you," Ariel kept flirting. "I would love to be with you right now, but I'm sure you have something you have to do today, and what I want to do could take all afternoon."

"And if I wanted to cancel, so you could come over?"

"We both know you won't cancel, sexy. No matter how bad you want me, there are things that take priority."

She had me, and she knew it. I closed my eyes and cursed, wishing that I didn't have the film session with the team in an hour. I lamented my overly-developed sense of leading by example as I contemplated the next words I wanted to say. I closed my eyes, wishing there was a way she could be here with me, even if it was for a few moments, I ached for her that much. She had me in so much lust I could feel her touching me, caressing every sensitive spot that drove me crazy.

Wait a minute … someone *was* touching me. I opened my eyes and stared directly into Ariel's eyes. I watched her body as it hovered over mine, feeling her fingers touching my skin. I tried to touch her, but my fingers slipped through hers, exacerbating my frustration to have her there with me in her physical form. After the madness I dealt with last night with Javon, I didn't have the energy to go through it again with someone I wanted to be there with me now.

Hi, sexy.

How is this happening, aren't you on the phone with me?

You wanted me here, so here I am, Kee.

Are you really here? Am I dreaming?

You're not dreaming, Keenan, you're wide awake.

I sat up for a moment, continuing to stare at the ethereal version of the object of my desire, knowing in my rational mind she was miles away in the confines of her apartment. She placed her lips against mine, and I felt the fullness of her lips pressing my flesh. Her hands caressed my cheek as she did her best to calm my confusion.

But you're not here, Ariel. How can I feel you if you're not actually here?

Maybe you want to believe I'm here so badly that you conjured a version of me to help get you through the day.

You know I want you here. I need you. Last night was scary, I had a full-blown conversation with my former nemesis, but he told me he was dead. He said I needed to make a choice to ... never mind.

What is it, baby? Don't shut me out, please?

It's nothing, I just need you so badly right now.

If you play your cards right, there's a way we can be together. Do you want that?

Yes.

I gave in to every emotion, every sensation that I had to

give her. Nothing else mattered to me except being in this moment with her, even if we weren't physically together.

Javon was right. We can't be together until you make a choice, Keenan.

What choice?

I didn't want to say this, but you know Ella isn't the one for you. She never was. She tried to keep you from me, the hold on you is strong. You need to choose, but in making that choice, you need to make sure you want what you want, not what someone else wants for you.

My emotions were raw and wide open; I was vulnerable. She knew it, too, and I wanted Ariel to claim what I now felt belonged to her, all she had to do was say it was hers.

You know what's in my heart, Ariel. I can't hide it from you, and I don't want to. It's yours.

I know it is, Kee, but you still have something that needs to be done first. Only then can we truly be together.

She began to dissipate into nothingness, and for a few moments it was silent. I heard my heart slow to a steady beat, my Bluetooth still in my ear.

"If you want to see me, you know where to find me, baby." Ariel's voice caressed my ear. "It doesn't have to be today, but I would like to see you before the game this weekend, if that's okay with you?"

"Will you be at Ballers later today?"

"No, I have another obligation tonight, Kee," she sighed. "There's an issue that needs to be handled and I can't get out of it."

I was frustrated; even if she got home at a decent enough hour, Ella would be home by then and I wouldn't get to call her or accept her call. I began to understand what Ariel meant by making a choice. If I chose to still be with Ella, I would be sneaking around on her, trying to steal moments with Ariel. I couldn't have my cake and eat it, too.

I straightened up in bed. "I will see you before game time on Saturday, one way or the other."

"Okay, baby, I'll clear the rest of my schedule as best I can," Ariel told me. "I'll see you soon."

"Oh, Ariel?"

"Yes, Keenan?"

"I can't help but ask, and I know it sounds crazy, but I really want to know," I rubbed my hands together to get the courage to ask what I knew was a weird question. "Were you really here with me earlier while we were on the phone?"

"That depends on what you believe. If you believe I was there with you, then I was there with you. Bye, sexy."

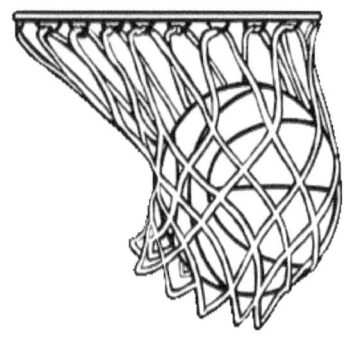

CHAPTER TWENTY-THREE

We were in the film room after practice this afternoon, preparing for the game against Kent. I was bored out of my skull. I already knew the game plan well enough to be Coach's eyes on the floor, so I let my mind wander a little bit.

By April, I'd have a second ring on my hand, which was something to say this day and age. Yeah, the UCLA dynasty will never be duplicated, so getting two rings in one college career was special, and I was going to be special. Lottery-bound and a game changer for whichever franchise that drafted me.

I had feelers out there, thanks to L.B. and Ella, and I was a definite lock for the top three picks in the draft. Even with the rookie wage scale, I would still have the dollars to make everyone around me happy. That was all I cared about.

Hell, the shoe deal with Nike would be killer—or maybe Adidas—or maybe go across the pond and rock with Reebok. Not to mention my charisma and ability to sell a product. The camera loves me! The possibilities were endless.

"Keenan, do you think you can join the rest of us down here and get your head out of the clouds?" Coach Bolden interrupted my thoughts. "We do have a pretty good opponent coming up in a few days."

"Coach, you act like I don't already know what's going on?" I countered in my dismissal. I was irritated that he crashed through my dreams like that. "We got this, Coach. We're the top-ranked squad in the country for a reason."

"Is that right?" Coach Bolden retorted, turning the film on to showcase my defense in a half-court set. It wasn't one of my better sets. I got burned on an isolation where my guy went baseline. Luckily, I recovered before Javi could rotate and pinned the layup on the backboard. "Let's see, that would be you, getting lax on defense, letting your man slip under you on the baseline and nearly posterizing you, right?"

"Yeah, but I ended up making him a *SportsCenter* highlight!" I yelled back as the rest of the team chuckled. "Come on, Coach, why are you riding me?"

"Because you're not hungry, Kee!" Coach snapped.

"Yo, Kee, ease it back a few, you got caught snoozing, it happens to all of us, that's why the rotations have to be tight," Javi tried to calm me down, but I was already in third gear and ready to punch it.

"Since when?!" I yelled back, feeling the room get quiet. "I'm the one everyone is gunning for! I'm the one that can carry this team on his back any time I feel like it! I've done it all since I stepped on this campus, so who are you to tell me I'm not hungry?!"

Coach Bolden's eyes were fiery, but his calmness should have been what put fear in my heart. "You. Me. Outside. *NOW!*"

"What is your problem?"

Coach Bolden was an imposing man; six-foot-nine and in good enough shape to still be able to run with us even in his sixties. I should have known better than to challenge him in the film room.

The heat I felt dissipated quick once it was the two of us talking in the hallway. I did not want to back down, but I did feel he singled me out for no reason. "Sorry, Coach, I guess I'm feeling the pressure a little more than I let on."

"This ain't like you, Keenan. We've been together nearly four years and you've never blown up like that, even when I've been on you."

"You know what it's like to have the target on your back, Coach, I thought you'd feel me more than anyone else," I remarked. "You were the man in the seventies when you balled for Coach Wooden."

Coach Bolden ran his hands over his beard. "Sooner or

later, Kee, you're going to have to understand the concept of grace under pressure. Last year, you were the best player in the country … there was no doubt in that at all. But you lacked humility. You acted like the college basketball world owed you instead of the other way around."

"Coach, you don't get it—"

"Yes, I do get it, son," he cut me off. "You got women running after you on campus, the spotlight is on you, *SportsCenter* and radio talk shows can't keep your name out of their mouths."

"Yeah, but that's not all of it, Coach." I tried to explain, but the words wouldn't come out at that point. I was ashamed of what I'd done, but it was too much to give up going back to before the injury, and I didn't want to let my family down. "You really don't get it."

Coach Bolden stepped away for a minute, took a long look at me like he was assessing me all over again. I stood there, trying to keep from feeling like that fresh-faced high schooler, trying to gain his respect, but the truth was, these last four years, I wouldn't be anywhere near ready for the next level without him.

Before the deal, and before the injury, he was preparing me for the next level, period. There was no way for me to think otherwise. He was the sole reason I came to Temp-State. I was not about to be gut-checked for no reason when I was a major reason we both have a ring on our fingers right now.

"Keenan, we've been together four years. You could have gone pro last year after we won it all, so why did you come back if you were gonna give me this half-assed effort?" Coach earnestly inquired after a long pause.

"I came back ... I want my legacy remembered, Coach," I shot back, straightening up to make my point. "I want to be remembered as being one of the best ballers the college world has ever seen. Alcindor ... Jordan ... Laettner ... the Fab Five ... I want to be mentioned with them."

"But that's the problem, kid, you're forgetting the bigger picture." Coach placed his hand on my shoulder. "You're good, damn good, but you're too damn arrogant for your own good. You were cocky when you got here, yes, but you had a humility that was mixed in with that, and that's why the fans loved you."

"Now, ever since your recovery from your knee injury, you've changed." His eyes never left mine. "You act like the fans, the university, everyone owes you something, and I'm here to tell you, no one owes you shit."

"Coach—" I tried to interject, but Coach kept on with his lecture.

"You may have the media fooled, Kee, but you don't have me fooled," Coach dropped the hammer on me. "Whether you like it or not, superstar, I still have the power to bench you whenever I see fit, regardless of what you've done in the past. The Keenan Ellis I know would've taken the gut-check I gave him and used it to wreak havoc on the court the first chance he got, not mouth off like he's some punk on the street."

He had me dead to rights, and I knew it.

"I know the old Kee is in there somewhere, not this manufactured nonsense that ESPN is painting as the next big thing." Coach did what he did best after ripping a player to shreds. In the next breath, he was building them back, sometimes even stronger than before. "God gave you the talent to do whatever you want to do on that floor. You're one of the best kids I have ever coached, hands down, but it's up to you to figure out if you want to waste your time listening to the hype, or if you truly want to re-write the record books. The choice is yours."

He left me in the hallway without another word, but he left me with a lot to think about. Had I really changed? Was I becoming something other than what I thought I was?

I wasn't sure I was ready for the answers to those questions. In fact, I was outright afraid of them. I didn't want to believe that I had gotten so far that I had forgotten who I was. I decided some extended time in the sauna would do me some good, maybe clear my head and figure out where I had gone wrong. Maybe I could get back to the old me before it was too late.

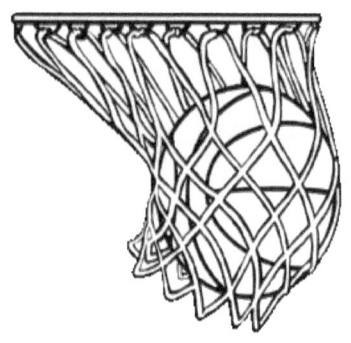

CHAPTER TWENTY-FOUR

I honestly thought I was alone for a little while, and I hoped it would last for a little while longer, at least long enough for me to clear my head of the clutter that swirled around up there.

I was in a good head space as I allowed the heat and the mist of the sauna envelop me and shield me away from the world for a moment or two so I could be me.

Not Keenan Ellis, All-American, but the regular kid who enjoyed playing games on the Xbox One or running World of Warcraft on my laptop. The one who enjoyed his mom's homemade peach cobbler and Brunswick stew while running his mouth with his uncles on the back porch in the summer months. The one who shot ball with his Uncle Dale until his arms were tired, before coming home and watching old videos of Dr. J, Magic and the other legends with Tyler.

I almost forgot how much fun it was to be that dude. Even then I was one of the most sought-after players in the country, but I still managed to have fun with my family and friends. To have those deep conversations with my father and grandfather, soaking up every possible pearl of wisdom they had to give me to help make this life a little easier to live when I got to be their ages.

That's what's missing, I scolded myself. I was so busy trying to be something I wasn't that I forgot how to be the man they molded me into. I had to get that back. But how?

"Well, well, well, if it isn't the Jesus of college basketball."

I lifted my towel over my head, not recognizing the disdain in the voice cutting its way through the dense mist. Once my head cleared and I listened to him speak again, I should have left the sauna right then and there.

Damn. Just when I thought it was safe to come out of my zone.

"I was good by myself, Pops, what do you need?" I scoffed, trying to find my zone again so I could leave without any more stress than I came in with.

"Wow, rough day in the film room, huh, kid?" He acted like he wanted to sympathize with me, but I wasn't feeling it. "That's what happens when you think you're perfect every game. You start slipping."

"I am not slipping!"

"Temper, temper, youngster, it's not my fault you've lost your way."

That got my attention, but he didn't need to know. "What do you think you know about it, huh, Pops?"

"I know more than you think I know, kid."

I slipped my towel over my shoulders this time, determined to figure out what the beef was between us, so I could get it over with and move on. I let it all hang out to clear the air. "You've been on my ass every time I come into your place lately, Pops. I never said two words of any disrespect in your direction, but yet you always stared at me like I'd done something wrong to someone in your family. This can't be about Ariel; I didn't even know she was your niece until recently, and a couple years ago when we were getting close, she never got the chance to mention you. So, what's your problem with me, Pops?"

Pops sat down across from me, leaning forward as the mist continued to surround us. All of a sudden, the mist cleared, and I could see him as clearly as if we'd stepped out of the sauna. How the hell did he do that?

"I have no ill will toward you, kid, but I know a troubled soul when I see one." His first statement rocked me to my core, sending chills down my spine. He couldn't possibly know, could he? "I've seen youngsters like you come and go for decades in my spot, and none of them had what it took to take their talents to the next level. You do."

"So, why are you giving me so much grief, Pops? If I have what it takes, why are you throwing salt in my game? Hell, Ariel had to fake interest in me because of you."

"You're right, this has nothing to do with Ariel, she can make up her mind the way she wants to," he replied. "I saw her slip the note to you, and yet I didn't say anything. She sees something in you, something that you don't see in yourself, and that's my problem with you. Ariel doesn't mess around with anyone, so there must be something about you—something *in* you—that she feels is worth the trouble."

I started laughing, not to spite him, but he sounded too much like my grandfather when I was growing up. "Okay, so break it down for me, what can I do to get you off my back, Pops? Everyone else on this campus worships the ground I walk on, but you're treating me like I'm some kind of pariah or something."

"I want you to make a choice, Keenan Ellis." The deadpan tone in his voice resounded off the walls. "You don't know it yet, but you have the power within you to do some great things, and not just on the court. I want you to stop acting like a boy and start acting like the man you've been made into by the people who cared enough to get you here."

I felt rage coming on within me. He was the second man in the last twenty-four hours to question my maturity. I was twenty-two years old and I wasn't about to be talked to like I was twelve years old with no clue in hell of how to be a grown man. "Pops, I don't know what you've been smoking, but I'm not about to sit here and take this from you, when you've been nothing but hostile to me ever since—"

"Ever since you made a choice that you didn't have to make." Pops stopped me dead cold in my tracks with that statement. "Let me tell you something. For every sucker who makes it, for every LeBron and Kobe, for every Kevin Durant, Steph Curry, there are thousands of pitiful excuses for ballers you never heard of. I mean, sure, the game has taught you how to swag, how to talk shit, how to shoot and dunk. But what else has it taught you? Sooner or later, there's gonna come a time in every athlete's life when there's no more money, no more adulation. The dream will be over, and yours hasn't even started yet, that's what you don't get."

I tried to interrupt him before he got into some pseudo-sermon, but he held his finger up to silence me before he continued on his "enlightening" words of wisdom.

"This is what I'm trying to say to you. When a man looks back on his life, he should be proud of all of it. Not just the years he spent in the limelight. Not just memories of when he was great. You gotta learn that in here, here in your mind, Keenan. The difference between a boy and a man is the choices he makes and the lessons he learns."

The mist in the sauna began to thicken again, which closed the gap between us. This time the mist was so thick that I couldn't see him or any silhouette of him to talk at. It unnerved me to no end that he would lecture me and then disappear. The problem was, I never heard the door open or shut to let me know he actually left.

"Why do you care so much, Pops?" I challenged, my voice booming against the walls. "Why does it matter to you if I succeed or fail? All I can do is play with the hand I've been dealt, and that's what I'm doing. I don't have a choice anymore, okay? I gave that up years ago!"

There was no response to my question. The only thing I heard was the insipid hissing of the mist in the room. He was gone.

I couldn't stop shaking, I was so irritated. I was trapped in a cage with no way to be freed, and it left me with an empty feeling as if I'd given away my future, and for what? So I could be the man? I was already the man before I got hurt.

Instead of trusting the process, I had to go and tell someone that I hadn't known a half-second that I would do anything to get my revenge on the people who were ready to close the door on my basketball career. In hindsight, I may have assumed that they were ready to close the door on my basketball career. Maybe Pops was right; maybe I made a rash decision based on information that I hadn't even confirmed yet, and in my haste—oh, my God, I may have made the mistake of a lifetime.

It didn't matter now. I couldn't take that choice back. How could I? Was it even possible? Why was it that everyone around me insisted that I still had a choice to make?

I left the sauna to get dressed and ready for one of my evening classes, when I noticed something written on a slip of paper on top of my bag. I took a closer look at what was scribbled on the paper: *You ALWAYS have a choice!*

I wanted to believe that. I made a choice that I regretted with each passing day, if I was honest with myself. I didn't think about the risks I was taking, and now I was no longer sure of anything I thought I wanted. If I had a choice, the chance to do it all over again, knowing what I knew now, I would have never agreed to L.B.'s proposal.

But I made that choice, and I have to see it through to whatever end it would take me.

I wasn't sure if some choices could be unmade. I had faith they could be, but there wasn't much I could do about it. At least, that's what I thought.

Maybe that's all I ever needed … my faith. Faith in my own ability to get out of this mess—and get righteous again.

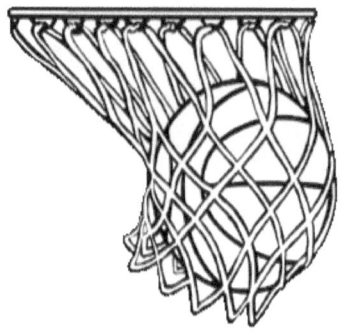

Chapter Twenty-Five

"Thank you for speaking with us today."

I loved the cameras, but I was beginning to wonder if I loved them all that much. The past few days had me questioning a lot of things.

I was in the gym with all these lights surrounding me and the ESPN college basketball analyst, Jay Bilas, chatted me up about the different things we were doing during the preseason and some of the things I was up to personally, which I felt was a little invasive, but this was what happened when you're the favorite for the Naismith Award as the nation's best collegiate player.

It was a taped interview, which was a good thing; I didn't want to do a live take. Anything could happen.

Still, I wanted to get this first take done so I could get back to my teammates and practice and prepare for the first game of the season. Second-ranked Kent was coming to our house for a top-ranked rumble.

They had a couple of players on that squad who had been running their mouths about taking us down, including a guy by the name of Dennis Markson, who was one of the other Naismith finalists this year, even though he was a junior.

Give him credit, he could ball, but he was dirty. That's my opinion on the matter. Last year I schooled him to the tune of a career-high sixty points, and he might still be a little salty after being reminded about it this week. In fact, that was one of the first question out of Jay's mouth when the interview began.

"Tempest State is the top-ranked team in the country and many have you as the odds-on favorite to win it all again," he began, trying to set the stage for the rest of the interview. "This is rarified air if you can win another title before heading to the draft. What are your thoughts heading into the season?"

"Well, I'm enjoying my senior year," I started. "My teammates and I have been working hard, but we've been having fun with it."

"I can appreciate that, Keenan. What have you learned about taking that approach?"

"Appreciating the moment, life is short. Even though we have a lot of pressure to win it again, we hope to entertain this year with our title defense. It's business, but it's fun, too."

It was going pretty well, and it felt that it would be a

softball type of interview, but I knew that sooner or later the other questions would come out. I never expected what would come next.

"Okay, I have to bring this up because he made the comments," he leaned forward for a second before broaching the subject. "But Dennis Markson, the star guard for Kent, has basically said that last year was a fluke when you scored sixty on him and said that this year he will definitely shut you down. What do you want to say in response?"

I couldn't hold the laughter in. "Jay, seriously? Look, he's a good player, not as good as I am, but he's a damn good player. He couldn't shut me down last year when we went at it, and I held him below his average at the same time. He can't guard me. There aren't many guards in the country that can, period."

"Fair enough, but he did mention an incident that happened to you a couple of years ago and alluded to the possibility of it happening again," Jay stated soberly. "I mean, I understand there's trash talk, but that was a rough time for you back then when Javon Leggett swept your legs from under you, causing your devastating knee and shoulder injuries. Do you want to escalate this bad blood between you two?"

"Look, I didn't say a word to him back then when I dropped sixty on him, and I didn't say a word to the press other than it was a good night for the team because it kept the streak going," I retorted, growing more agitated by the second.

This was going nowhere fast, but we both knew that the news outlets would have a field day with it. There's nothing like a good rivalry, right?

Until someone gets hurt…

I wasn't about to let that happen to me again, no way in hell.

We ended the conversation on a decent note, so it wouldn't look like Jay had it out for me or anything, but I was spooked. I managed to get through the rest of practice without anyone noticing that I was off-balance, and I hoped I would be able to sleep tonight.

The first thing I planned on doing was calling L.B. to make sure that nothing happened to me that night. I stopped short of wishing ill will on Dennis. It was nothing more than trash-talking; nothing more than what we did on the blacktop during the summer months. I couldn't shake the feeling that something crazy was going to happen that night. I didn't like it, and I was going to do something about that, before history repeated itself.

We stopped at Ballers to grab something to eat before heading home, and Rome could feel the tension on me. No matter what I tried to do to keep him from starting in with his questions, it seemed to make matters worse. He studied my body language, shaking his head over what I could assume he saw as me not being myself.

"Yo, you all right, man?" he asked as he took a sip of

his beer. "What happened with the interview? Did the trash-talk with Markson get mentioned?"

"Yeah, and something else," I confessed. "Jay brought up the thing with Leggett."

Rome nodded, waving his hand in a dismissive manner. "Don't sweat it, that was two years ago, bro."

"It's been two years, Rome, and some nights it feels like it happened last week."

"It's nerves coming from this game with Kent, Kee, don't worry about it. Stick to the game plan and try not to show Markson up too bad and we'll be home free."

I looked over at the bar and saw Pops staring in our direction. This time, he motioned for me to come over and talk. I got ready to head in his direction when Rome grabbed my arm to stop me. I looked back at him, confusion written all over my face.

Rome tried to make light of the situation, masking his concern that I was walking into a trap. "Yo, did you and Pops square-up or something? He isn't looking at you with that crazy father eye anymore. You must have gotten a few good ones in, I hope?"

"It's all good between me and Pops, for real. We had to come to an understanding," I replied. "Pops has his ways, you know how these old school bruhs do their thing."

The minute I was within earshot of Pops' voice, it got interesting. I could feel the stares around us, wondering if we were going to have a verbal war of words. I wanted to laugh at the spectacle of it. I understood where they were coming from, it had been chilly between him and me for over a year.

"Are you okay, youngster? I heard the interview got a little tense earlier." Pops queried as he poured a beer for a customer. "Must have shook you up really bad to stop by here after practice. That's not your usual pattern."

Leave it to Pops to have my tendencies committed to memory. I shook my head, acknowledging his suspicions, doing my best to play a shell game with the reason I stopped by the spot. Hiding my disappointment proved futile, so there was nothing more to do but to come clean. I didn't have time for pretenses.

"To be honest, Pops, I was hoping to see Ariel here so we could talk." I tried to hide the grin on my face at the mere mention of her name, but that wasn't going to happen, either. "I hadn't really seen her in a couple of days."

"Ariel's been off campus taking care of something for me," Pops told me. "But she should be home later on tonight if you want to call her."

"Uh, Pops, umm, I don't know that I'll be—"

Pops picked up on my hesitation and tried to calm me down. "You're not married to her, Keenan. Yes, she's been there for you, but she doesn't own you."

She acts like it, sometimes.

"Ariel likes you, kid, but don't tell her I told you that, she'll kill me," Pops let out a hearty laugh that caused everyone in the bar to turn in our direction. He shook his head and let the crowd go back to what they were doing before he continued. "I understand the need to feel obligated to someone when they were there for you, but that's not love, son, that's friendship."

She was more than a friend. Friends didn't do the things we did, but I wasn't about to disclose that information, either. "So, what are you saying, Pops? Ariel's trying to be more than that?"

"You ain't heard nothing from me, kid, I've said enough already."

"She hasn't given me any reason to believe what you're saying, so why should I believe it?"

"You really don't know much about women, do you, kid?" He laughed again, shaking his head at my apparent naïveté. "She stood toe-to-toe with that girl, even after she said that you pushed her out of your life in favor of that girl. Women do what they want to do when it comes to the people they believe in. Throw the L word into the mix and there's no telling what they will be willing to do for you."

"Whatever, Pops, I'm about to head home and put this day behind me." I gave him pound before I walked back to my table with Rome and Javi. "Thanks for the advice, I'll try to take it under consideration."

I headed back to the table, noticing that Javi had joined the party. He was having a conversation with Rome when he noticed I had returned from my engagement with Pops. He held his hands in the air, clapping them at their apex over his head. "So, you're not a hell spawn after all?" Javi laughed at his attempt at a joke. "I thought Pops was gonna inhale you and spit you out for a minute there."

"Nah, we came to an understanding," I offered, but I

didn't say any more than that. Sometimes less was more.

I went through my conversation with Pops, slowing the exchange between us down so I could understand everything he was trying to say to me. He had my attention when he told me about Ariel.

Was I really that blind? We had that brief exchange at the Quad, but by the time we had a chance to figure anything out, Ella showed up. Earlier this morning, there was a stronger connection between us, but she said I had to be willing to choose. I wanted her, but I wasn't sure she wanted me. I wasn't sure if she still held a grudge after I blew her off. It wasn't of my own volition, but that wasn't enough of an excuse. A lesser woman would have dropped me without hesitation. I knew what I felt, but I didn't trust my feelings.

Did she want me and I was too scared to give up the comfort that I knew Ella represented? Maybe Pops was right. Maybe I was so consumed with dealing with Ella that I might be blinded to another woman being interested in me?

I didn't want to think about it; Ella had only been showing her true colors over the past few weeks. I closed my eyes for a moment to take inventory of that statement. Was I blind to that, too? Was she so busy smashing me on the regular that I didn't want to care about another woman?

I didn't want to let Ariel go, despite everything that had happened. There was something in me that told me that we belonged together. I wanted to curse Ella for interrupting that inevitability, but I still had myself to blame for setting the events in motion that put Ella in my path in the first place.

I needed to find a way to set things right. The feelings I had for Ariel were too strong to ignore any longer. If I didn't figure this out soon, I'd end up losing everything.

I was at a crossroads, and it felt like I was lost. "Earth to Mr. Ellis? Yo, you there, bro?" Rome snapped me out of my thoughts. "Damn, where did you go?"

"Don't worry about all that," I brushed him off as I got up from the table. "I was envisioning dropping seventy on Markson Saturday night for the primetime folks to get a taste of what's coming this season."

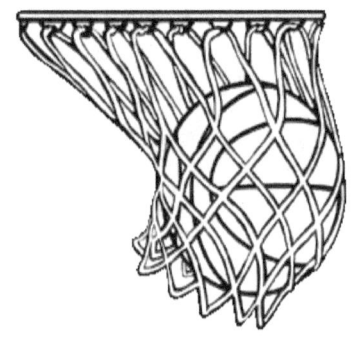

CHAPTER TWENTY-SIX

"Hey, mom, how is everything?"

I didn't know what made me call my parents, but if I checked my ego at the door, I'd admit that I was a little more freaked out than I thought. I had a habit of calling them when I felt I was having a difficult time or I felt like I had gotten stuck in a corner or something. This qualified on more than a few levels.

Having that incident with Javon come up during the interview, I knew my father and my brother would see it, so I wanted to call them to let them know I would be okay.

"Everything is fine, baby, how are you doing?" Hearing her soothing voice on the phone was exactly what the doctor ordered.

I did my best to calm my voice, to keep her from worrying too much. She would regardless; she's my mom.

"I'm okay, mom, I'm getting ready for the game this weekend, are y'all gonna be able to come up?"

There was silence on the phone for a few seconds, and I could tell something was up from her hesitation alone. "Mom, what is it?"

"Baby, it's nothing." She still hesitated. She cleared her throat and changed her tone when she realized that I would persist until she relented. "It's your father; he had a minor accident at the job. He's okay, but they took him off the trains for a while until he mends."

My heart sank. "Put him on the phone."

"*Alton! Keenan's on the phone, baby!*" I heard my mother yell in the house.

"Hey, Kee, what's good, youngster?" He tried to sound like he was oblivious to what my mom might have told me. "You ready for your senior season to start?"

"What happened, Dad?"

"Oh, it was nothing, son, I had a fall and twisted my knee, nothing to concern yourself over," he mentioned. "Not thrilled about this cane I gotta walk with, but all things considered, I'm good. I saw your interview on *SportsCenter* earlier. You good, kid?"

"I didn't expect him to pull that question out of the pile, but yeah, Dad, I'm good." I wasn't sure if I was lying to him or myself. "Are you going to be able to make the trip up for the game? You can't be ready to travel, yet, are you?"

"Keenan, I haven't missed too many of your games, or your brother's, for that matter, either on TV or in person, so I'll be there with your mom and Tyler," he affirmed, calming my nerves. "There's not too much that will keep me from cheering my boys."

I fell silent for a moment after he said that, and true to our bond, he picked right up on it. "Kee, talk to me, son, I can tell something's up."

I had the opening I needed to try and explain myself, but I couldn't squeeze the trigger. I still didn't think either he or mom would believe me, so I didn't bring it up. "Dad, I—"

"Son, I know you have a lot of pressure on you and everything but try not to let it get to you so bad." Dad began one of his infamous lectures, and I already knew where it was going to end up. "I was going to call you after you looked irritated after that question."

"Dad, about that incident—"

"Let me finish, Keenan," Dad cut me off, ruining the momentum I tried to build up to tell him about the events that happened that night. "You will have plenty of time once you get into the league to treat this like a business, but have fun while you still can in school, finish your degree. You're acting like you're already employing people."

I wanted to argue the point, but the truth was I did act like it, at least to some degree. I didn't act like a kid on campus doing my thing, I acted like the CEO of Keenan Ellis, Inc., and Ella and L.B. were a part of the Board of Trustees. That's what was going to change ASAP. I was no one's puppet anymore.

"You know what, Dad, you're right, I think I need to handle that and have fun this season." I felt like a weight had been lifted from my shoulders. I loved my father for his ability to make things feel a little less stressful. "And I plan to rid myself of some dead weight while I'm at it."

"That's good to hear; I wasn't exactly all that thrilled when you started hanging around with that nurse when you were in the hospital." His laughter infected me to the point to where I couldn't help but laugh, too. He never liked Ella, that wasn't hard to figure out, but he was of the mindset that unless I proposed marriage, he stayed out of my affairs with women. "And that dude, L.B. I think? He needs to go, too. There's something not right about him."

I laughed even harder, trying my best to wipe the tears from my eyes. Without me telling him everything, he still managed to figure out what advice to give. "All right, Dad, we'll get that done right away."

"Yeah, you do that, son; you need a good, strong-willed woman by your side that can handle all the craziness that the NBA has to offer and smile like she ain't got a care in the world."

When he said that, one woman came to mind: Ariel. Yeah, fathers definitely knew best.

"I'm glad you feel better, Keenan. I think you'll be okay now."

Yeah, I thought so, too. But what I needed to do and what I had the courage to do would be two different things. "I'll see you Saturday, Dad, and tell that little brother of mine that we'll talk when he gets up here, okay?"

"Will do, Kee. He's threatening to break all your records at school, you know?"

"Is that a fact?" I beamed with pride; I knew the work I put in over the summer with Tyler was paying off. "That's fine. Records were made to be broken, right?"

"Yeah, something like that. Now get some rest, son, we'll see you Saturday."

"Ahhhhhhhhhh!!!!" My body tensed up like I was having a seizure. The pain was so intense, I couldn't figure out whether my heart or my lungs were going to explode. If Rome wasn't at Angela's tonight, I would have woken him out of whatever slumber he was under.

I felt hands on my back as I struggled to catch my breath. I was so disoriented that I almost forgot Ella was in bed with me. "You okay, baby?"

I sat on the side of the bed, away from Ella so she couldn't see my face. I needed a minute to breathe before she tried her usual routine of getting me to calm down. Even that began to bore me now. This nightmare was different from the others, and it was triggered from that ESPN interview. I was a little more than freaked out; the only thing I saw was paramedics asking me if I was okay, and I couldn't move anything, my arms or my legs.

I thought that maybe it was the pressure I put on myself to put on a show for the home crowd and on national television that was triggering these episodes, but I wasn't sure if something deeper was going on or not.

Ella and I were okay, but we weren't where we were before the incident with Ariel at the Quad. I had never seen her so enraged about one woman before. When I got home later that night, she apologized so sweetly for letting her emotions get the best of her that I almost gave in and let her back inside. Key word: almost.

I couldn't trust her to not flip out like that again. I hadn't told her yet, but for the ESPN broadcast of the game, the producers told Coach Bolden that it would be a good idea to have the cheerleaders escort us out at half-court to receive our championship rings before raising the banner.

Angela wasn't thrilled, either, but at least she understood it was the nature of the beast of dating a baller. After that near-fight the other day, I wasn't sure what to make of Ella's reaction once I did tell her.

I had another day to figure out how I wanted to handle things, but I was at the point in my mind to where I was getting used to the idea of Ella being more of a friend. I no longer saw her as my girlfriend or a potential wife.

Pops was right, even with the sex that was involved in our relationship I really wasn't in love with her. The connection with Ariel showed me the difference. I was sorry it took two years to figure that out. It wasn't fair to Ella, and it wasn't fair to me.

"Keenan, are you sure you're okay, baby?" Ella asked again, rubbing my back to try to calm me. "Was it that same dream again?"

"No, this was different, Ella," I explained. "I was

paralyzed from the neck up in this dream. The other times weren't as bad as this one. It felt like this one was really going to happen."

"Kee, come on, you know nothing has happened since the last incident, and that was two years ago," Ella kneaded my back. "You gotta let it go sooner or later."

"I can't just let it go," I snapped. "If I landed any other way I would have been paralyzed or I could have died."

Ella slid across my lap, but I wasn't in the mood for the type of "healing" she wanted to indulge me into. Realizing that her feminine wiles weren't having their desired effect, she exhaled and reached for the phone.

"Who are you calling at this time of night?"

"Uncle L.B. You obviously need something to help you sleep. Maybe talking to him might do the trick?"

I shuddered every time she referred to him as uncle, like there was some perverse incestuous relationship between the two of them.

Within seconds, she was on the phone with L.B.

Within minutes, he was in my ear. "What seems to be the problem, Keenan?"

"These nightmares keep creeping up. I've tried to shake them, but they won't go away."

"What are these nightmares about?"

I proceeded to tell him about the latest one about me being on the floor looking up and not being able to feel my extremities before I woke up. I didn't bother telling him about the recurring one; it involved him.

"So, you're thinking this dude from Kent is trying to

cause a bit of déjà vu, huh?" L.B. chuckled over the phone. I didn't find it all that amusing. "I don't think you're getting it, kid. No one can hurt you, you're a beast on the court, and the college basketball world knows it. Nothing's happened to you since your injury, and you've come out better than ever."

"Look, L.B., the ego boost is not what I need right now," I slammed my hand against the nightstand. "I'm too close to getting what I want to worry about some fluke accident, okay? I need a guarantee from you that nothing will happen to me."

There was silence on the other end of the phone, and I had a feeling that I had overstepped the line, but I didn't care anymore. My sanity was hanging by a very thin thread now, and I needed assurances that the ledge I was on wasn't crumbling beneath my feet. In my mind, if he wanted me to get with his agent, he needed to prove that he wanted me to be where he wanted me to be, period.

After the long pause, L.B. spoke, but there was an edge, an irritation to his voice. "You have my word no harm will come to you, Keenan."

The line went dead before I had a chance to respond.

"Are you happy now?" Ella tried to kiss me; it was obvious she was still in a mood to be handled, but I wasn't in the mood to handle her.

This routine bored me to tears and I needed out. Besides, based on L.B.'s tone before the line dropped, sex was the last thing on my mind.

I had hoped to be able to sit down with her and have a

civilized conversation with her before she decided to go all nympho on me. I no longer believed that she had my best interests at heart, which was saddening; I liked her and appreciated everything she'd done for me to get me back on top. But she never had my heart. Somehow, I'd kept that from her all this time, not realizing that I had been holding space for someone else—Ariel.

I stood up and put on my practice gear, ignoring the glare that Ella gave me. "Where do you think you're going? It's after curfew, mister."

"Save it, Ella, I'm not in the mood. It didn't bother you when I was handling business earlier in the summer, right?"

That shut her down. "Baby, just let me put you to sleep, okay? I promise I won't beg too much for you to take it."

It was funny; once upon a time, that routine would have made me putty in her hands and it would be over before it started. The first time she did it, I thought it was one of the sexiest things any woman had ever done for me. Now, it wasn't even cute.

I didn't budge when I saw the tears in her eyes. She was losing her hold over me, and she was getting to the point to where she realized it. No matter what she tried, there was nothing she could do to regain her hold. Maybe this conversation might be easier after all.

I felt like a new man the moment I closed the door, like a weight had been lifted from my shoulders. I felt light, airy, like I could jump into the stratosphere, no longer burdened by things I thought I had no control over. That's what I wanted to tell myself, but I needed to be a man about things first before I moved on.

I called Ariel by the time I got into my car.

"Well, this is a lovely late-night surprise. I hope you're not calling thinking you're going to get some, Keenan. I'm not *that* easy."

I felt Ariel's smile over the phone and couldn't stop grinning. This was what falling in love was supposed to feel like. "Nah, nothing like that, sexy, but I was wondering if you were okay with me coming by. I know it's late and all, but I needed to talk, and you were the first person on my mind. Besides, I did promise to try and see you before game time, right?"

She giggled a little, and for a moment I thought she would say no, but she stifled a yawn instead. "Okay, superstar, I guess I can let you come by. Since all you want to do is talk."

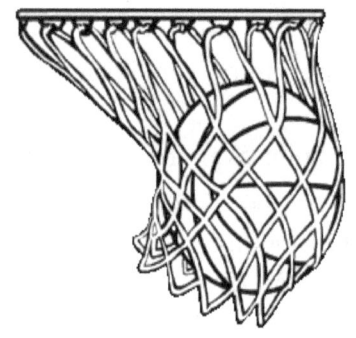

Chapter Twenty-Seven

"Oh, my goodness, you look horrible."

I thought I felt better than I looked, but if the expression on Ariel's face was any indication, I was fooling myself big time. I allowed her to lead me into her apartment. "I guess I haven't been sleeping all that well the past few days."

I took a look around, impressed with the décor and the niceties that surrounded us. It was a lot bigger than I thought it would be; she was working part-time for Pops at Ballers. I couldn't resist my curiosity, and I wanted to know what I wanted to know. "Okay, you're really going to have to tell me how you can afford all of this on the tips at the bar."

"Well, I work for Pops part-time, yes, but my other employer takes very good care of me," she teased as she led me to the couch in her living room.

"Well, whoever your employer is, they are definitely balling out big time," I tried to hide my awe of all of the lavish surroundings. "Maybe I can do some side business for them once my playing days are over."

"You never know what the future may hold for you, Keenan Ellis," Ariel smiled as she caressed my face. I closed my eyes and gave in to her touch, feeling her penetrate my mind. This time I offered no resistance; I wanted to show her everything—including my greatest fear.

"So, what did you want to talk to me about?" Ariel queried while getting comfortable on the couch. I was so mesmerized by her body draped in nothing but a silk sleep shirt that I almost forgot the words I wanted to say. She caught on to my momentary distraction, trying to lighten the mood and get me to focus. "Keenan, I know I'm gorgeous and all, but tell me what's on your mind."

"Ariel, I don't know how to begin to explain." I fumbled through the first few words, frustrated with myself that I couldn't at least say what's on my mind and let the chips fall. "I did something a couple of years back…you know that thing you did at the Quad, when I tried to keep you from seeing something?"

"Yes, I remember."

"Well, the reason I didn't want you to see it was … it was something that I … God, why is this so hard to say?"

"Kee, whatever it is, we can get through it, okay?"

"But it's horrible, and I was weak, and—"

"Tell me, Keenan, you're starting to scare me now."

"Okay, I signed a contract with a dude named L.B. Prince." I let the words flow, knowing there was no turning back. "He came to me when I got hurt a couple of years ago and the doctors said I might not play ball again. He asked me if I was willing to do whatever it took to get back on the floor, and I took him up on it. That's how Ella and I got together. She claimed she was his niece, but I don't know what she is to him anymore."

"Go on, let it all out." Ariel encouraged me, her hands entwined with mine, her gaze never looking away from mine, despite my wanting to hide from her with each passing word. "Tell me everything."

"The next thing I knew, my knee was healed a couple of weeks later, and I didn't think or care how it happened, I was glad I could get back to doing my thing. By the time I figured out that other parts of my body had been enhanced, it was too late." I continued to purge, baring everything to her. "Now I'm having these crazy dreams that feel more real each time I have them, and I feel like I'm trapped because if I try to break my contract with L.B., I know what was given to me will be taken away, including my repaired knee. I'm scared; I don't know what to do."

Ariel's grip on my hands slipped a bit, and I was hyper aware of it. "I understand if you want me to leave, and I understand if you don't believe what I'm telling you. Hell, I don't believe it sometimes, but it has been my reality for the past two years. I was so worried about taking care of my family and doing the things I needed to go pro that I deluded myself into thinking that it was worth making the deal. I don't want to be scared anymore, Ariel."

"Kee, you'd be amazed at what I might believe, and no, I don't want you to leave." She smiled for a moment, her eyes never leaving mine. "I knew there was something keeping you from me, and some of this is making sense in my head. I just didn't know what it could have been that made you push me away."

"But I just admitted that I made a deal with the devil for my own selfish reasons." I tried to understand why she was so calm. "You said it yourself, I pushed you away. I would have never done that if I was in my right mind. I wanted you then, and I want you now, but I don't know if you still want me."

"Keenan, relax, I told you whatever it was, *we* can get through it." Ariel took my hand again, slipping her other hand and placing it against my cheek the same way she did that day on the Quad. "This time, give it all to me. No holding back, no more running."

I nodded as I wiped the tears from my eyes. I braced myself for whatever might happen once she was done going through everything I'd done the past two years. There was no turning back. I had to have faith that she would believe me.

She held my hand tight as she slipped inside my mind again, and I held her hand with both of mine, wishing I didn't let her go this time. I was still scared she would tell me to leave, but I had to give it all so she would understand what I'd been through.

She blew past every original proverbial lock and door that I possessed with ease, smiling as she remembered her way around the recesses of my mind. She found herself at the door I didn't allow her to touch, the one that led to the other thing I didn't want her to know yet. This time, the door opened itself, allowing her to walk through.

The moment she walked through the door … there was no other way to explain it, but all fear and doubt dissolved. I wasn't afraid anymore, of anything, nor anyone. Not of what I needed to do to give closure to my relationship with Ella; not of taking the necessary steps to break my agreement with L.B., regardless of how hard I knew it would be to do.

It all made sense as long as Ariel was in my world.

Are you ready to go down this road now?

Yes, Ariel, I am. I love you.

This time, Ariel broke the connection between us. "What did you say to me?"

"I love you, Ariel. I fell for you from the moment I saw you, but I didn't know if you would want me after I told you what I'd done. Once you'd seen for yourself, I was sure you were gone."

She kissed me before I could say another word. Her lips felt like warm honey over mine. I gave in to the embrace, losing myself in it. I felt her pull me into her mind as we kissed, and at first, I felt a little out of sorts, but she took my hand to steady me. *I love you, too, Keenan. I had to be sure you would let me see everything. Now, it's my turn to show you something.*

Ariel pulled me on top of her, continuing the kiss we shared, never once breaking the connection between us. Inside her mind, I saw things I wasn't sure I was prepared for. I saw Ariel, but instead of the clothing she wore before we kissed, I saw her wearing an Egyptian headdress and cloth that barely covered her body. In the distance, I could see the Great Sphinx being constructed.

In a flash, her clothing and body had changed to reflect The Middle Ages. I looked at the dress and recognized the location as Constantinople, which put her somewhere in the fifteenth century or so. In yet another flash, Ariel's clothing and the surroundings changed, this time showing her wearing clothing from what looked like the Victorian era, taking in the sights of Great Britain.

Thank God I paid attention in World History class.

I wasn't sure if my mind was playing tricks on me or if she was playing tricks on me, but I watched with complete wonder as her body and clothing and face transformed as the times and surroundings changed. The last change showed her in nineteenth century America, sitting in the Ford Theatre before President Lincoln was assassinated.

How could she possibly show me all of this? How was it possible?

I'll explain when the time is right, baby, I promise.

It felt like an out-of-body experience traveling with her, and by the time I got back to my own mind and body, we were still on the couch like we never left the confines of her apartment. Needless to say, I needed answers. "What in the ... I mean, how?"

"Shhh, relax baby, I told you I'll explain in due time," Ariel whispered as she took my hand to lead me upstairs to her bedroom. "Right now, I want to be yours completely, if you still want me?"

I lifted her in my arms as her legs wrapped around my waist, kissing and caressing her as I walked to her bedroom, ready to consume her essence without hesitation.

"Make love to me tonight, Kee, that's all I want. It will all make sense to you soon, trust me," she cooed as she squirmed under my touch. "We'll deal with the storms tomorrow, together."

I smirked, doing my best to keep the sarcasm at bay. "I thought all we were going to do was talk?"

"Oh, shut up and give it to me."

She was right, there would be time to understand what she showed me, and I was willing to find out. She was also right about the pending storms on the horizon. I hoped I was strong enough to face them head on. I remembered a passage from a novel that I read for a literature class, *The Count of Monte Cristo* was the name of the book. There was a part that stuck with me that I didn't think would be so appropriate.

Life is a storm, my young friend. You will bask in the sunlight one moment, be shattered on the rocks the next. What makes you a man is what you do when that storm comes. You must look into that storm and shout as you did in Rome. Do your worst, for I will do mine!

This was about more than the upcoming season. More than the decisions that I made that got me where I am at this moment in time. This was about something I was ready to fight to get back because it belonged to me.

Looking into Ariel's eyes as we lay on her bed, it all made sense. My life was mine to live, not what someone dictated to me. I wanted my life back, but this time, it would be on my terms, not based on a contract that I was coerced into signing. It was time for me to do my worst now.

I wouldn't be doing it alone. I had all the help I needed.

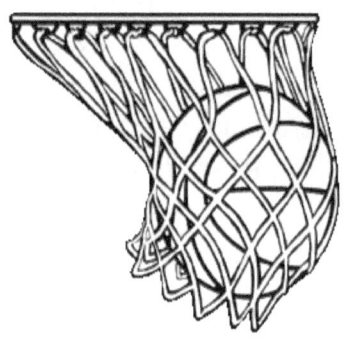

CHAPTER TWENTY-EIGHT

"I called you three times, Keenan. Where were you?"

"Your point would be what, exactly, Ella? I wasn't answering my phone, and you weren't the only one who called me, okay?"

This conversation was going to be a little more interesting than I had anticipated. Ella was sitting on the living room couch waiting for me with red-rimmed eyes. It was obvious she had been crying all night, and I would have colored myself concerned under normal circumstances. These weren't normal circumstances anymore.

I never bothered to mask Ariel's essence. Her scent lingered on my body. The moment that our bodies merged, I knew she was the one for me. I was willing to deal with the consequences of leaving Ella, as I was no longer afraid of those consequences.

From the look on her face, being friends was a long shot, too. "So, where were you last night? You sure as hell weren't here with me."

I didn't hesitate with my response. "I was at Ariel's apartment."

I didn't know if the flatness of that statement shook her or if her imagination of what did or did not happen while I was there disturbed her more. I half-expected the roof to get blown off the room.

Ella did not disappoint. *"You sonofabitch! How could you do this to me? After all I did for you?!?!"*

I stood in the face of the storm brewing around us, and all I could think about was the bliss of last night's events. The calmness of the aftermath of the passion that Ariel and I shared last night was beyond description. One night with her compared to countless nights with Ella and the various women that popped up for some of the more intense nights we enjoyed?

At this moment in time, there was no comparison.

I felt some guilt for not ending things with Ella before I began any type of relationship with Ariel, but that was something I'd have to live with.

"Did you fuck her? Tell me, motherfucker!"

"Ella, I understand you're upset, and you have every right to be, but this thing between us is over."

"Oh no, it isn't over until I *say* it's over, bro," Ella ranted. "You got it twisted if you think I'm giving you up without a fight."

"Ella, I don't know what you're thinking, but it won't

help matters. I don't love you."

Ella's eyes widened when she heard that statement. She laughed hysterically, spitting at my feet. "This was *never* about love, you idiot. This was about getting paid. Did you think L.B. would let a hot commodity like you get away because you tore up your knee?"

It was my turn to look shocked. I was being used the whole time?

The disappointment must have shown on my face; Ella continued to pour salt in the wound. "I told L.B. that you weren't the one we needed, but he was convinced that you were the perfect baller to turn the odds in our favor."

"What are you talking about? What odds?"

"Damn, you really aren't as smart as you look." Ella shook her head in disgust. "I'm over this anyway. You were too weak to handle the responsibility, especially when you fell for *her*."

I was confused on levels that she didn't have a clue about. I didn't feel as confident as I did when I stepped through the door. I grasped at straws to help make sense of it all. "So, everything you told me: being Catholic, being placed in my life for a reason, the St. Jude reference, all of that was faked?"

"Well, I'll be damned, give the man a hand." Ella clapped. "Hell, I was right about one thing; you are a lost cause. You're a fucking joke, and you don't deserve anything L.B. gave you."

"What do you mean, he gave me?" I found myself getting angry once the blinders were taken off. "He didn't give me a damned thing. The only thing he did was heal my knee, everything else was God given, or now you're going to tell me you don't believe in God now?"

"This ain't about His passive-aggressive ass," Ella shrieked. "Or do you remember the words you said about God letting this happen to you when He could have stopped it?"

Hearing that phrase thrown back at me after two years felt like hot coals being placed on my skin, and I felt the sting of every word. I was so angry back then, so pissed off that He had left me that I no longer had faith that He had my back.

"I thought so. L.B. enhanced your skills so much that your God-given skills have probably withered and died by now. If I know His sorry ass, He allowed your skills to erode, simply to teach you a lesson." Ella laughed again, taking pleasure in breaking me down. "So, what are you going to do now, superstar? Don't even think about breaking your contract now or you'll kiss everything you built up to this point goodbye."

"No, I don't believe that," I offered. "I was the man before you came into my life, and I'll be the man once I've rid myself of you."

"Oh, you'll be the man all right, with a bum knee and no vertical jump." Ella giggled at her little joke. "I'll tell you what, I'm willing to forgive you for your little misstep if you promise to leave Ariel alone. Otherwise—"

She touched my knee, and the excruciating pain that I felt two years ago when I first injured my knee coursed through my body, this time it felt ten times worse than I remembered. *"Okay! Okay! I'll do what you want! Ahhhhh!"*

Ella took her hand off my knee, grinning as I struggled to breathe after enduring the last few minutes. She tried to kiss me, but I jumped from her grasp. "I see we have an understanding. I'll see you at the game later on tonight, sexy. You have a national audience to shock and awe. You're gonna knock 'em dead!"

She made her way to the door and blew a kiss; her self-satisfying grin still present on her face. "I'm actually glad that this is finally out in the open. I was getting tired of playing the dutiful little girlfriend. Later, baby."

I sat alone in my apartment, realizing my world was not anywhere near what I thought it was, terrified of the unknown and not knowing what to do. I looked at my watch and noticed that I had an hour before game time and I needed to get to the arena in time for shoot around.

I thought about the promise I was forced into, to never see Ariel again or face the consequences of breaching the contract. I signed up for more than I bargained for, and like I fool I took the bait.

I wasn't even sure if it was worth it anymore.

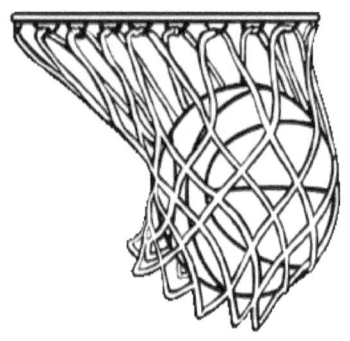

CHAPTER TWENTY-NINE

"Yo, Kee, you're late, bro."

I walked into the locker room and was met by Javi and Rome, both with concerned looks on their faces.

"Coach is pissed, you almost missed shoot around," Javi mentioned. "We didn't know what to think when you didn't pick up your phone."

Rome chimed in, "We got him to calm down, but he still wants to see you, ASAP."

"All right, I think there are some things that he and I need to talk about anyway," I told them both, trying to manage a smile. "Look, I want to say I'm sorry if I have been a jerk the past year or so. I have some things to atone for, and hopefully I will before it's too late."

"What the hell, man, you dying on us or something?" Rome raised an eyebrow. "Look, just get things square with Coach so we can do some damage tonight, all right?"

I walked into Coach Bolden's office and saw him sitting behind his desk as he finished a call. He motioned for me to sit down until he hung up the phone. "Keenan, are you okay, kid?"

I wanted to lie and say I was, but I was too tired to try to put up a poor excuse. "Coach, I've had better days, to tell you the truth. Some things went down last night and earlier today and it has my focus all screwed up."

Coach Bolden gave me the once-over, stroking his beard the whole time. "I should have known it had something to do with that girl you've been hanging out with. I take it you two aren't together anymore?"

"Not exactly, Coach," I replied. "Look, I'm going to try to lay this as straight as I can, and I really don't expect you to believe me because I still don't know if I completely believe it myself, and it's been two years."

"Okay, kid, say what's on your mind."

"Remember two years ago when I ripped up my knee?"

"Yeah, how could I forget? The staff and I went through every doctor in the country trying to figure out what to do."

That caught me off guard. "Wait a minute, you did what?"

"We called every specialist in the country to see what we could do with your knee to get you on the mend," Coach Bolden replied. "It took a few days, but we found someone who could perform the procedure, and it would have had you back by the summer with aggressive rehab. When we got to the hospital to tell you, the doctors told us you were already on your feet and moving as if nothing happened."

I felt nauseous. I had no idea they were working on surgery for me. If I had waited instead of taking the easy route, I wouldn't be in this mess right now.

"You were saying, Kee?"

I thought about spinning the truth to keep me from sounding like I was insane, but I thought better of it. I had to trust my coach. "There was this dude that visited me, his last name was Prince, and—"

"L.B. Prince?" Coach's look was incredulous. "My God, I thought I had heard the last of that dude once and for all. But that's impossible, he couldn't have visited you. We took care of that."

"Yeah, well, he kinda got me to sign with him in exchange for healing my knee." I got the part that I expected him to not believe or understand. The thing that threw me off-balance was the last words out of his mouth. "Wait a minute, what do you mean you took care of it?"

Coach continued to shake his head, looking at me like I needed to be committed. "Pops said something was up with you, but I didn't want to believe it. I didn't want to believe that you would take the easy way out. No wonder he said you reminded him of—"

"Of who, Coach? What in the world is going on that you're not telling me?"

"Listen to me, Kee, we'll figure out how to get you out of this mess, let's get through tonight and we'll work it out in the morning, all right?"

"You're not making sense, Coach, what's going on?"

My question was interrupted by Javi coming into the office. "Sorry, Coach, but it's time to head out."

"We'll discuss this later, Keenan," Coach stated, grabbing his suit coat as we headed out the door. "Do me a favor and stay away from L.B. until we can figure something out."

I was still trying to make heads or tails of what he said about L.B. when the sight of Ariel standing at my locker threw me further off balance. She wrapped her arms around me, kissing my lips. "Hi, baby, good luck tonight."

I held her as tightly as I could, willing my tears away.

"Hey, I'm here, I'm not going anywhere, okay?" Ariel reassured before getting a good look in my eyes. "What happened, Kee? What did Ella do to you?"

"It's not important. We'll talk after the game."

She didn't let me go, even after the coaches tried to pull me away from her. I held them up, letting them know I would be out in a moment. "Kee, something's wrong with you, I can feel the stress of it. What did Ella do to you? Tell me."

"Please, baby, don't make this any more difficult than it already is. She won't let me go, and she—"

I tried to break from Ariel's hold, only to realize that her grip was stronger than I'd ever thought possible. Her eyes flashed; I saw a fire that I hadn't paid attention to before. Then again, she'd never been as irritated and upset as she was in that moment, either. "Listen to me, baby. There's nothing Ella or L.B. can do to you now. I promise you we will get through tonight and this will be behind us, do you hear me? Do you trust me?"

"Yes."

"Good, now be the superstar that the world is expecting and come back to me when you're done. I love you."

I kissed her, walking out onto the floor to join the rest of the squad in the shoot around. I was so focused, so dialed in, that I didn't bother noticing Ella in her usual spot, behind the bench courtside. I couldn't figure out whether the sweet smile she gave me was genuine or not. It gave me an uneasy feeling, but I had to focus on the task at hand.

Beating Kent.

"Watch the screen!"

The game with Kent was intense, and it was obvious they came to play. Markson was left on an island with me in Kent's Diamond-and-One defense, where the primary defender was one-on-one against the player they wanted to stop while the other four players helped on the penetration.

Coach Bolden hated that junk defense; they only work if the top player was off his game. I was not off my game tonight, drawing my concentration by finding Ariel in the crowd after every shot I made.

I didn't bother penetrating during the first half because Kent left the middle soft for Javi and Rome to exploit their size advantage. That was the difference between last year and this year, and Kent's head coach should have recognized that.

He expected me to shoot over the top of the defense and hope my bigs would be able to get a lot of offensive rebounds, but this year I wanted to focus on my passing ability to show the scouts that I was more than a scorer. The strategy worked; Rome and Javi led the team in scoring and I had double-digit assists and a modest twelve points, too.

Markson tried to bark the whole time that he had me locked up, but I didn't pay him any mind. We were up by about eight points, so all I did was point at the scoreboard while I continued to shut him down to make other people beat us.

Yeah, like that was going to happen.

Seeing Ariel in the stands despite Ella's ultimatum was a comfort to me. Tonight, I felt like I was playing for more than myself, and that muted the trash talking that I did on the floor.

I couldn't say the same for Rome. He was in rare form; the focus turned away from me and toward him as the man tonight. He glared at me after I threaded the needle in the defense to get an easy dunk for Javi. "Okay, D, quit with this Magic Johnson routine and shut this clown up, please?"

Markson heard the chatter between us and remarked, "Nah, dude, let the wannabe superstar pass the rock, he can't get by me anyway."

"You need to quit worrying about stopping me and

worry about calling the cops," I yelled as I stripped the ball away from him on the bounce. "Got him!"

Markson tried to come after me to measure my shot for the block when Rome ran between us to take him off balance as I rose for the dunk. The crowd went crazy.

I jogged back down on defense to get ready for whatever Markson had coming for me. Sure enough, he came down jawing again, "You won't be ripping me again, partner."

He attempted a three-pointer that hit the front of the rim. I shot down court, waiting for him to catch up with me. "Tired already, Markson? Come on, it's just the first half, playa!"

I wanted to abuse him on the pick and roll with Rome, so I took him down the left sideline and nodded at Rome to set up for the pick-and-pop. After hesitating on the dribble, I headed back up to the top of the key, setting Markson up for one of Rome's patented screens.

He never knew what hit him.

The crowd reacted as Markson hit the ground hard after getting hit with one of Rome's forearms. We kept the play going as I kicked the ball over to Rome and he hit a baseline jumper to put us up by twelve.

The refs called timeout on the floor because Markson was still on the floor holding his nose. Blood was dripping from his fingers; Rome had got him good.

One of the Kent big men tried to jump in Rome's face to take up for his teammate, and Rome laughed it off. "Come on, son! This here is a man's game, right?"

The other two refs tried to break up the quick exchange of words, with the Kent big that started the beef yelling something about dropping Rome off in a body bag. I didn't sweat the words, though; the refs kept the extra stuff under control for the most part.

Coach Bolden called a twenty-second timeout to bring us over. "Rome, watch the extras on the screen, that could have been called offensive."

Coach got the nod from him before he turned to me. "They're going to drop back to the zone coming out of this timeout, Kee. Scorch the nets a few times to make them go back to the junk defense they were playing."

He didn't have to say another word. For the next three series, I didn't bother to set up for any half-court sets, draining threes from the top of the key, the wing, and one on the baseline, putting the lead at twenty-one points.

Javi got into the fun, blocking a shot to ignite the break, putting me and Rome in a two-on-one against the big Rome was jawing with earlier. I knew he couldn't rise with me, but I wanted to give my big man some time to shine, too.

Rome raised his arm up to give me the cue to put the ball up for the alley-oop, and I let the ball fly off my fingers, waiting for the familiar quiet before the rim rattling dunk that Rome would drop through once he caught the ball.

Only thing was, he never got the chance.

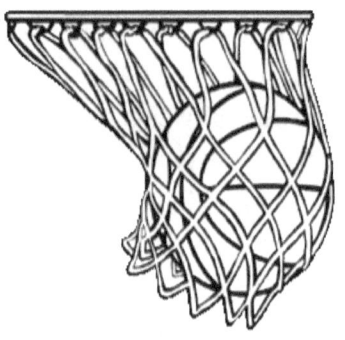

CHAPTER THIRTY

This couldn't be happening. I wanted to punch myself, anything to wake up from what I witnessed. My nightmare came true in the form of Rome lying in a heap under the basket, unconscious and not responding to treatment the paramedics were giving him.

I never thought the big from Kent would undercut Rome like that. Watching him fall and hit head first was like watching a bad movie in slow motion. The crowd went silent. I heard Angela's screams pierce the air as the crowd waited for some sign that Rome was okay.

This wasn't like what happened to me. This was worse—a lot worse.

I kept hearing the medics say that Rome wasn't breathing, and I feared he wouldn't wake up. I looked in the stands and searched for Angela. The look on her face sent chills down my spine.

Is he okay?

I shook my head, looking back at the scene in front of me. I felt as helpless as anyone in the building. The tears I wanted to shed, I wiped away before anyone could see them. I didn't want to panic Angela or give the cameramen anything to make newsworthy.

I looked at the bench, expecting to find Ella in her usual spot. I was surprised to see L.B. sitting with her. His hands were in a very inappropriate location between her legs for an *uncle* to have his hands. I didn't like the smirk on his face. It stoked an anger inside of me that would have had me run over to the bench and choke the life out of him, if he had a life to choke.

But I had to concentrate on my friend.

The gurney was called for, and Javi and I helped the paramedics get him strapped onto it. The crowd clapped softly as we walked with him to the locker room, with the paramedics still feverishly working to get Rome conscious.

Once in the locker room, Coach Bolden took me by my shoulder to try and shake me out of the fog I was in. "Let the folks work on Rome, I'll keep one of the assistant coaches back here to let us know how he's coming along."

"Yeah, but Coach—"

"You know Rome would not want you here sulking while your team needs you," he insisted. "You said the same thing to him when you got hurt."

"This is different, Coach. He's not breathing." I didn't

want anyone to talk me out of leaving the area until I knew Rome was okay. "I'm not going back out there."

Coach sighed for a moment, realizing the seriousness of the situation himself. I could tell he didn't want to go out there, either, but he had to go and inform the president of what was happening. "Listen to me, Kee, stay here with Rome until the paramedics tell you he's okay. Once you know, I want you to call me immediately. You got me?"

"Yes, sir."

He headed out the door, already surrounded by the flashing lights of the cameras. I didn't want to imagine what I would have to deal with once I got the final confirmation from the medics, but my feet felt like concrete as I moved to where Rome was being worked on. He was so still; he hadn't moved at all since we brought him back. I feared the worst, but I leaned in and tapped his heart, hoping that I could will him back to us.

"Get back, bro, Javi and I can't do this without you."

We were up by twenty, and the refs, on advice from the league commissioners who were there on campus, called the game, giving us the win. The player who caused the incident was taken into custody on assault charges, based on his threats heard by the refs and other players earlier in the game.

It didn't matter to me in that moment. Rome was still unconscious; the word got back to us that Rome's concussion was more severe than we thought. His brain was bleeding and swelling at a rate that made the doctors nervous about surgery. The doctors also said that he'd broken his neck, and they had to induce him into a coma to keep him from dying.

I sat by his bedside waiting for him to blink, twitch, anything to let me know he was coming out of the darkness. The coaches and Rome's parents were talking to the doctors to figure out the next step. Angela was with his parents, too, and she was inconsolable. I didn't try; I was running on auto pilot for the most part.

I couldn't remember one thing I did once we got back on the floor. I went through the motions, doing enough to keep my teammates encouraged. We sat there for what seemed like forever as the officials tried to figure out what to do. It wasn't like there wasn't a precedent, either; Hank Gathers collapsed on the court over twenty-five years ago, and they cut the game quick. That was what I wanted; I didn't want to be out there on the floor while one of my best friends was fighting for his life.

Markson tried to offer condolences on what happened to Rome, but I was too far gone to accept them, graciously or otherwise. All I cared about was getting to the hospital to see about my friend.

This wasn't how I pictured this night to go at all. I was angry at myself for putting him out there. I couldn't shake the play from my mind, and it began to eat away at me. I wanted him to wake up, and I was dying inside, watching him lying there like that.

The doctors felt inducing him into a coma would help them assess things better, maybe help to stem the swelling. I hoped he would come out of the coma in one piece. I needed him to, for my own sake and sanity.

I tried to focus on something, anything that might help him come back. I remembered reading somewhere that if you read something or talked about something a person in a coma was passionate about, it would help fire their brain up and bring them back to consciousness. I figured talking about the game before the injury would help matters a little bit.

The only problem: the passion in my voice was gone. I couldn't get excited about one of the biggest wins in the program's history due to the Pyrrhic nature of the win.

"Rome, I know you can hear me, bro," I started as I moved closer to his ear. "You need to get back here, all right? You have a good woman waiting for you, your team needs you, and your family loves you. This is not how your story is supposed to end, you hear me?"

"I beg to differ, Keenan."

I whipped around ready to fight; the familiarity of that voice was not welcome, not around here. "What in the hell are you doing here, L.B.?"

"You're in no position to question anything, Kee," L.B. spat. "Besides, it's your fault that he's here."

I wanted to tear his throat out. "How is this my fault? For all I know, you probably set this whole thing up."

"Let's cut the BS, Kee, you didn't want to get hurt in this game, and you didn't get hurt," L.B. grinned. "I made sure of that, but what happens to the rest of your team … well, you have to be careful who you talk shit to on the court, right?"

The laughter that bellowed from him cooled the blood in my veins. My mind began working a mile a second, taking me back to that night two years ago.

During the game, yeah, Javon and I were trash-talking on the court, but it was nothing out of the ordinary. I had him shook from the moment we took the court, but he kept looking over at someone in the stands, and every so often, I would take a look at who he was looking at.

"I see the wheels are turning in your head, playa," L.B. sneered at me. "Ready for the big reveal?"

I ignored him to focus for a minute. In my mind's eye, I recalled noticing L.B. and Ella that night, but they weren't wearing Temp-State gear, they were wearing Trent gear while they sat in the stands.

The light clicked and burned so bright I could have cut through the darkest night. "You set me up, you bastard!"

"Ella was right, you really aren't very bright," L.B. crossed his arms as he rested against the wall. "Javon was supposed to be the man that night, taking you off your pedestal because he was supposed to be the next big thing in basketball … and he was willing to do whatever it took, too."

I wanted to yell in frustration, but I didn't want to draw attention in case someone was listening for any progress from Rome.

"I saw the potential in you, but I had to put you in a

position to where I could get you and get rid of Javon at the same time," L.B. explained. "It was the perfect set up, if I do say so myself. Catching you at your weakest point when He couldn't reach you was too good to pass up."

"You can have your damn contract! I wish I'd never agreed to it!"

"But you did agree to it, partner, and you're going to fulfill your contract the minute you're drafted as the top pick in the draft later on this summer."

I took a swing at L.B. and hit nothing but air. I shook my head, forgetting that tactic never worked when dealing with him. It didn't stop me from wanting to find anything to bash him over the head until I cracked his skull.

L.B. smirked, but I could see the annoyance in his body language. He wasn't used to me being this belligerent. "Now you're trying to be rude. Is this how you treat someone who's helping make your dreams come true?"

"My dreams? You've turned me into a puppet! This isn't a dream. My free will has been taken from me!"

"Oh, quit being so dramatic, Keenan, it was your free will that got you into this mess, and it just might get your boy out of his."

"What are you talking about?"

The answer to my question came in the ethereal form of Rome, sitting up in his hospital bed as his body continued to lay while hooked up to the monitors. He looked around, seemingly aware of everything and everyone around him. His gaze turned toward me, his eyes piercing through me. "Where am I? Kee, what's going on?"

L.B. spoke up before I could try and calm him down. "Jerome Dantley, I think you might remember me from the summer camp at Zeek Taylor's place. I have a proposition for you."

"Rome, don't listen to him," I begged. I didn't want him to get caught up in the same hell I willingly put myself in.

"Jerome, you might want to listen to me," L.B. interjected, cutting me off. "Your injuries are too far gone, but the doctors haven't told your parents or your girlfriend yet. The machines are the only thing keeping you alive, but I can change that."

Rome looked back at his body, further adding to his confusion of what was happening to him. "How can you do that? You ain't no magician, so how you gonna pull that trick off? I remember you, too, and I warned Kee to stay away from you. I knew something was ill about you."

"There's nothing ill about me, I am simply a fan who wants to see a young man reach his full potential," L.B. smiled as his eyes flashed. "I can bring you back, good as new. How badly do you want to get back?"

"Don't listen to him, Rome!"

Rome looked confused, and I couldn't blame him; it looked surreal from my perspective, too. He thought he was dreaming like I thought I was at the time. "What do you mean by that? You mean I'm dead?"

"In a manner of speaking, yes," L.B. affirmed. "At least, you will be once they pull the plug on your life support."

"So, what's the catch? The way my boy is fighting you,

I might wanna let Him have the final say and whatever happens is whatever happens." Rome's form began to glow, its radiance slowly blinding me. "I'm sure there's another option. There's always another option."

L.B. was undeterred, continuing through his spiel like he'd been through this routine before. "He wouldn't have let you get stuck in the position you're in. I'm offering you a chance to get back in the game, be on my team and handle some business."

Rome's form began to glow brighter by the second, and I couldn't understand why that was in the moment. The way he was illuminating, it was only a matter of time before I couldn't look at him without hurting my eyes. He shook his head, stepping away from L.B. before he took one more look at his earthly form.

"Nah, I think I'll pass. The business you got going on isn't what I would have rocked with in life, so I know I'm not dealing with it in death." Rome looked up for a minute and smiled. "Besides, it looks like He's got a spot in His starting five for me, and the way things are looking, I think I'll be seeing you again, and soon."

L.B. shook his head as he walked out of the hospital room. "It's your loss, but it doesn't matter, I still have *him*."

"Not anymore!" I yelled in his direction before I felt the pain in my knee begin to rage. "I'll be rid of you soon enough, I promise you!"

"You're still under contract, Keenan Ellis, whether you like it or not," L.B. stated before he disappeared. "You still belong to me. There's nothing you can do about that."

"So, this is what you've been caught up in?" Rome asked me. I couldn't bring myself to look him in the eyes, I felt so weak and guilty. "Damn, the offer was tempting, though, I ain't gonna lie. I can understand why you did what you had to do."

"So, why did you turn him down? You're going to die, Rome." I shook as tears streaked down my face. "It's my fault that you're hemmed up like this, bro. This isn't supposed to go down like this."

He shrugged for a minute, and he looked up again before his eyes met mine. "None of this is your fault, things play out the way they play out sometimes. I'm not salty about it, there's other work to do. I wasn't playing when I said He had a spot for me. This might not be how my story on earth was supposed to end, but my story won't end, Kee."

"At least you're free now," I choked my words. I was frustrated—and angry. "I don't have a choice in the matter. I may have to deal with this nonsense the rest of my life."

"You always have a choice, Keenan, you always did," Rome replied. "You felt like He left you in a lurch, and I can get with that. For a moment, I felt that way, too, that's how L.B. was able to show up."

"Yeah, but you didn't choose to rock with him, I did."

"That doesn't mean that you still can't change your mind," Rome's form began to glow again. "Look, He never lost faith in you, don't lose faith in yourself. That's not how this works."

"I wasn't playing, Rome, I can't do this season without you," I confessed. "Even with the things L.B. gave me, what if he was right? What if my God-given ability withered away while I was dealing with him the last couple of years?"

"Keenan, you were on your way to being the best baller on the planet anyway," Rome grinned. "You got caught up in the easy road, but being the best is never easy. That was the lesson that He wanted to teach you."

I started to laugh a little; he began to sound all Zen-like. "When did you start getting so enlightened? This ain't the Rome I know."

"Being your new Guardian Angel tends to have that effect on a brotha." He tapped his chest as his grin got wider. "That's what made the decision so much easier. I get to help you out of this mess and get you back to what you were meant to be."

"And what is that?"

"That's up to you to find out, once you choose to have faith in the path laid out for you." His image dissipated as he laid back down into his body. "Tell my parents and Angela I'm sorry it had to go down this way, but I'll see them soon and often. I promise."

His image faded, and so did the monitor that kept up with his vital signs. The nurses and doctors rushed into the room to try and revive him, but I already knew he was gone.

He was at peace. I, on the other hand, would have to go through hell to find mine. I was willing and ready to, but I couldn't do it alone.

The phone call I made would set me on the path into the unknown, but with her by my side, I would be able to conquer whatever lay in that path. No more running … not anymore.

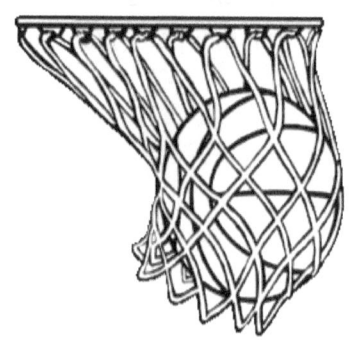

Chapter Thirty-One

"I'm outside, baby."

That was all I needed to hear as I walked out of the front door of the hospital lobby and towards the parking lot. I kissed Ariel as I slipped inside of her car. I made sure to avoid anyone spotting me leaving the hospital. The news would hit soon that Rome had passed away, and it was liable to be crazy in the building.

I made sure Ella didn't see me, either. She had been keeping a close eye on me the entire time we were there, but it was hard for her to get close. She wasn't familiar to the family, and there was no way Angela was about to allow her anywhere near him or me. It was one of the few times I was grateful she was as protective as she was.

It was a media circus outside. ESPN had a reporter on the premises, and the local sportscasters and radio hosts were all over the place, trying to get sound bites and interviews from wherever they could. All of the frenzy and confusion made it easy for me to slip out.

Once we were away from the hospital, I let loose the flood of emotions that I kept bottled up until I could get away. Ariel sensed what was wrong with me as she kept her left hand on the wheel and her right hand against my shoulder, rubbing my back. "Rome?"

I nodded.

"Baby, I'm so sorry."

Her phone chimed, letting her know a text message came in. She read it and a smile spread across her face. I was too involved in my grief to pay attention to why she was smiling. I didn't think she was being insensitive, but it threw me off that something had her attention at such a difficult time.

I tried my best to get it all out of my system so I could get words out of my mouth without them sounding incoherent. "L.B. showed up before he died. He tried to get him to commit to the same deal he roped me into. Thank God he turned him down."

"I know, baby, that was what I was smiling about." Ariel picked my hand up and kissed the back of my palm. "Don't worry about Rome right now, he'll be fine. We need to get you back to my place. We need to prepare."

"What's wrong?"

"Let's get you home first, and I'll explain when we get there."

I smiled; I needed to feel safe somewhere for a change,

and my apartment might as well be ground zero for whatever battle was about to take place. Once Ella found out I wasn't at the hospital anymore, she was bound to start the hunt to see where I could have run off to.

We got to her apartment, hurrying into the foyer like we were being chased. Ariel locked the door and told me to sit on the couch as she chanted something in a language I couldn't make out, but I had never heard it spoken before.

As she chanted, the creases in the door began glowing bright blue, and I heard something that sounded like glass crystalizing around the door frame. I looked at the windows, noticing they were crystalizing also at the sound of her chants. "What did you just do?"

"I had to safeguard the house tonight so we could rest without any interruptions. Tomorrow's going to be a trying day."

"Why are you going through all of this for me, Ariel?" I needed to know as she closed the blinds on the windows and led me upstairs to the bedroom. "Am I really worth all of this?"

She kissed my lips and held my face in her hands. "Keenan, you're worth all of this. You have no idea how much. You're worth it to me because I'm in love with you, with everything in my being. Now, let's go to sleep so we can be ready."

"Ready for what, exactly?"

Ariel shook her head and closed her eyes for a moment or two before opening them to meet my gaze. She kissed my lips again and continued to move toward the bedroom.

"In due time, sexy, it will all make sense."

Once in her bedroom, she chanted again, sealing the doors and windows shut. I tried to get comfortable in bed, but my mind was a mess. So many thoughts flooded in, and I couldn't shut them off, no matter how hard I tried.

"Kee, what's wrong?"

"I'm tired, Ariel. I feel like, with everything that has happened, it's not worth it anymore. Now that Rome's gone, I don't have it in me to ball anymore. My passion for the game isn't what it used to be. It feels like work now, and it was never work for me."

"Keenan, listen to me," Ariel slipped under the sheets with me, placing her hand on my chest, over my heart. "Rome will be here when you least expect him to be, and you will get through this season, but it won't be without him."

"How is that possible, baby? He's dead."

"Do you trust me?"

"Yes, more than I care to admit."

"Do you love me?"

"Yes, more than any woman on this planet."

"Then understand when I say Rome will be there, okay?" Ariel kissed my shoulder and snuggled against my body. "Now, let's see if we can't release some of that tension so you can rest, baby."

As I lay with her, this calmness swept over my body. I felt her energy wash over me, giving me a warmth that I remembered a few days ago. She hummed, vibrating against my chest, causing my heart to slow to a steady pace.

Before long, my breathing lumbered, sinking me into a deeper zone. I didn't worry about anything, my troubles felt light, at least for the moment, and all that mattered was being in that moment with her.

I'll see you in my dreams, baby. I'll be waiting for you, she whispered into the depths of my mind. *I'm with you, no matter what happens. I believe in you. We will get through this, I know we will.*

I didn't care anymore about the future or what would come. She was convinced that we would conquer it. Regardless of what happened, I was ready for it.

"That was a helluva game, Kee."

"Rome? What are you doing here?"

"Well, we never got a chance to finish our conversation. I had to take care of some business."

"I didn't think there was anything left to talk about, bro."

"Actually, I figured I'd stop by since I wanted to make sure my baby was okay and my parents understood why I had to go."

"Ariel kinda explained some things to me, but I still don't understand."

"Here's the deal: things happen for a reason, and it might not seem like it's the right thing that should happen, it was supposed to happen."

"What happened to you wasn't supposed to happen."

"Yes, it was, and I'm okay with that. I get to try and keep the people I love out of harm's way a lot better now, bro."

"But it was supposed to go down differently, Rome. What am I supposed to do now? You're not on the court with us."

"Right now, that's not important. What is important is getting you out of this mess. You're too important to Him."

"I'm confused, what makes me so important?"

"Look, Kee, you have the type of talent and charisma to influence a generation of players to do it the right way. To understand how to not take short cuts, use their talents to get to the next level."

"Yeah, some role model I turned out to be."

"You don't have to be perfect to be a role model, Keenan. You only have to be strong when the chips are down. Michael Vick figured it out, and he had the ability to help thousands of kids coming up to not go down the road he took."

"How do I do that?"

"Tell your story. All of it, including how you came out of this mess in one piece."

"But I won't come out of it in one piece, Rome. I'll lose everything."

"Not everything. You'll lose what you never needed in the first place. That was a false sense of security, for real. You have more than you think you do, Kee. I promise you that. But first, there's the matter of you and Ariel

confronting L.B. and Ella tomorrow and starting with a clean slate."

"All right. I just won't be able to tell this part of the story, bro. They'll think I'm crazy and have me committed."

"Look, Kee, trust the process, and know that there are ways to tell a story."

"I got you, Rome. I'll trust the process. Keep this up and you'll have me thinking I'll be drafted by the Sixers or something."

"Nah, I wouldn't do that to you. You're meant to be somewhere where you'll make the biggest impact. Don't just trust the process, bro. You have to have faith. In the end, I know you will know exactly what to do."

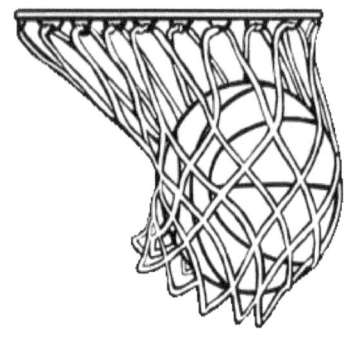

CHAPTER THIRTY-TWO

"So, you've made your choice? It's about damn time."

Ariel smiled as we walked into Ballers to talk to Pops. The look on his face seemed to brighten the place up. What amazed me was that the connection between he and Ariel seemed to intensify the illumination.

I was still confused from the events that occurred last night: the incantations to secure the apartment from God knows what. Talking to Rome in, what I thought, was a dream, and having him acting and talking like he could see the future. Ariel's ability to take every care away with a simple stroke of her hands over my mind and heart. Pops' ability to pop in and out of the sauna when we were talking without a trace.

I needed answers.

The bar was closed in the mornings, which gave us a

little more privacy to hash some things out. I felt like the blindfold was still over my eyes and I was stumbling in the dark. I thought I'd rid myself of that when I broke things off with Ella, but I was sadly mistaken.

"Yes, I've made my choice, Uncle Solomon." Ariel turned and kissed me. "But he deserves to know everything."

I whipped my gaze in Pops' direction, noticing the spreading grin across his lips. He moved from behind the bar and motioned for us to take a seat at one of the tables in the middle of the main area. I found it odd that he would do that, and even stranger when he positioned us in a way that he could still see who was coming in.

He took a sip of the beer in his hand and began to speak to what Ariel alluded to. "Okay, kid, I will admit that I haven't been completely forthcoming with you, but it was for a reason. Ariel and I are not what we seem. In fact, neither are Ella nor L.B., as I'm certain you found out the hard way."

I thought back to the confrontation between Ella and me in my apartment. The memories of that incident caused a knee-jerk reaction to grasp at my knee. "Yeah, that's putting it mildly. So, what are you?"

"Well, kid, that's where the answer becomes ... well, complicated." Pops continued. "Some tend to call us Guardian Angels, others use terms that have similar meanings for those that serve Him. We prefer the term emissary; although we are not warriors on the front lines, we do tend to get our hands dirty from time to time here on earth."

"Is that why I saw you in different times when you showed me the depths of your mind?" I asked Ariel. "Are you even human?"

"Yes, of course I'm human. Angels do take human form, silly," Ariel smiled, trying to soothe my discomfort. "We have the ability to be mortal when necessary, and we do have the capacity to die, be hurt, to love someone who loves us."

I smiled when she mentioned that last part, but I found myself questioning everything in front of me. "Pops, Coach Bolden mentioned something about me reminding you of someone. What in the world was he talking about?"

Pops slumped in the chair and blew air out of his nostrils, looking like he did not want to speak about the connection. "He mentioned Darius Proctor, did he? Proc was a teammate of mine back in the seventies, when I was assigned to help him through something similar to what you're going through. I tried to help him, too, but he was so damn arrogant and wanted things easy."

"Wait a minute, I remember that dude." My memory was jogged from all of the pictures on the Wall of Fame, which was how I found out about Pops. "He died in some freak accident on the field during the championship game against Notre Dame that year, right?"

"Yeah, it was the craziest night of my life." Pops stared off into space, pulling the memories out like they could physically manifest themselves. "There was this cat that showed up right before the game, his name was Bazaar. He tried to propose a deal to Proc and me, not realizing what I was. I had to reveal myself to Proc before he was ready to understand what was going on."

"Let me guess, he freaked out, like I'm trying not to do but I *really* want to do right now." I squeezed Ariel's hand to balance myself. "What happened to him, why did he die?"

"Well, he was given a choice, and he made it that night," Pops recalled, shaking his head the entire time. "I told him not to do it. It would only cause him strife if he did. He was so enthralled with the women that Bazaar had around him, and I couldn't compete; it wasn't what we were supposed to do back then. Using women as objects against their will was against the rules, but as we know, the other side doesn't play fair, and probably never will."

The words Ella said to me about never having been in love with me, they rushed to the surface, flooding my emotions. I hated myself for thinking that I ever had the upper hand, that I could turn my own emotions on and off when she had me played for a fool from the first words she said to me. "You didn't answer my question, Pops, but let me answer it for you. Proc is L.B. now, am I right?"

"You catch on fast, youngster."

I froze. I didn't want to be right. Dammit.

"L.B. kept hanging around campus after he gave up his mortality to become Bazaar's student. Eventually, he took over where Bazaar left off, trying to use the college basketball world as his playground. He knew I would sniff him out in a heartbeat on the football field."

"How come Coach didn't know about L.B. before? Is he like you two?"

"Bolden is human, through and through, but He has a plan for him when he's done with this life." Pops recounted. "Bolden and I thought we had him taken care of when he tried to go after one of his stars back in the nineties. I set different protections all around campus, and we thought it worked for a while, until you got hurt. It never occurred to me to wrap the individual players because L.B. always tried to come to games before."

The blank look on my face was a clear giveaway that all of this was above my pay grade. L.B. caught me at my weakest point while in the hospital, while Coach was elsewhere trying to find a way to get me back on the mend. If I could have crawled under a rock, I would have.

"We were ready for L.B. at Temp-State, but Eldora was something else entirely. That was a different school, and we came in too late," Pops wiped his brow. "It wasn't until Ariel came into the fray that the scales were balanced, but the unfortunate part was we couldn't get to him, either. I think you met him over the summer, Kee. Does the name Isaiah Taylor mean anything to you?"

There was no two ways about it. L.B. had me pegged and dead to rights. The only thing I could figure out was he saw something that I gave away that set the plan in motion. I was ripe for the picking because I confused my confidence and swagger for pure arrogance that I couldn't be touched. I needed to be taught a lesson in humility and understanding that what can be given can be as easily taken away.

"So, wait, if Ariel was there, and the stakes were even, how did you still lose that battle?"

"It all came down to the choice he made, Keenan. It always comes down to that, no matter what we do to try to influence. We won some others, but the only way that the scales could be balanced was if the women were active participants in the conflict," Pops said, looking at Ariel. "Whenever the women were targeted, we had men on the front who could assist where they could, but He felt that the women were needed in another capacity. That changed when we began losing the more influential targets. He began asking for volunteers, and they jumped at the chance. However, it came at a price."

"What price?" I asked.

"The same price that the men pay when they fall in love with the women they are assigned to," Ariel grinned. "They give up their ability to be emissaries and become mortal."

"Which is not an easy decision to make," Pops' eyes focused on me before moving to Ariel again. "That is why I asked Ariel if she'd made her choice. Not only is she choosing you, she is choosing to be mortal."

I shook my head in defiance. "I won't ask you to give that up for me, Ariel. I love you, He knows I do, but I can't ask you to give all that up for me. I haven't done anything to deserve it."

"Yes, you have, Keenan," Ariel countered, pressing her hand against my chest, over my heart. "This became mine the moment you told me you loved me. You can try to deny it, but it's not possible, and you know it. It was the one thing Isaiah wouldn't give to the emissary he was assigned to; he wanted the fast life and faster women. He didn't want to be anything more than what he is right now. Think of all of the great things you can do with me by your side, baby. It's all there for you."

"Ariel—"

"No more running, Kee."

I closed my eyes and sighed. "Okay, no more running, baby. I love you, with everything I have."

In the next few seconds, Pops hopped out of his chair, moving his hands behind his back. In a flash, I saw matching swords in his hands as he switched into a defensive position. "They're here."

I turned and saw Ella standing at the door, dressed in a black pant suit, with a look that could kill. After everything I'd witnessed and heard, I shuddered at the truthfulness of that thought.

"Maybe you should be running, Kee," Ella sneered. "There's no telling what might happen if you stay."

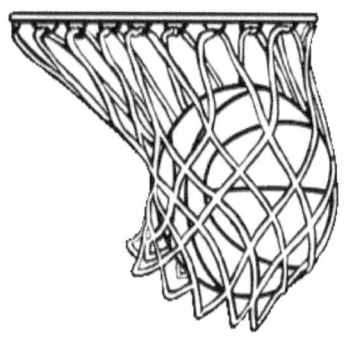

CHAPTER THIRTY-THREE

"Don't you ever get tired of losing?" Ariel clenched her fists as she moved in front of me. I was taken aback by the sudden show of protection over me. In the game of chess, the queen protected her king when threatened, but this was taking on a whole other connotation.

"By my last count, Ariel, I think I won the last two rounds, or am I missing something?" Ella laughed. "Just because you might have fallen for this pathetic excuse for a man doesn't mean you have the upper hand here, trick."

"I guess we'll have to see how things play out, won't we?"

I tried to look like I at least had a backbone, not realizing that I might be in over my head. "Ella, why don't you do us a favor and raise up, huh? I get that you're still pissed about us not being together, but damn."

"Aww, Keenan, you still think this is about you?" Ella turned her attention to me. "Look, you were a good lay and all, and I get that you think you're God's gift to women or something, with those pretty eyes and that 'White Chocolate' persona, but I can end all of that right now."

In the next instant, I felt the familiar searing pain in my knee that I felt when I injured it. I crumpled to the floor clutching it, wishing the pain would go away. No matter what I tried to calm the surge coursing through me, I was powerless to stop it.

Ariel dropped to where I was, trying her best to help me ease the pain. "Keenan! Listen to me, you're okay, you're going to be okay."

"You see? You should have stayed out of this, superstar." Ella stared at me as I continued to rub my knee like I could somehow rub the pain away. "No pain, no gain, right? And there's nothing she can do about it. She can't do for you what I can do for you, but you made your choice, and you chose wrong."

Ariel stopped long enough to slip her hands over my knee. She made me focus on her, despite the fear of what Ella might do behind her. I closed my eyes to block out the pain, but she forced my eyes open and trained on hers.

For a few moments, it calmed the intensity of the pain I felt, but Ella interrupted the process by kicking her, sending her flying across the room. "Nah, what you're not about to do is undo what has already been done. I don't care what L.B. wanted, I'm about to end you now."

"That's it! I should have dropped you where you stood

in the Quad when I saw you!" Ariel yelled, reaching behind her back in the same manner as Pops did earlier. "I guess the only way we'll ever get this over and done with is to send you back to where you came from!"

"How sweet, she's taking up for her man. But let's do away with the swords, shall we? It's so barbaric, and I know you've been dying to get your hands on me." Ella scoffed. "Once I've sent you back, I'll make sure he joins you!"

Pops rushed over to me, trying to assess my ability to move. "Come on, kid, the ladies have a bit of a score to settle."

Ella rushed Ariel with a punch toward her face. The blow glanced past her cheek as Ariel slid to the left. With the skill of a mixed martial artist who had sparred with Rhonda Rousey, Ariel popped a spin kick to the side of Ella's head, sending her staggering against one of the tables.

Before Ella could recover, Ariel moved in on her, launching an overhand right that connected flush against her jaw. A flurry of punches to her rib cage sent Ella screaming in pain. Finally, a swift kick to the sternum sent Ella flying toward the wall, crashing the paintings down with her. Ella gave an incredulous look as she struggled to her knees, trying to figure out where Ariel had learned to fight like that.

"Welcome to the twenty-first century, darling," Ariel taunted. "Are you sure you don't want to go back to the old school? It makes no never mind to me. We can go however you want."

Ella growled as she lunged toward Ariel, scraping across her stomach. Ariel cried out and immediately grabbed for the spot where she was injured. As blood canvassed her hand, her eyes narrowed and she gritted her teeth to try to push through the pain.

Ella quickly withdrew the claws protruding from her fingers, laughing at her handiwork. "The more things change, the more they stay the same. Old school or new school, you always try to fight fair."

"Ariel, watch out!" I screamed out for her. Pops continued to hold me back, and I was surprised at the strength he had for an old man.

"Don't get into it, Kee, this is her fight, let her handle it."

Ella's claws extended again as she lunged, aiming for the jugular. No matter what I tried to do to escape Pops' grasp, all I could do was watch the fight unfold. I honestly couldn't move much anyway; the excruciating pain in my knee kept me at bay.

Ariel spun to avoid Ella's second lunge, and as Ella flew past her, the other move she made happened so fast I couldn't believe my eyes. Ariel grabbed the swords from her back and in one swish through the air she connected with the back of Ella's neck. From where I sat, it looked like the blade cut through paper, the slice was that quick. All we heard was the blade cutting through the air and the unnerving crunch as the blade connected with bone.

"How's that for fighting fair?" Ariel retorted as Ella's

head rolled under a table. The rest of her body continued to flail for a few more moments before it finally expired.

"Is she dead?" I hesitated to move near the body, and I was nauseated from the sight of Ella's decapitated head, her eyes still opened and looking directly at me.

"Yeah, I think it's a safe bet she's back where she belongs." Ariel walked over to the bar to wipe the blood from her blade before she slipped it behind her back again. I watched as the blade flashed before disappearing. "There's no telling when or where she may turn up next, but that's not our problem right now."

"You're right, but you have a bit of a larger problem now." L.B. appeared out of nowhere, startling the three of us. "And a very serious problem at that."

L.B. frowned as he knelt over Ella. "What a shame. It looks like there is a bit of house cleaning that needs to be done before we get to it."

With a wave of his hand, he dissolved Ella's remains into dust, watching it scatter away toward the front door.

"L.B., you have no business here."

"Oh, but I do, Solomon," L.B. countered. I looked around trying to figure out who he was referring to, when it dawned on me that Pops was the only other person in the bar with us. "Whether you like it or not, I have a contract with Keenan, and I will collect on it the moment the season is over."

I got to my feet and limped over to the bar to where Ariel sat. I looked in her eyes to make sure she was okay before I addressed L.B. She nodded as she dressed the cuts across her abdomen and softly kissed my lips.

"I am rescinding the contract, L.B.," I stated. "I have no plans on moving forward with anything as long as we are bound by that contract."

"Oh, that's so unwise," L.B. mentioned as I felt a new level of pain surge through my body. I cried out as it coursed through every part of me, bringing me back to a heap on the floor.

Ariel tried to comfort me, forcing my eyes to connect with hers. "I'm here with you. I'm not going anywhere, Kee. I'm with you no matter what happens, do you understand me? I need you to focus on me, he wants you to beg him to take the pain away, don't let him win."

Each second brought more unbearable pain, to the point where I thought I would pass out. I desperately wanted this to end, but I didn't know what else to do. I kept my eyes trained on Ariel, doing my best to draw as much strength from her as I could, but even that became more difficult to do.

"Do you really want to go through life as a cripple?"

"If it means I don't have to deal with you, yes!" I screamed. "You'll have to kill me to get what you want!"

"That can be arranged, my dude." L.B. derided as he increased the pressure on my knee. "I had such hopes for you, but you had to go and fuck it all up, you and that bitch of yours."

Pops pulled his swords from behind his back and began to head toward L.B. "I've had about enough of this shit. Let him go, L.B. or you'll have to deal with me."

"Are you serious right now?" L.B. laughed, focusing his attention in my direction. "He's mine, and there's nothing you or anyone can do about it. He can't rescind the contract, no matter how badly he wants to. In his heart, he knows what he wants to do."

I began to lose consciousness. The little energy I had left to fight dwindled away to near nothing. In that moment, a voice came from almost nowhere, telling me to repeat after him.

Though I walk through the valley of the shadow of death, I will fear no evil ... repeat, Kee.

Though I walk through the valley of the shadow of death, I will fear no evil.

Again, Keenan.

I chanted, even in my weakened state, and it sounded like I was babbling, at least to my ears. I wasn't sure whether it was working or not, but there was nothing left to lose anymore. I wanted to be released from this prison, and I was willing to do anything to do it.

Ariel heard me, and she tried to shake me to keep from losing consciousness. "I hear you, baby. Keep chanting. Don't stop!"

This one, Kee: The Lord is my light and salvation, whom shall I fear?

God is my light and salvation, whom shall I fear?

Again, Kee!

God is my light and salvation, whom shall I fear?

Pops grinned at L.B. as he picked up the faintness of my voice. "There might not be anything I can do about it, but someone else can."

At that moment, I looked at L.B., focusing on his face, as I continued the chants the voice told me to repeat.

Though I walk through the valley of the shadow of death, I will fear no evil...

God is my light and salvation, whom shall I fear?

The pain began to slowly subside, but the voice wasn't satisfied. He continued to cheer me on as I felt Ariel's grip on me tighten, unwilling to let me slip from her.

Louder, Kee, so He can hear you!

THOUGH I WALK THROUGH THE VALLEY OF THE SHADOW OF DEATH, I WILL FEAR NO EVIL!

GOD IS MY LIGHT AND SALVATION, WHOM SHALL I FEAR?!?!

"What the fuck?" L.B. shouted as he noticed something burning inside of his suit coat pocket. He pulled out the contract I signed and noticed its glow. He did his best to keep the paperwork from bursting into flames, placing his hand over it to cool the parchment and slow the burn. It was a futile attempt; the paper glowed a radiant orange, a telltale sign that it would soon light up.

I continued the chants in rapid fire succession, trying to let my voice ring out as loudly as I could. I saw the paper catch fire, and I continued chanting to get the flame to grow larger.

"No, this ain't happening!" L.B. lost his concentration,

lessening his torturous grip on me. "You're not getting away that easily!"

"Come on, baby, keep it up," Ariel cheered as she heard me chanting. "Almost there."

The flames around the parchment grew, and soon he had no choice but to drop it on the floor. "Damn it! That's some BS!"

I was undeterred as my eyes focused on watching the papers disintegrate into dust. Once the pages were no more, L.B. yelled like he had been cheated. I glared at him as I struggled to my feet. "I told you I was done with you, dude. Now, you're welcome to leave. Now."

"Do you really think this shit is over, Kee? You belong to me!" L.B. rushed toward me, growling as his eyes glowed bright red.

Ariel tried to step between us, but I slid her out of the way, preparing for the onslaught coming for me. I wasn't afraid anymore. I was more than ready for it, and I had something for him.

L.B. threw a punch and was stunned when his hand was caught before it could reach its intended target. "Oh, I believe it's over, Lucius Prince. You no longer have power over me."

L.B. stared into my eyes and nearly cowered at what he saw. I stood, this time without pain, and I released his fist as I pushed him a few feet away from me. Ariel watched with a grin on her face as I grabbed L.B. and lifted him off the floor like he weighed next to nothing.

"Put me down!"

"I don't take orders from you anymore, bruh."

He tried to break the hold I had on him, but to no avail. I had him right where I wanted him. He couldn't do anything but face me. I wanted him to see and hear everything I had for him.

"Here's what's about to happen, and I want you to hear me clearly on this," I clenched my teeth as I locked eyes with him. "Temp-State is off limits to you, forever! Do you hear me?!?!"

"Fuck you!"

"Nah, I don't flow like that, playa," I kept my grip firm against his arms. "If I see you anywhere near *my* school again, you *will* deal with me."

The more he struggled to break free, the firmer my grip was on him. After a few more minutes, he figured out he couldn't break unless I let him go. "All right, damn you!"

I released his arms from my grasp, dropping him to the floor. L.B. began to rub his arms from where I held him and spit in my direction. "That's okay, I got another one coming down the pipeline, and I'll still get what I want. Besides, this one's damaged goods now anyway. Good luck trying to rehab that knee without me!"

"That's no longer your problem, I'll be fine. I promise you that." I picked up the dust that used to be my contract. "I think you dropped something, do you want it back?"

L.B. shook his head as he walked out of the bar as quietly as he slipped in.

It was finally over.

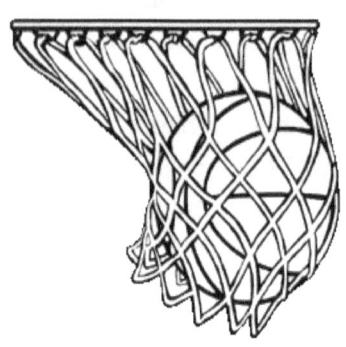

CHAPTER THIRTY-FOUR

I looked around the bar for a few moments, wondering if the whole thing was a figment of my imagination. The quiet and calm that followed the melee only moments ago felt like a murderous night giving way to the peace of the morning sun rising. It was an eerie feeling, and I wondered if something else needed to happen before I was convinced that the nightmare was over.

Ella was gone. So was L.B. The contract I signed still remained as ashes on the floor. My nightmare was over, the proof was sitting at my feet.

"How did you do that?"

"How did I do what?" I asked Ariel as she kissed me. "One minute my knee hurt, the next minute, it didn't hurt anymore."

Pops glanced over at us and smiled. I swear it was the

first genuine smile I had seen from him in years. "You made your choice, kid, and it looks to me like someone gave you a little help."

"Don't look at me, I didn't do it." Ariel put her hands up and shook her head.

I grabbed my knee as I tried to walk, stumbling to the ground. "Yeah, a lot of good that choice will get me now. I'm back to where I was sophomore year."

"That's not entirely true, Kee," Ariel countered as a blue radiance surrounded her body. "You're not alone anymore."

I hobbled backward, unsure of what was happening to Ariel. I admit I was a little scared that she would turn into, I didn't know what, but I wasn't entirely sure I wanted to stick around to find out. I'd obviously been watching too many horror flicks.

The radiance dissipated moments later, and Ariel looked the same. Her caramel skin maintained its sexy glow, her eyes were as mesmerizing as the first day we met, and her assets, for lack of a better word, were more pronounced than before.

"Okay, tell me what happened before I freak out again."

"She made her choice, too, Kee," Pops smiled wider, acting like a proud father who had watched his daughter make the proper choice in a mate. "She chose to be with you and live a mortal life."

"Wait a minute, does that mean she—"

"Yes, baby, I did, but it's only temporary." Ariel pressed her fingers to my lips to quiet me before she kissed

287

me. "I am still one of His emissaries, that won't change, but I also get to live one mortal lifetime. Once that life has been lived and we transition to the next, I will resume my duties."

"You did all that for me?"

"Yes. I love you, Keenan."

"I love you, too, Ariel."

I still couldn't walk very well, and I grit my teeth with each painful step I tried to take. "How am I going to explain how I got injured again? There's no way I can rehab in enough time to finish the season."

The answer to my question manifested itself in the form of a man walking into the bar. He wore a black suit and matching tie, and I had to admit, dude was clean. I watched Ariel as she admired his gait, tripping every jealous bone in my body. I gave her a look, but she simply waved my concerns away with a reassuring kiss.

"Okay, where did the extra from *Men In Black 3* come from?" I asked, trying to make light of the growing gloom over my situation. "Who are you supposed to be, Agent Double-O Negro?"

"Who do you think I'm supposed to be, Keenan?" He took off his glasses, and while I couldn't recognize his facial features, his eyes were unmistakable. Yeah, this day was about to get nuttier.

Rome gave me pound like he was still among the living, and my mind couldn't comprehend how he could be here, flesh and bone, in front of me. "What is this, 21 Questions or something? I asked how I'm gonna get my knee worked on, and you come waltzing up in here like you didn't just die last night. You don't even look like you, bro. Is this a joke?"

"It's not a joke, Kee, and considering what you were able to do about twenty minutes ago, I would think you'd understand that anything is possible," he grinned as he greeted Pops and gently kissed Ariel's hand. "We'll get your knee worked out, but I told you, you got to have a little faith."

Yeah, I had faith, all right. I had faith that I was losing my mind and I was in a deeper state of grief over losing my best friend than I thought. "Yeah, that's all good and whatever and you can try to convince me that you're Rome all you want, but unless something happens in the next day or so before practice on Monday, I'm going to have a lot of explaining to do."

Rome gave a look to Pops, who nodded in agreement to whatever inside joke they had between them, and he motioned for me to sit down. "After all that just happened, after the talk we had the other night in your dream, you're telling me you can't go on a little faith and try to understand what's going on?"

"Seriously, put yourself in my shoes, bro, and tell me you wouldn't be losing it right now?" The last thing I needed was my intelligence being insulted. "All three of you are looking at me like I was supposed to know all of this has been going down the whole time. I only had one side of this equation, and none of this is adding up."

"All right, I feel you, it can be a trip trying to make

sense of all of this, but I'm telling you to have a little faith. At the very least, trust that I have always had your back," Rome leveled with me. "Who do you think was the voice in your ear helping you with the incantations to break the contract?"

I cracked up laughing. He'd had my back from the minute we met, so I couldn't help but put on my big boy pants and try to act like all of this was normal to me. "Okay, let's rock with this, Rome. You were the voice in my ear telling me what I needed to say, I got that part."

"Yep, you probably didn't recognize my voice because I changed it, just like I changed my appearance so that family and friends won't recognize me and I can still do my thing."

"Give me one good reason why I should believe you are who you say you are?"

"Okay, fine, how about this: who was the one who covered for you sophomore year when you thought you got Kira Parsons pregnant? You know, Angela's soror? Or what about the time—"

"All right, all right, I got it, you're Rome, all right?" I tried to shut him up before he gave away too much other stuff I would have to explain to Ariel.

"No, I want to hear about some of this, Rome." Ariel teased as she stepped in front of me. "And since I outrank you, I can force you to tell me."

Rome laughed out loud at the threat. "Ariel, you may outrank me, but you're mortal now, so you can't hold me to it for another few decades."

Ariel looked over at Pops, and the first words out of his mouth made him look like Switzerland during World War II. "My name is Bennett, and I ain't in it."

Rome's focus switched to me, his eyes serious as he looked down at my newly-swollen knee. "Good, now that we got that out of the way, I need to get to work on this knee. I ain't gonna lie to you, Kee, this is gonna hurt a little bit."

He moved toward me, and I flinched. This was the same way L.B. "fixed" my problem. "Yo, I trust you and all, Rome, but I ain't gonna lie to you. I'm a little hesitant, even if you are my Guardian Angel."

"How did you figure that out, baby?" Ariel asked as she held my hand to calm me.

"I'm not as dumb as I look," I smirked as she slapped my shoulder. "Nah, seriously, Rome and I had a conversation last night, he kinda hinted at a few things, and the rest of it I figured out on my own."

I shot a look at Rome, who cracked up laughing. "I told you I would look after you, bro. Now, I get to take that to another level. So, quit bitching up and let me handle this, please?"

"I thought angels weren't supposed to be so vulgar?"

"When did you become an expert on being an angel, bro?"

I laughed through the pain as Rome moved his hands over my knee. He wasn't playing, it hurt like hell and beyond, but after about ten minutes or so, the pain finally subsided.

"Okay, try out your new knee, playa."

I stood up and walked around for a minute or two, and when I didn't feel the pain from earlier, I looked at Rome and grinned. "Now that's what I'm talking about! So, how did you pull this off?"

Rome sat down for a moment and clasped his hands together. He finally looked up at me to offer his explanation. "Let's just say, I signed my donor card in the unlikely event of my passing. My parents made sure that my organs were donated to those that needed them, including you. That's how I ended up becoming your Guardian Angel."

"Yep, we got word that same night," Ariel chimed in. "Pops gave the okay for him to come to Temp-State, with a bit of a makeover so no one would recognize him, to help with the protection of the campus."

Now that all of that was said and done and we all knew how to proceed, I stared at Rome for a moment, the sadness evident in my eyes. "I'm still pissed that you won't be there, dammit. You're supposed to be on the floor with us."

Rome stared at me, and I recognized the look. "Lawd, this man is using my moves on me!" I threw my hands up. "Fine, let me guess, I'll be seeing you in the stands."

"Yep, and I'll watch you and Javi lead our team to another championship, just like we planned," Rome advised. "My memory will be all the motivation you need to get back to where we belong. I'll be there, in the stands, cheering right along with Crimson Hurricane nation."

Pops put his hand on my shoulder, looking down at me with a knowing grin. "He's right, kid. The road is there for you to travel, but only you can influence where the journey will take you, no one else can do that. Just make sure you have faith in the steps you take."

"And I'll be by your side, every step of the way, just like I told you I would be." Ariel slid in my lap. "No matter what happens from here on out, I'm with you."

I looked at the three of them, all smiling at the way things turned out, and I couldn't help smiling, too. I'd been given a clean slate, and it was all because I made a choice to no longer let someone else control my destiny. I was ready to face the unknown without fear instead of letting someone else move the obstacles out of my way.

Pops was right. The difference between being a boy and being a man was the lessons he learned and the choices he made. Well, I learned my lesson, and I vowed to myself to make better choices in the future, now that I knew I had a future of my own making. I had too many people who depended on me and helped me to get where I was, and I owed it to them to become the man I was meant to be.

I was ready for the journey and I couldn't wait to see what would be around the bend. I was the master of my fate, and I was the captain of my soul once again.

Thanks to Him.

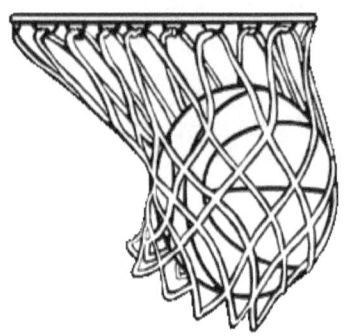

EPILOGUE – ROOKIE YEAR

"Welcome back to *SportsCenter*."

The past nine months had been like an absolute dream! Things couldn't have gone better if I'd written the script myself.

To give you a bit of a recap, let me rattle off some of the stuff that's happened to me:

Second National Championship!

Naismith National Player of the Year…

Top pick in the NBA Draft…

Tournament Co-MVP with Javi…

To say it's been crazy would be an understatement.

We won the national title, although it was closer than it would have been if Rome was still alive, but a win was a win and another piece of hardware for me and Javi and for Temp-State.

Javi and I also caught a bit of historical luck in the draft, too; I went with the top pick to the Hawks, my hometown team, and Javi went nine picks later, joining me in Atlanta. I didn't think it'd ever happened before that college teammates ended up getting drafted by the same team. To start my career in the A, and having Javi with me, too? Perhaps an NBA title would be in our future on top of that? Who knows what the future holds?

Fairytale ending? Maybe, but I didn't really play all that out too much. The most important thing was I had my life back … and my soul, too.

"We're back with the phenom, Keenan Ellis, for our Sunday conversation, and Keenan, I wanted to ask you about a few things that have happened over the past season," Stephen A. Smith began with his questions that we talked about. "You and Temp-State went through a lot this season, starting with the death of one of your best friends and teammate, Jerome Dantley, during the first game on national television. How did you and your teammates get through the season and still win a national title?"

I paused for a moment as I took a breath to figure my thoughts on his question. He was right, a lot happened during the season. A lot happened before the season ever began.

After collecting my thoughts for a few more seconds, I leaned forward in the chair and answered his first question. "Stephen, the thing we tried to do, and my boy Javi helped out with this more than anything, was help the rest of the team understand that Rome wasn't gone. Yeah, he was gone in body, but not in spirit. Every time Javi and I went out on the court, we hit half court and stood in silence, the way the three of us did when Rome was alive. We didn't want the team to think that we would change the routine, even though we were a man down. Rome was with us every step of the way. I truly believe that."

I wasn't about to tell him that I had proof of that, or he would have thought I was nutty. Rome was in the stands every game, the way he said he would be, sitting next to Ariel and my family. I saw the pride in his face over the way his backup took to his new role as starter and shot into the national spotlight.

"You had a slight knee injury right before conference play, and it was the same knee you injured during your sophomore year," Stephen continued his interview. "It was serious enough to keep you out of more than a few games, even though the doctors said you would be out until the NCAA tournament. How did you come back from that injury? Are you simply a fast healer?"

I laughed at the last question. What he—and the rest of the country, for that matter—didn't know was the knee injury incident was a well-scripted smoke-and-mirrors ploy to take some busy-bodies off the scent of how I was able to come back from the first injury so quickly. That, and we had to figure out how to adjust from the resolution with L.B. "Well, I have to thank Rome for the assist with that, actually. Before he passed away, he signed his donor card, which gave permission for his organs to be used.

When I hurt my knee, they flew me down to see Dr. Andrews and get the surgery done. The ligaments used to help with the surgery came from Rome's body."

"Wow, so even in death, your best friend was able to take care of you," Stephen quipped. "Is that part of the reason why you took some of your signing bonus to help renovate his parents' home?"

"Yes, it was the least I could do," I replied. "I owed them a lot, too. They could have gone against their son's wishes and buried their son, but they didn't. Not only did it help me, but I believe there are a few other people that are thankful to them also because a piece of Rome gets to live on in them."

"You kind of stole the spotlight on draft night when you immediately proposed to your fiancée, who's sitting in the studio with us today." Stephen sat back as he prepped the question. "You have made it known that she is your angel, that you couldn't have gotten through this last year without her. How true is that statement?"

"One hundred percent true." I stole a quick glance in Ariel's direction and grinned. "She's been awesome this past year, and I never thought she would be able to handle everything that came with being with me. Proposing on draft night was the icing on the cake."

"Spoken like a soon-to-be newlywed."

I laughed again. "I'm a lucky man."

"Okay, enough with the mushy stuff." Stephen got set for the last question. "Now that you're in the league, and you can finally look back on your collegiate career and how you withstood all of the madness, good and bad, what do you take from all of this to move forward and do what you always dreamed you would do?"

The smile I had on my face slowly faded to something more stoic as the weight of the question hit home. "I took a lot of things for granted before I got hurt during my sophomore year, and I made a few questionable decisions that almost derailed the plans I had for myself. Thankfully, with the help of people that He placed into my life, I was able to make the right choices and learn the lessons that He wanted me to learn."

"What were those lessons, Keenan?"

"That there is always time to make the right choices in life," I stated. "No matter what the road looks like once you've made that decision, there is still time to correct the course. You simply have to believe you can."

"Well, that's a good way to end this conversation, Keenan, thanks for sitting down with us," Stephen leaned forward and shook my hand.

"Thanks for having me, Stephen, and I'm looking forward to the start of the season. Hopefully we can have Atlanta in the playoffs this year."

Back in the A...

Ariel and I were watching Tyler get ready for the start of his senior season, and it was crazy to say the least. He was definitely better than I was in high school, and this season would see my career scoring mark fall on the very first game of the season.

Tyler was on every magazine cover imaginable, and he came into the season as the top-rated player overall in the country, with damn near every school trying to make him the centerpiece of their recruiting class.

As much as I wanted him to sign with Temp-State, I told him he needed to be his own man and make the best decision for him.

As long as it wasn't Kent or Trent State, of course.

When he decided to stay close to home and commit to North Carolina, I didn't know what to say to that. Yeah, I was glad it wasn't a conference opponent, but I didn't think they had the juice to recruit him away from Duke or Kentucky or even my alma mater after coming off a national title. He truly was his own man and I was proud of him.

This same night, my high school jersey would be retired, and coupled with my jersey being retired at Temp-State as the National Player of the Year, this would be an interesting season, that was for sure.

Even though he committed to Carolina, a Who's Who of coaching was still in the stands to take a look at Tyler play tonight. I tried to keep a low profile to keep the cameras at bay, but that was going to be hard when ESPNU was there to broadcast the game because Lake Grove's first game was against another nationally ranked high school. I already knew I was in for a lot of interviews tonight.

I left Ariel and my parents in the stands while I went into the locker room to chat with the team before game time. As I walked down the hallway, I picked up a strange vibe that didn't sit well with me. I turned around and notice the source of my discomfort. L.B. stood toe-to-toe with me.

"You have some nerve showing your face here."

"Like I give a damn what you think?"

"Do we really need to do this dance again? I don't think you liked the way it ended last time, Lucius." I smirked, staring him down.

"Oh, you think you bad now because you managed to breach your contract? Don't get the big head, partner."

"I didn't breach anything, partner. Otherwise, we'd still be connected, or did you develop amnesia or something?" I was growing more agitated by the moment. "Let me see if I can spin this another way, since you have a hard time listening."

I grabbed him by the suit collar and slammed him against the wall. The thud echoed so loudly the security guards peeked into the hallway to find the source of the trouble. I turned my gaze toward them for a second or two, and the guards recognized me and nodded before disappearing from view.

I stared directly into his eyes to make my intentions clearly heard. "Leave, now, before this gets messy."

"Well, look at this? Keenan Ellis thinks he has the balls to actually throw down," L.B. scoffed as I let go of his shoulder. "Well, check this out, playa, your girl ain't here to save your ass, and neither is Solomon, so you might want to rephrase your words before it does get messy."

As I kept my grip on him, L.B. noticed an aura surrounding me. I sneered as I dropped a punch to his gut that sank him to his knees. "I don't think so. What I do think is that you're going to find the nearest exit before things get a bit more interesting."

"Fuck! That actually hurt! How the—?"

"Yeah, I thought it might." I cracked a smile as I stood over him. "What you thought you took from me was given back to me tenfold, and while I might still be mortal, I'm definitely much more than human now."

I lifted him to his feet with little effort, catching him off guard. His eyes searched for something that was no longer there—hesitation.

"Yeah, well, this thing is far from over, bro," L.B. dusted off his pants as he walked away. "I'll still get mine, you can bank on that!"

"Yeah, but it won't happen here!" I shouted back as he disappeared from sight.

I finally walked into the locker room and saw Tyler and the rest of his teammates in the midst of a huddle and prayer before they headed out on the floor. Once they finished, I shook Coach Al's hand and remarked, "You have another big-time squad on your hands this year, Coach."

"Yeah, they're pretty good, but they'll be great before the year is over," Coach Al replied. "What about you, Kee? It looks like things have finally played out the way you always talked about. I'm proud of you, kid."

"Thank you, sir," I beamed. "I owe a lot to you, and I hope to support the program for as long as I can."

I gave Tyler pound while the team was on the way out the door, but I pulled him to the side for a quick pep talk. I locked eyes with him to make sure he heard the words I said. "I remember what Dad told me after I first made starter, and I'm going to say the same thing to you, Ty. No matter what happens, kid, always know that He has plans for you."

"I know, Kee, I couldn't agree with you more," Tyler replied, letting a smile spread across his face. "Make sure you remember that now that you're a big-time NBA baller now. He still has plans for you, too."

"Okay, little brother, I'll keep that in mind. You know you can call me if you need anything, right?"

"Yeah, I know. I always have."

"Good, now go out there and show them what I taught you."

"I got a few things I learned on my own, big brother. You'll see when the game starts."

I nodded as I walked out into the gym, watching the crowd go wild as the cameras were everywhere from ESPNU. I did my best to blend into the crowd as I headed back into the stands to watch the game with my family.

When I got back to Ariel, she raised her eyebrow as she looked from head to toe. I leaned away from her for a moment, trying to gauge her observations. "What's that look about?"

"There's a strong aura around you, baby," Ariel grinned. "It looks good on you."

I smiled and kissed her. "That's because I've got angels looking out for me."

"Yes, you do." She returned my kiss before we focused on the tip-off. "You've become His All-Star now."

www.ingramcontent.com/pod-product-compliance
Lightning Source LLC
Chambersburg PA
CBHW031035120726
47905CB00007B/2194